TREVOR DOUGLAS

Cold Comfort

Bridgette Cash Mystery Thriller Series – Book 1

Version 2.0 (July 2023)

Second edition

This book was professionally typeset on Reedsy.
Find out more at reedsy.com

*This book is dedicated to my Advanced Reader Team.
Thank you all for your support, encouragement and honest
feedback.*

Contents

Chapter 1

The rancid smell of decaying human flesh shrouded Bridgette like a mist as she opened the door of the unmarked police car. Suppressing the urge to vomit, she stared out through the windscreen at the police tape that surrounded the shallow grave fifty feet in front of her. Bridgette recalled the words of several seasoned detectives from her final year lectures as she sat and tried to compose herself. Their confessions that they often needed to shower three and four times after attending a murder scene before they felt clean again was something she'd never understood. But now, as the overwhelming stench of death began to settle on her, she understood why.

As she felt bile rise in her throat, she knew nothing she had learned during her four-year degree would prepare her for this part of the job. In only her second week on the force as a rookie detective, the real learning was about to begin.

Her thoughts were interrupted by a short laugh. She turned and looked across at Lance Hoffman who was already out of the car. At sixty-one years of age and three months short of retirement, the tall, slightly overweight and balding detective had an official reputation on the force as being a competent investigator who held the record at Vancouver Metropolitan Police for the most murder cases solved.

With an amused look, her partner of less than two weeks leaned down and said, "You know, it's much easier to do the police work when you actually get out of the car, Detective."

Hoffman's reputation had been tempered by Bridgette's new boss, Chief Inspector Felix Delray, who had given her a slightly franker assessment of her partner when making the assignment.

'I'm putting you with Hoffman for your first three months, Bridgette. He's old, doesn't like change or women much, but he's one hell of an investigator and he'll teach you a lot.'

As a throwaway line at the end of their conversation, Delray had confided that if she could stick it out with Hoffman, she could probably work with anyone on the force. Bridgette had taken this as a challenge and as she sat staring back at her partner who clearly found her misery amusing, she silently admonished herself to hold it together.

Bridgette ignored the condescending jibe and pulled a small tube of Vicks VapoRub from her leather satchel. Determined not to appear weak or overwhelmed, she took her time spreading a liberal smear of the lotion just above her top lip.

Hoffman watched with amusement for several seconds before asking, "They teach you that in police school?"

The whiny tone in Hoffman's voice as he said, 'police school,' was yet another subtle reference to her criminology degree. Hoffman had made it clear on their first day together that he thought university courses were hopelessly inadequate in preparing anyone for real police work. To his surprise, Bridgette had readily agreed.

Bridgette had quickly learned that her training partner was

rude, overbearing and opinionated. She had been miserable for the first three days of their partnership as she had tried to placate the crusty, aging detective. On day four, she was tired of being polite and found Hoffman seemed to respect her more when she was rude back to him.

Ignoring his question, Bridgette finished applying the Vicks and then asked, "Do you ever get used to it?"

The grin vanished from Hoffman's face as he looked across towards the grave. The medical examiner and two other technicians were already in position and ready to start the recovery.

In a slightly more reflective voice, Hoffman replied, "You learn to tolerate the smell, but you never get used to the violence."

Bridgette said nothing in response as she got out of the car. As they walked in silence through the sparse tree line towards the police tape, the smell intensified. Bridgette was thankful the Vicks was masking the worst of the odor, but as she fought the urge to gag, she knew she would need to remain totally focused to get through what was ahead of her. Hoffman put his hand up to stop her just short of the tape.

"You wouldn't be the first recruit to puke on me, but we can't afford to have the crime scene contaminated. So, if you're going to puke, do it now."

Hoffman studied her waiting for a response.

Bridgette had deliberately not eaten breakfast and now felt that had been a wise decision, as she responded, "I'm good."

Hoffman didn't look convinced and replied, "You look terrible. Right now, you're green enough to pass for an avocado."

Bridgette shook her head as she replied, "I'm alright. It's

just going to take me a while to get used to the smell."

Hoffman kept his hand up and said, "As I explained in the car, the medical examiner and his techs will be doing most of the work here with the recovery. We keep out of their way and learn whatever we can from the crime scene. You let me do the talking—just watch and listen."

Hoffman looked across at the medical examiner and held up an index finger to signal he needed a moment more, before turning back to Bridgette again.

"If it's who I think it is, she's been missing for two weeks. You'll have learned enough from that fancy school of yours, to know decomposition will be well advanced. You think it smells bad now—it's going to get a whole lot worse when they move the foot of soil that's currently covering her."

Now getting slightly more used to the smell, Bridgette held Hoffman's gaze and said in a more confident voice, "This is what I signed up for."

Hoffman nodded and said, "Remember who's in charge. You don't touch anything without my say so."

Bridgette was smart enough to realize that the three months until Hoffman's retirement would pass quickly and that picking a fight with him was pointless. Instead, she simply nodded and followed him as they passed under the tape.

Bridgette counted off six police officials at the crime scene—two uniformed police officers who remained outside the police tape, two technicians who were supporting the medical examiner, a photographer and the medical examiner himself. Hoffman ignored everyone but the medical examiner who was currently putting on a mask and gloves.

"Good morning, Ray."

The stout medical examiner, who Bridgette guessed was in

his late fifties, replied evenly, "Not much good about today, Lance."

"Ray, this is my new junior partner in training, Detective Casseldhorf."

The medical examiner nodded in Bridgette's direction and said, "Doctor Ray Warner," before asking, "Is this your first crime scene?"

Bridgette nodded.

Warner smiled and handed her his paper mask and said, "Put this on. It's got a perfume on it that ordinarily smells disgusting, but it works wonders with decomposing bodies."

Bridgette thanked Warner and put the mask on. The smell was strong and unusual, but it did significantly reduce the odor and her urge to vomit.

Warner smiled and said, "Better?"

Bridgette nodded again and said through the mask, "Much better. Thank you."

As the medical examiner retrieved another mask from a large plastic medical chest, Hoffman said, "I've briefed the detective on her role here today, but I'll get you to fill us both in on what you know so far, Ray."

Warner walked to the edge of the grave and stood looking down at the eight small blue flags that were pegged out around the mound of earth.

"So, we know a call came in from a Vietnam veteran who was out walking his dog early this morning down along this trail."

Warner paused and pointed to a small hole near one of the middle flags, before continuing.

"The dog gets excited and starts digging here and the guy knew by the smell and his time in Vietnam that the dog had discovered a body."

Hoffman interrupted, "The man's name is Seymour. I've spoken to him on the phone and got some basic details. We'll visit him later today and take his statement, but he seems straight up—no criminal record that we know of."

Warner nodded and then continued, "We've been here for about an hour. So far, we've removed and bagged the leaves that covered the grave and taken photographs of the area. This is going to take a while, but based on what we've seen so far, I'd say the victim has been here about two weeks."

Hoffman nodded and said, "It lines up with the disappearance of Monica Travers."

Warner's face turned grim. "Well, at least it will give her parents closure."

Bridgette had followed the story of Monica Travers' disappearance through the newspapers and in the detective's room at Vancouver Metro. Travers was a law student who worked part-time in a florist's shop. She had not returned home one evening after work and her parents had notified police immediately saying it was totally out of character for their daughter.

The word inside the department was that she was a quiet nineteen-year-old, who didn't do drugs or have a criminal record. After forty-eight hours with no leads on her whereabouts, most of the detectives within the division feared the worst.

Warner shook his head slightly and then continued, "I've got two extra lab guys on their way. The department's not going to like the Sunday overtime bill, but this is going to be a long day. We have seven large bags of leaf litter that we've removed from on top of the grave to examine as well as all the soil we still need to excavate. The body is under close to a foot of soil, so there's a lot to get through."

Warner looked from Hoffman to Bridgette and then said, "It might be hours before we find anything. If you want, you can go back into town and start your interviews? I'll call you if we find anything significant."

Hoffman shook his head.

"We'll stay for a while, Ray. I want to take a look around anyway and get an idea of the layout of the area. It looks remote enough, but you never know. If we find someone who saw something, we might break this wide open very quickly."

Warner nodded and then directed his two technicians to begin removing and sifting soil from the southern side of the grave. After fitting his mask, he made a few notes on his laptop and then joined his two technicians in their tedious endeavor.

Growing bored, Hoffman called out to Warner, "Hey, Ray, I'm going to check the surrounding area. I've got coverage on my phone here, so if you find anything significant, call me."

Warner looked up and briefly nodded as Hoffman moved away from the grave. Bridgette turned to follow. She was glad they were at least going to be doing something constructive, other than standing around and waiting. As Hoffman lifted the tape, he turned back with a surprised look on his face.

"What are you doing, Detective?"

Confused, Bridgette lifted her mask and said, "I thought I was coming with you?"

Hoffman let out a short laugh and replied, "You've got your little mask, so you stay here and watch. You'll learn more from watching these guys than you can possibly imagine."

Without waiting for a reply, Hoffman moved under the tape and made his way up the bank back towards the road. Bridgette refitted her mask and shook her head. She was still trying to figure out whether Hoffman was simply obnoxious or had a personality flaw when Warner called out, "Detective?"

Bridgette turned around to see the medical examiner walking around the edge of the grave towards her.

"I'm sorry, I didn't catch your first name?"

"It's Bridgette."

"Okay, Bridgette. And you can call me Ray or 'Doc'."

Bridgette nodded as Warner looked up and watched Hoffman disappear over the top of the bank.

He said, "There are a few things you need to know about Lance. Apart from being the crustiest bastard I've ever worked with, he's good—very good at his job."

Warner paused as if collecting his thoughts before he continued.

"He's easily misunderstood. I don't know how much you know about him or what you've managed to figure out yet, but he's actually a decent guy. He has almost no clue about common courtesy, but he means well and if you earn his respect, he'll never let you down or sell you out.

I'm not trying to make excuses for him, but he's actually one of the few people in Vancouver Metro I really trust, even though I don't always agree with him."

Bridgette thought about what Warner had just shared with her. She would make up her own mind in her own time, but she appreciated the gesture.

"Thanks, Ray. It pans out a lot with what Chief Delray said. I don't imagine we'll ever be friends, but I plan to learn as much as I can from him over the next three months."

Warner nodded and said, "That's a good attitude."

He turned to head back to the two technicians and said

almost as an afterthought, "Feel free to ask us questions, Bridgette. Lance is right, you'll learn a lot from this."

Bridgette thought she detected a smile beneath the medical examiner's mask. Most people she had met since commencing her new job with Vancouver Metro had been friendly. Several of the older male detectives had been cold and aloof and she still hadn't worked out if that was because she was a rookie, or a woman, or both.

She decided Doctor Warner was someone she could probably trust and watched in silence for the next thirty minutes as they carefully removed and sifted the soil. In that time, Warner and the two technicians made steady progress and had already removed about six inches of soil from the southern end of the grave.

Bridgette decided there was little to be gained by staying and watching until they exposed the body and said, "Hey, Ray, I think I'm going to take a walk back up to the road, just to get a better perspective of the site."

Warner looked up and nodded, "Okay, Bridgette, but stay where I can see you if you don't mind. It's not worth the grief if Lance returns and I don't know where you are."

Bridgette promised she would as she bent down to pass back under the police tape. She was not surprised by Warner's request but was amazed that senior people in Vancouver Metro allowed Hoffman to dominate them as much as he did.

The short walk back up the bank brought her to a long tall row of Katsura trees that flanked the left-hand side of the road. With winter fast approaching, the trees had lost most of their leaves and now looked more like a long row of gnarly wooden columns than a picturesque backdrop to the road. After zipping up her jacket to keep out the cold wind, she walked to the edge of the road and stood thinking for several minutes as she looked back at the scene below. The site of the grave was barely a stone's throw from the roadway, yet it was almost completely hidden from the passing view of motorists by the steep descent of the bank.

Bridgette looked across to the woods beyond the walking trail. The wooded area was much bigger than she had first assumed and looked like it would take several hours to walk around as it stretched out deep into the green valley below. She could not see any tracks or lane ways that connected the woods to any of the surrounding farmland and wondered how much of it Lance Hoffman planned to explore on foot.

Her thoughts were interrupted by an approaching car. Bridgette moved back from the edge of the road and stood amongst the trees as the car passed by. She watched as the car's slipstream disturbed a few of the remaining leaves on the road, causing them to lift and flutter before they were carried over the bank and down the hill by the prevailing breeze.

As she watched the leaves float and swirl, she moved back to the edge of the embankment where her eye was immediately drawn back to the grave-site below. Warner and his technicians were making good progress and she could now see the outline of the top half of the body in the exposed earth. Deciding there was nothing more that she needed to see from the roadway, she made her way back down to the grave-site and placed her mask back on as she passed under the police tape.

Warner motioned Bridgette to join him as the technicians moved back away from the grave to allow the photographer better access.

With a grim look on his face, Warner said, "It's her. I

remembered reading in the missing person's report that she wore a monogram gold ring on her right hand. I homed in on clearing soil around her arm and hand, and sure enough, there's a ring on the right ring finger."

They watched in silence for several minutes as the police photographer took photographs from different angles before a voice behind them broke the silence.

"You find something, Ray?"

They both looked around to see Lance Hoffman standing behind them.

Warner replied, "We have, Lance," before going on to explain what he had just told Bridgette.

He concluded by adding, "I brushed away enough dirt from the ring to read the engraving. Just one letter—'M'."

Hoffman nodded and said, "It's definitely her then."

They watched the photographer take a few more photographs before Hoffman said, "Ray, I'm thinking Detective Casseldhorf and I will head back to the office and start planning some interviews. I've scoured the area and there don't appear to be any residences close by. If we leave now, we can spend all afternoon working up a list of people who knew Monica Travers and hit the ground running when we get the formal ID."

Warner nodded and said, "No problem, Lance, I'll keep you posted on anything else we find here, and I'll email you photographs of the ring shortly."

Hoffman nodded and turned to Bridgette, "Let's go, Detective."

Bridgette removed her mask and as she passed it back to Warner, she asked, "How long do you think the leaf litter has been on the ground, Ray?"

Warner looked up briefly at the Katsura trees and replied, "It's close to winter, so maybe four weeks?"

Bridgette nodded as she responded, "It's odd, isn't it? If this is the grave of Monica Travers, who we know has only been missing for two weeks, why would the killer pick a spot covered in leaves to bury the body?"

Hoffman replied evenly, "Murderers do strange things, Detective, many of which defy logic. Let's go."

Bridgette stood her ground and pointed to the woods beyond the walking trail.

"We're less than forty yards from the woods. It wouldn't have taken him any longer to bury the body in there where it might not have been found for months or even longer."

Hoffman was getting agitated and asked, "Where are we going with this, Detective?"

Unfazed, Bridgette continued, "This spot is right next to a walking trail and was discovered by someone who probably walks it regularly."

Hoffman replied, "Your point being?"

"It doesn't make sense. If the murderer wanted to keep the body's location a secret for as long as possible, surely he would have chosen the woods? If he just wanted to dump the body and get out of here as fast as he could, there would have been no burial?"

Warner asked, "I'm not sure I follow?"

Bridgette looked up the bank to the row of Katsura trees and then back at the grave again and continued.

"It almost looks like he deliberately chose here so the body would be discovered once it began to smell. It's just a theory, but why else would you pick a spot where you have to remove a lot of leaves before you dig and then go to the trouble of replacing afterward?"

Bridgette looked from Warner to Hoffman but didn't get a response to her question.

She continued, "It only makes sense when you're using the leaves to temporarily hide where you've buried a body?"

Warner nodded and then added, "Until it starts to smell."

Bridgette nodded, "Yes, until it starts to smell."

Hoffman asked, "Okay, so the murderer may have wanted the body discovered. So, what does that prove?"

Bridgette looked down at the grave again.

"If the spot was deliberately picked, it implies planning. That doesn't fit well with a spur of the moment crime of passion and potentially opens up a much wider group of suspects beyond friends, family, and acquaintances. It may—"

Hoffman interrupted, "What kind of suspects?"

Bridgette could see by Hoffman's body language that he was growing increasingly impatient, but she wasn't about to be rushed. She considered the question for a moment before she answered.

"I can think of two. Organized crime figures occasionally want their crimes discovered. I'm sure you've covered crimes where someone's death is used to send a warning message."

Warner was now intrigued, "And the second group?"

Bridgette looked from Warner to Hoffman and then replied, "The second group are serial killers."

Chapter 2

Hoffman let out a belly laugh and responded, "Well, now I've heard everything, Ray. Detective Casseldhorf has been on the case for five minutes and we've got a serial killer on our hands."

Bridgette kept her anger in check as best she could and replied, "I didn't say it was a serial killer, Detective. I simply answered your question."

Hoffman turned serious and asked, "How old are you, Detective?"

"I'm twenty-seven, but I don't see what—"

Hoffman interrupted, "This is your first murder case. Don't you think you should be leaving this to the experts?"

Bridgette looked from Hoffman to Warner. She was the rookie and knew she should back down, but that wasn't in her nature.

"Surely I'm entitled to ask questions?"

Hoffman replied, "Do you know what percentage of murders are committed by serial killers, Detective?"

"Between one and two percent."

"I retire in less than three months, and in my time as a police officer, I've solved seventy-one murder cases. Do you know how many of those have been serial killers?"

Bridgette held Hoffman's gaze but said nothing. She was not familiar with the breakdown on Hoffman's record and wasn't going to give him the satisfaction of an 'I don't know' answer.

Hoffman continued, "Metropolitan Vancouver has a population of just over two million people—big enough to have a full cross section of scumbags that commit murder. I've arrested everyone from crime bosses to little old ladies for murder, but never once have I arrested a serial killer."

Hoffman turned to Warner and asked, "How many serial killer cases have you be involved with, Doctor?"

Warner mumbled, "One that I know of."

Hoffman nodded and looked at Bridgette.

"Detective, this is the real world here. It's not your police school or some Hollywood movie. Vancouver Metro doesn't have unlimited resources and I need a lot more than a few leaves put back on top of a grave before I go to the Chief and tell him we think it might be a serial killer."

Even though she knew Hoffman was probably right, the location for the burial bothered her. She decided now was not the time to argue.

"Detective Hoffman, you're the lead on this case, not me. I simply asked a question."

Hoffman replied, "Let's go, Detective," before pausing to look at Warner again.

"Ray, I'd like a close-up photo of the monogram ring and the grave-site sent to my email ASAP. I'm going to brief the Chief as soon as I get back and the photos will help paint the picture."

Warner nodded, "No problem, Lance."

As Hoffman turned to leave, Bridgette said to Warner, "Would you mind also sending through some photos of the shovel marks around the edge of the grave?"

Hoffman turned back and said sharply, "Are you trying to tell Doctor Warner what to do as well as me, Detective? Because if you are, our meeting with the Chief will be more than just—"

Slightly irritated, Bridgette cut him off and said in a louder voice than she had planned, "Go take a look for yourself, Detective."

Hoffman looked at Warner and then walked back to the grave. As he bent down to examine the shovel marks, Bridgette watched Warner walk across to join him.

Bridgette gave them a moment and said, "You'll notice the shovel marks at the edge of the grave are only about seven inches wide, consistent with the size of a small portable shovel—like campers carry in their backpacks."

Hoffman looked closely at the edge of the grave for a few seconds.

Without looking up he said, "Okay, Detective, what am I looking at apart from shovel marks in the soil? You know as well as I do that shovel markings are measured and documented as part of standard procedure."

Bridgette walked over and stood beside Warner. She took a pen from her pocket, bent down and pointed at more of the exposed shovel marks.

"Do you see that?"

Warner adjusted his glasses and looked down but shook his head.

"I don't see it, Bridgette."

Without replying, Bridgette moved the pen to the next

shovel mark and pointed at a narrow, almost undetectable score in the earth.

As she traced the score mark as it ran in a vertical line down into the soil, Warner replied, "Son of a bitch."

Warner gently scraped more soil away from the edge of the grave and pulled a small magnifying glass from his top pocket.

As he began investigating the other marks left by the shovel, Hoffman leaned forward slightly and asked, "You find something, Ray?"

Warner looked at Bridgette. She nodded at him as if to say, 'this will be better coming from you'.

Warner pulled his mask up and pointed at the shovel mark and responded, "The shovel used to dig the grave has what looks like a burr on it."

Warner pointed to several of the other shovel marks as he continued.

"You can see here that the shovel marks all show a faint vertical indentation in the soil in the same spot. It's not easy to make out, but you can definitely see a faint score in the soil where the blade has been pushed into the ground."

Warner rose to his feet and continued, "We'll get this all photographed properly for you, but based on what I'm seeing here, we have a way of identifying the shovel that was used to dig the grave."

Warner looked at Bridgette and continued, "This is great work, Detective. Provided the burr hasn't been filed off, if you find the shovel, we should be able to positively match it to the crime scene."

* * *

Traffic was heavy and the trip back into Vancouver took longer than expected. Bridgette had lived most of her life in the city and normally wouldn't have minded, but Hoffman had insisted on eating two pastrami and onion sandwiches that he had made earlier that morning as he drove back.

Still feeling slightly nauseated from the smell of the crime scene, she found the car trip miserable as she fought the urge to vomit. She was thankful when they pulled off the freeway and headed back in through the outer suburbs towards the South Metro police complex.

After Hoffman had finished the last of his sandwich and began to lick his fingers, he said, "The leaves bother me."

Bridgette wasn't sure how to respond. Hoffman hadn't said a word to her since they had left the crime scene and she wasn't sure where he was going with the statement.

Playing it safe, she replied, "How so?"

"I'm not buying your serial killer angle, but the question about why the killer picked a spot where he had to move leaves before digging the grave concerns me. That takes time and exposes him to a lot more risk of being caught."

Bridgette thought about Hoffman's analysis as the un-marked police car drove across the four-lane iron bridge. It had rained heavily the previous evening and turned the river below a dirty brown color.

She looked down at a ferry making its way slowly down the river and replied cautiously, "Maybe?"

Hoffman shot back, "Maybe?"

"Even though it's only just outside the city limits, there's probably only a few houses within a half mile radius and you can't see the grave site from the road. If the murder took place in the middle of the night, the killer could have been there for hours with nobody knowing."

Bridgette turned to face Hoffman.

In an effort to keep the conversation going, she said, "Let's assume for a moment that the killer wanted the body discovered. Why bury it at all? Why go to all that trouble if you want the world to know what you've done?"

Hoffman frowned for a second and then answered, "Maybe the killer wanted to get out of town, or even leave the country? Two weeks buys you more than enough time for that."

Bridgette considered Hoffman's answer, but didn't respond straight away.

Hoffman pulled up at a set of traffic lights and then asked, "So what are you thinking, Detective. Are we back in criminology school reviewing the latest crime theories by some professor who's never done a real day of police work in his life?"

Bridgette replied, "No. I was actually thinking about what you said?"

Hoffman laughed and mockingly said, "Something I said?"

Bridgette ignored the taunt and said, "I think you're right. I think he was buying time—maybe not to leave the country, but maybe enough time to make it safe?"

Bridgette watched Hoffman for a moment before she continued. He was clearly uncomfortable when she agreed with him.

She looked out the front of the vehicle at the traffic that was making the trip impossibly slow and said, "We know DNA evidence at any outdoor crime scene needs to be collected almost immediately. Even a slight breeze or a downpour of rain like we had last night can virtually destroy any chance of gathering usable evidence."

Hoffman did a right turn into Canyon Street and started the final drive past a series of modern office blocks towards the Central Precinct building.

He was quiet for a moment as he thought about Bridgette's analysis and then mumbled, "Bury the body close to where people walk and shallow enough so that the smell alone will ensure its discovered sooner rather than later..."

Hoffman turned left at the side entrance of a large glass and concrete four-story complex. He drove down a concrete driveway past a sign that read Authorized Vehicles Only, before pulling up at a boom gate. He flashed his police ID at the security guard who nodded back as the boom gate rose.

As they drove around to the rear of the building, Hoffman continued, "We've got a few different angles to work on. We'll talk to the Chief when we get inside and start on the list of people who knew Monica Travers and interacted with her."

Hoffman pulled the car up at another boom gate at the back of the building.

After swiping a plastic security card to gain access to the underground parking lot, he said, "After we talk to the Chief, I'll get you to ring someone from the City Council—a botanist or head gardener. I want an expert to tell us how long those leaves have been on the ground. We can't assume anything and need to make sure it's three or four weeks like Ray suggested, otherwise your theory of the killer intentionally picking that spot starts to look thin."

Bridgette replied, "Okay," and was pleased that Hoffman wasn't dismissing her theory entirely.

Hoffman parked next to a group of identical late model dark Ford sedans.

As they headed for the elevator, he said, "When we get those pictures from Ray, I want you to scan our databases and see if there are any other crimes that mention a shovel with burr marks on the blade."

Hoffman pressed the button on the elevator and as the door opened, he continued, "It's most likely a dead end, but Monica Travers' parents deserve the most thorough investigation we can put together."

Bridgette followed Hoffman into the elevator and they rode up to the second floor in silence. She thought about what they knew so far. In a way, she hoped she was wrong about the murder being planned. Whoever killed Monica Travers would be far easier to find if they had just snapped in a fit of rage, lust or jealousy.

She shuddered to think who they were up against if the killer had been able to orchestrate the discovery of his work when it suited him.

Chapter 3

Hoffman knocked on the door to Chief Inspector Felix Delray's office. The door remained opened most of the time and Bridgette could see Delray sitting behind his aging wooden desk concentrating on his computer screen. This was the first time she had seen him wearing casual clothes and figured Delray had things other than work originally planned for his day off. She was quickly learning Hoffman and Delray weren't afraid to work long or irregular hours. Without looking up to see who his visitors were, Delray said, "Come on in," and kept reading.

As Hoffman and Bridgette settled into their chairs on the opposite side of his desk, Delray said in a quiet, distracted voice, "Have a seat guys, I'll be with you in a minute."

They both watched in silence as Delray continued to read his computer screen, mouthing some of the words and sentences to himself as he went. Bridgette marveled at how Delray's heavy, black frame reading glasses remained perched almost on the end of his nose, seemingly defying gravity. She had only been in his office twice before and had quickly developed respect for the veteran Detective's inclusive and practical style of leadership.

Delray finally pushed back from the screen and said, "Okay, I got the email from Ray with the photos from the crime scene. He's put together a short report on what he's found so far. It looks highly likely that it's the body of Monica Travers."

Hoffman nodded. "We need to go through a formal proce- dure, but I expect we'll have enough information late today to be able to advise the parents ahead of a formal identification."

Delray frowned and said, "She's been in the ground for two weeks. So whatever we do, she's not going to look pretty for an identification."

Hoffman grimaced and answered, "We may be able to spare the parents the need to formally ID the body. We already have her DNA on file, and we can clean the monogram ring up and show them that to start with."

Delray pondered Hoffman's response for a moment and said, "Good plan, Lance. They've got enough bad memories without us adding to them if we don't have to."

Bridgette was slightly surprised by Delray's empathy. Now in his early fifties and a veteran with over thirty years on the force, she had expected Delray to be more detached.

Delray sighed and then asked, "Okay, Lance, what have we got."

Hoffman spent ten minutes providing his boss with a full summary of what they knew so far. He went into detail about Monica Travers' last known movements before she disappeared and then gave a full run down of the crime scene. Delray nodded occasionally and scratched a couple of notes on a pad while Hoffman gave the briefing but didn't interrupt.

When Hoffman had finished, the room became quiet for a moment before Delray looked at Bridgette and asked, "Do you have anything to add, Bridgette?"

Bridgette looked across at Hoffman who said bluntly, "Now's not the time to be shy, Detective. If you think there's substance to your theory, then share it."

Bridgette turned back to Delray who had an 'I'm waiting' look on his face. Hoffman hadn't gone into any real detail on the leaves on the grave or the shovel marks. She took two minutes to go through her observations before concluding with her theory that the killer deliberately chose the spot so that the body would be discovered.

Delray scratched a note on his pad and then turned to Hoffman and said, "Lance, what's your take?"

Hoffman shifted slightly in his seat. Bridgette thought, here it comes, expecting Hoffman to shoot down everything she had just said.

"I don't agree with all elements of the Detective's theory but going to the trouble of re-covering the grave with leaves bothers me as well, Chief. The more I think about it, the more I think he wanted the body discovered once decomposition had set in."

Delray thought for a moment and said, "If he planned it ahead of the actual murder then Bridgette's right. We are potentially looking at a much wider pool of suspects."

Hoffman replied, "We plan to start with relatives and known acquaintances and if nothing comes from those interviews, we'll widen the pool."

Delray ran his fingers through his short, curly dark hair as he stared down at his notes. Bridgette had seen him do this in a previous meeting and knew he was in deep concentration.

Finally, he looked up and said, "If this is Monica Travers as we expect, then it's going to get wide media coverage. I expect I'll be asked to give the Commissioner a briefing on this as early as tomorrow ahead of a formal press announcement. It's going to get political and we're going to be under a lot of pressure from above to solve this quickly."

Delray looked at Hoffman and said, "Needless to say, Lance, if that happens, the Commissioner is going to want a team on this, which I'd like you to lead?"

Hoffman nodded and said, "Okay, Chief."

Bridgette could see the reluctance on Hoffman's face. From what she had heard and observed, she knew Hoffman preferred to operate on his own, or at best with one partner he could control.

Delray said, "Work up your list of potential suspects as quickly as you can. I'd like to have something to show the top brass tomorrow morning to show we're on it. The last thing we want is one of them breathing down our necks because they don't see enough progress."

Hoffman nodded and replied, "Got it."

Delray replied, "Also, I'd like to get that monogram ring back here and cleaned up as a priority. If we can get a positive ID from the parents, it will help us hit the ground running."

Hoffman replied, "I'm on it, Chief."

Delray nodded and said, "Okay, we're done for now."

Bridgette took this as her cue and rose from her chair, but Delray motioned her to sit again.

"Detective, I'd like you to stay a minute?"

Hoffman gave Delray a nod and headed for the door.

Delray called after him, "Close the door as you leave please, Lance."

Bridgette immediately assumed she was in trouble and wondered what she had done. She wondered whether Doc Warner had said something in his email to the Chief. As she began to run through other possibilities, Delray opened up with a question.

"How are you settling in, Bridgette?"

"Fine thanks, Chief."

Delray looked at Bridgette for a moment and said, "Relax, Bridgette, you're not in trouble. Everyone knows when I'm angry—something to do with steam and my ears I've been told. You see any steam?"

Bridgette smiled and said, "No, Chief."

"Good."

Delray put his glasses back on the tip of his nose and opened a paper file on his desk.

As he began reading the first page, he said without looking up, "So you know how this works. As a graduate, you get the option to rotate through several sections of Vancouver Metro in your first twelve months. Gives you an opportunity to find out what you're really suited for."

He looked up from the file and said, "You saw the body up close today?"

Bridgette nodded, not entirely sure where he was going with the question and answered, "Partially. The bottom half of the grave hadn't been fully excavated."

Delray nodded and asked, "Did you puke?"

Bridgette shook her head. "No, but it was close. I saw quite a few autopsies in the lab while I was studying, but nothing prepared me for what I experienced today."

Delray nodded again. "How do you feel now?"

Bridgette thought for a moment and said, "I'm not sure. Mostly I'm thinking about the killer and how we narrow down the suspect list. And, the family of course."

Delray removed his glasses and leaned back in his chair.

"I've had people in your position who have requested transfers out of Homicide after seeing far less than what you saw today. I make it a point to check in with all new starters after their first crime scene. I can't afford to have people on my team that don't want to be here, Bridgette."

Delray let the sentence hang and watched for Bridgette's response. Bridgette understood the Chief was going to rely more on her body language than what she actually said to know whether she was cut out for Homicide or not.

"I'm good, Chief. As I said to Detective Hoffman, this is what I signed up for. I might have to shower a couple of times tonight to feel clean again, but I don't plan to let it get me down."

Delray nodded but didn't say anything straight away. He studied Bridgette for a moment and said, "And how are you getting on with, Detective Hoffman?"

Bridgette decided there was no point going into too many details and simply said, "He's not the easiest guy to work with, but I'm managing."

"Like I said before, Bridgette, he's never going to win any prizes for his social skills, but I think you will learn a lot from him before he retires."

Bridgette nodded.

Delray asked, "Is he still eating those pastrami and onion sandwiches?"

Bridgette tried not to roll her eyes as she said, "Mostly in the car."

Delray smiled and said, "He's been eating those things for thirty years. We were briefly partners back in the day, and we fought about his sandwiches more than anything else."

Delray turned serious again. "So, Bridgette, the door is

always open. Come and talk to me anytime you feel the need. I think you have the makings of a very good detective, and I want to make sure you get every opportunity to develop. If there's anything else I can do, you let me know—okay?"

Bridgette nodded. She was about to rise from her chair to leave but decided Delray's offer was too good to pass up.

She hesitated a moment and said, "Chief, there is one thing I'd like to talk to you about."

"Okay."

"My father."

Delray's face turned serious.

"I don't know a lot about him, Bridgette, but what do you want to know?"

Bridgette wasn't sure where to start and now wasn't even sure she had made the right decision bringing this up when she had only been a probationary detective for two weeks.

"I know my father used to work here once. I just wondered if you ever worked with him?"

Bridgette watched as Delray got up from his chair and walked across to his window. As he stared out at the parking lot below, she knew she'd raised a subject he wasn't comfortable with.

Finally, he turned back and said, "We worked on the same team together—for a short period, before his transfer. By all reports, he was a very good detective."

Bridgette nodded. In a voice barely above a whisper, she asked, "Do you think he murdered my mother?"

Delray's complexion darkened.

Bridgette realized she had overstepped the mark, and quickly added, "Sorry , Chief, that was out of line."

To her surprise, Delray shook his head and said, "No,

actually it's not," before returning to his desk.

Bridgette watched as Delray sat down and then began typing on his keyboard.

Without looking at her, he said, "All our old case files are in our database now—including your mother's murder case. I'm giving you read access to it. In your spare time, you can read the file for yourself and make up your own mind."

Delray made several more swift keystrokes and then pushed back from the screen again.

He held Bridgette's gaze for a moment.

"It doesn't matter what I think, Bridgette. This is one you have to work out for yourself. Read the file on your own time and when you're done, I'm happy to talk if you want to. I—"

Delray was interrupted by his telephone. He held a finger up to Bridgette to signal her to hang on a moment as he looked at caller ID before answering the call.

"I'm just finishing up a meeting, Danny, can you hang on a minute?"

Delray covered the mouthpiece, "I gotta take this, Bridgette. Come back to me when you've read the report. There are a few things you'll need to know that aren't in there."

Chapter 4

Bridgette walked into the homicide detective's room and over to the pod she shared with Lance Hoffman. She still felt like an outsider even though most of the twelve detectives in Delray's team had been friendly enough. She sat down in her worn office chair that didn't roll so well and half lifted it to move it closer to her desk. Her chair was like most of the other furniture and decor in the homicide room—old, tired and in need of replacement. She looked briefly across at Hoffman as she switched on her computer. He was currently on the phone, with his head down, immersed in deep conversation.

After logging on to the Vancouver Metro computer system, she Googled the information number for Vancouver's City Council and then dialed the number from her desk phone. She wasn't surprised when her call went through to an answering machine that told her the call was important, but nobody was available until Monday. She left a polite message explaining who she was and asked for a horticulturist to call her back as soon as possible.

With her fingers hovering over her keyboard, she thought for a moment about how she could quickly find out when

Katsura trees shed their leaves in Vancouver. She typed a few keywords into the Google search engine and pressed enter. The search result was much larger than she wanted. She thought for a moment and added another two keywords and pressed enter again. The search result was narrowed to fifty-two matches and it took Bridgette less than two minutes of scanning web pages to find the answer.

She smiled as she bookmarked two web pages from her search results and decided to check her email while she waited for Hoffman to get off the phone. With a couple of keystrokes, she opened her email program and clicked on her inbox. There were several unread messages, but Bridgette focused on the most recent, which was from Ray Warner.

Bridgette opened the email and counted nineteen photo attachments from the crime scene. She decided to read Warner's preliminary summary of findings first but only got through the opening paragraph before she heard Hoffman's voice behind.

"Nobody at City Council today?"

Bridgette turned to face Hoffman and answered, "No. I left a message for them to call me back tomorrow, but I checked a couple of local gardening websites and they say the same thing about Katsura trees—in this area they all shed their leaves about four weeks ago."

Hoffman scratched his chin and thought for a moment. "It still doesn't prove it was premeditated. Or that the spot was chosen. It might still be just some whacko who wasn't thinking straight. He parks his vehicle on top of a thick pile of leaves and doesn't think to look around for an easier place to bury the body."

Bridgette wasn't sure why Hoffman was now backing away

from the tentative support he had just given to her theory in Delray's office. She knew she wasn't likely to get a straight answer and instead steered the conversation in a different direction.

"Doc Warner has sent through the photos of the shovel marks from the crime scene. Do you want me to start checking for matches in NatTrack?"

Hoffman nodded as he reached for the phone.

Bridgette decided to push it further as she watched him punch in a number and said, "I think I'll check national as well as state. We want to be thorough."

Hoffman mumbled, "Don't spend too much time on it. Focus on Vancouver—I've got other things we need you to do."

Bridgette was about to clarify what he meant by 'focus', but Hoffman was already onto his next call. While she listened to Hoffman speaking to the lead detective in the Missing Persons division about the Monica Travers' case, she decided to start with a routine NatTrack search for shovels used in crimes over the last three years.

She was still learning how to use the new database system but was impressed with its ability to allow police agencies across the country to share information on criminal investigations. The system had only been recently commissioned but was already proving invaluable in helping police officers quickly access information from other jurisdictions to help solve crime.

Bridgette started with just a search of greater Vancouver. The search took just a few seconds, but only returned a handful of hits. Bridgette browsed through the search summary screen but didn't see anything that looked close. One crime involved a man beating a dog to death with a shovel, another involved a man committing a robbery using a small shovel as a weapon and there were several other matches for assault and battery where a shovel was involved. She quickly browsed the summary information on the felons associated with each crime before deciding none of them looked worthy of immediate investigation.

She was hesitant to widen the search parameters to cover the complete national grid. She knew enough about NatTrack to know that it would return a vastly larger group of random cases to trawl through and would be like looking for a needle in a haystack. She rested her fingers on the keyboard and thought about the keywords she needed to enter to narrow the search. She was positive the burial had been planned ahead of the murder and nearly as positive the killer wanted their work discovered. Her worst fear was this was not the first time.

She allowed her fingers to tap lightly on the keys as she thought about what were the important pieces of information she needed to feed into NatTrack. She kept the word shovel in the keyword search and added parameters to limit the search to murder cases involving victims who had been buried in shallow graves. She paused before pressing the enter key and changed the date range of the search from crimes committed in the last three years to five years and then pressed enter.

While she waited for NatTrack to return its search results, Hoffman ended his phone call.

"Okay, I've got it all sorted with Delaney from Missing Persons. After what I told them about the crime scene and the monogram ring, they're happy enough to hand over the file on Monica Travers."

Bridgette replied, "Okay. What do—"

Hoffman interrupted her and said, "He's got one of his team working today, so I'm going over to get the paper file right now. Most of it is already in the computer, but I don't trust those guys to have entered everything. Also, they've got surveillance video from the store where she worked for the two weeks leading up to Monica Travers' disappearance.

I want you to spend the rest of the day going over the video. Look for anyone that looks out of the ordinary—customers that seem more interested in the staff than buying flowers, for example. Also, anyone that keeps coming back in. You never know, the killer might just be on the video."

Bridgette nodded and looked back at her computer screen. The search had just completed and showed one hundred and fifty-seven cases that matched her request. She looked back at Hoffman and thought quickly about what she would say next. It was important to her that Hoffman didn't totally shut off what she was doing even though reviewing the security video footage was also important.

"I'll set the video up on a laptop here so that I can show you anything that looks suspicious."

"I'm not going to be here. I'm starting preliminary interviews on the key suspects right away."

Hoffman paused and looked at Bridgette's computer screen.

"You started searching on the shovel already?"

Bridgette tried to play down her response.

"I only got a handful of matches with the first search—nothing that remotely resembles what we're dealing with here. I've widened the parameters and I'll take a quick look through them when I need a break from the security video."

Hoffman grabbed car keys off his desk and said, "You're not going to solve this crime with a computer, so make the video footage your priority."

Bridgette nodded and said, "Okay," pleased that Hoffman hadn't out rightly directed her not to look through the search results.

Hoffman rose from his chair and said, "I'm going to visit Monica Travers' ex-boyfriend and then two delivery guys from the florist shop. They're the key suspects at present according to Delaney and I want to find out for myself if they're on the level or not. You find anything on that video that looks promising, call me immediately."

Bridgette watched Hoffman leave the floor and then turned back to her computer screen. She knew she should be getting across to missing persons straight away but became fixated on the number of matches her search had returned. One hundred and fifty-seven cases were still a lot to search through effectively in the limited time she had.

Bridgette let her fingers dance over the keys again as she thought about how she could narrow down the size of the haystack she was searching in. She thought about the profile of Monica Travers and further narrowed the search down to show only female murder victims aged between sixteen and thirty-five for crimes that were still currently unsolved.

She held her breath for a moment and then pressed the enter key. As she watched the computer process her search, she thought about the crime scene again and wondered when Hoffman planned on notifying the parents? She knew from reading the file on Monica Travers that her parents had loved her dearly and that she would be greatly missed. They deserved to know as soon as possible without being caught in any political games with the media.

She wondered how many people would truly miss her if

she had been the victim instead of Monica? With her mother dead and her father presumably dead, she didn't think the number would be very high. She was jolted back to reality as the NatTrack search ended. Bridgette stared at the screen, not sure of what to make of the results. There were currently eleven unsolved murder cases across the country involving young women who had been buried in shallow graves.

It seemed to be a high number of active murder cases for such a refined search. She stared at the screen for a moment before pushing back from her desk. The surveillance video had to be her priority for now, but she knew she would be back to review each case in detail before the day was out—even if it was on her own time.

Chapter 5

B ridgette leaned back in her chair and massaged the back of her neck. She checked her watch and realized she had been looking at the surveillance video for over four hours without anything more than a break to refill her coffee cup.

She thought she would find the process of checking video footage tedious and boring and was positive that was why Hoffman had assigned her the task. It had been confronting to start with as she viewed the first black and white video images of Monica Travers happily going about her job just two weeks before her murder. Bridgette became engrossed as she watched the young woman engaging with other staff and customers. It was hard for Bridgette to comprehend she was now dead and lying in a shallow grave after being brutally discarded by her killer.

While continuing to massage her neck, she reviewed the eight pages of notes and observations she had taken and was pleased with her progress. There had been long periods during each day of the recordings where there were no customers in the store. She had been able to fast forward through these periods reasonably quickly. With her review for the first three days now complete she was hungry and decided it was time for a break.

Bridgette grabbed her car keys and had almost made it out of her cubicle when her desk phone started ringing. She debated leaving it to go through to voice mail but returned to her desk just in case it was related to the Travers' murder.

"Detective Casseldhorf speaking."

"It's well after seven, I'm surprised you're still working?"

Bridgette rolled her eyes as she recognized Hoffman's voice.

"What can I do for you, Detective?"

"I just called in on the off-chance you'd still be at work. I've finished the preliminary interviews on the three suspects, and I think the old boyfriend may be hiding something. I'll tell you more tomorrow. How did you go with the surveillance video?"

Bridgette spent several minutes explaining what she had learned so far. Hoffman seemed disappointed when she informed him that there was nothing overly suspicious in any of the video she had seen so far.

"All right, pack it in for tonight—we don't pay you overtime. I've got a call with media relations in ten minutes and then I'm heading down to the morgue. Doc Warner has the body back there now and I want to catch him before he goes home. They'll do a formal autopsy tomorrow, but I'm hopefully going to get the monogram ring. I want to take it over to show Monica Travers' parents tonight. If we get a positive ID from them, there will be a press conference tomorrow morning where we'll be publicly announcing the Travers' case is now a murder investigation."

Bridgette tried to imagine Hoffman breaking the news to Monica Travers' parents. He was as subtle as a brick at the best of times. She couldn't imagine him being either gentle or empathetic.

"Detective, would you like me to accompany you to meet the parents? We know it's going to be a shock to them even though she's been missing for two weeks. It might be better if two of us there when we break the news?"

Hoffman replied flatly, "No need to bother, Detective. Delaney from missing persons has already met them, so I'm taking him."

Bridgette felt slightly frustrated by how often Hoffman was excluding her and replied, "It may be worthwhile having a woman there, Detective. Perhaps to comfort Monica's mother?"

"No, I don't think so. You're young and pretty and have long dark hair just like their daughter had. I've done this enough times to know that if someone like you shows up, they might resent us because you look a lot like their daughter."

There was a pause while Bridgette did her best to control her breathing. She had never felt belittled by someone calling her 'young' or 'pretty,' but Hoffman had managed to pull it off.

Before she had a chance to respond, Hoffman continued. "Clock off and go home, Detective. Tomorrow is a big day and I want you to complete the review of the rest of the surveillance footage, so you need some rest."

The phone went dead. Bridgette rolled her eyes. She had not learned anything from Hoffman yet, apart from getting some practice with anger management. She dropped her keys back on her desk—there was a small Chinese restaurant at the bottom of Canyon Street within walking distance of the office. Walking was what she needed now, both to clear her head and help her plan what she was about to do next.

* * *

Bridgette spooned a mouthful of Korean BBQ into her mouth as she switched on her PC again. She thought it ironic that the most popular dish at Ming's Chinese Restaurant was a Korean dish. Even though she had only been working with Vancouver Metro for two weeks, Ming's was quickly becoming a favorite and she knew she would be back there shortly as she savored each mouthful from the cardboard container.

The walk to Ming's and back had given her a chance to think as well as an opportunity to cool down. She'd thought about Hoffman's dismissive manner on the phone and had drawn the conclusion that nothing he did or said was personal—he was simply self-centered and opinionated like Chief Delray had warned and she was the one currently in the firing line.

The walk had also given her a chance to think about what she would do when she returned to the office. Hoffman wasn't expecting any further progress on the video surveillance review tonight, so she decided she would skip her usual gym session and spend a couple of hours reviewing the other unsolved murder cases in NatTrack.

With her login complete, Bridgette started the NatTrack system again and keyed in the same search parameters as she had used earlier in the day. While she waited for NatTrack to return the search results from the database, she finished the last of her meal and closed her eyes to relax for a moment. The call from Hoffman to say they had a new murder case had come through before six a.m. that morning. It had been a long day already, but she knew she wouldn't be able to sleep until she had reviewed the cases.

A small beep from her computer signaled NatTrack had finished the search. Bridgette opened her eyes and looked at the screen. The same eleven cases were displayed in the summary. She paused for a moment as she thought about how she should review each case. What was she looking for? It had all been theoretical during her degree—now it was real. She decided to start by reading through the basic synopsis for each case, noting down anything about the victims or the crime scenes that could potentially show a pattern.

She clicked on the first case and started reading the file on her screen. The victim had been a twenty-three-year-old school teacher who lived in Bolton, a city of seven hundred and fifty-thousand people three hours north of Vancouver. She started making notes as she read the file. The woman lived alone, enjoyed her job, and appeared to have lots of friends, but no boyfriend. She had no criminal record or history of drug use. The circumstances surrounding her disappearance were vague. She had left school at the normal time according to work colleagues but had not returned to work the following day.

Bridgette read through the rest of the summary of the file and then moved on to the second case, which involved a thirty-one-year-old mother from Rochford. Rochford was a five-hour drive west of Vancouver. Bridgette had only visited the city once but knew greater Rochford had a population somewhere above one million people.

She did her best to read the file objectively without drawing any immediate conclusions. The Rochford victim worked as a clerk for a local airline that specialized in charter flights. She had failed to return home one Sunday evening after work, and her husband had immediately raised an alarm. She had been found two weeks later in a shallow grave by three horse riders adjacent to a horse-riding lodge just out of the city.

She had only one minor infringement for being caught with marijuana as a teenager but had a clean record since then—not even a speeding ticket. Bridgette read the remainder of the file and made a number of notes as she went. After she had finished, she leaned back in her chair and stretched before opening the third file. She glanced at her watch as the computer retrieved the next file from its database. It was already nine fifteen p.m.—it was going to be a long night.

Chapter 6

Bridgette tried to hide a yawn as she walked through the detective's room towards the pod she shared with Hoffman. Hoffman was currently standing up and talking on his mobile phone and frowned at her as she approached. She ignored him as she walked past and sat down at her desk. After turning on her computer, she pulled the thick pile of notes that she had taken the previous evening from the locked metal cabinet under her desk.

Just as she was about to begin reviewing what she had written, Hoffman ended his phone call and walked up behind her.

"You got a lot of nerve turning up twenty minutes late for work when we've got a murder case to solve."

Bridgette swiveled in her chair to face Hoffman and said, "I'm sorry, Detective. I was here until almost two this morning and overslept my alarm."

Hoffman exploded, "What the hell were you doing here at two a.m.?"

"I was working on the Travers' case. I—"

"I told you to go home. Are you insubordinate or just thick, Detective?"

"Neither. I was using my own initiative and on my own time. And it paid—"

"I'm not interested in your initiative, Detective. You're a university graduate with no experience and a lot to learn. We've got a murder investigation going on here. How do I know you're not going to miss things today because you haven't had enough sleep?"

Bridgette looked past Hoffman and could see eight other detectives in the homicide room now watching their exchange.

Keen to take it down a notch, Bridgette replied evenly, "I'm sorry, Detective, it won't happen again. I believe I used the time constructively. I—"

"How many days' worth of footage did you get through?"

"I didn't use the time last night to look at the footage. I went through NatTrack looking for similar open unsolved cases that might—"

Hoffman's features turned even darker as he said, "I told you yesterday what I wanted you to focus on. You've deliberately gone behind my back. Do you realize that—"

"Lance!"

Hoffman turned around to see Chief Delray standing in the middle of the Detectives' Room with his hands on his hips.

"I'll see you both in my office."

Without another word, Delray turned and walked away. Bridgette grabbed the notes she had taken the previous night and followed Delray back to his office. Neither of them spoke until Hoffman entered.

"Close the door behind you, Lance. If I'm going to play referee, we don't need the world listening in on this."

Delray waited until Hoffman was seated and then looked at each of them in turn from across his desk and said, "Someone mind explaining to me what that was all about?"

Bridgette looked at Hoffman as if she didn't have anything to say.

Delray clasped his hands together and leaned his elbows on his desk and calmly said, "Lance, I think you should go first."

"Chief, I'd like to raise a formal complaint about the professionalism of Detective Casseldhorf. She does not follow my directions, is insubordinate and is seeking to embarrass me in front of my work colleagues. This morning she was late to work and I—"

Delray held up his hand and said, "Sorry, Lance, but let me get this straight. You want to put in a formal, as in a written, complaint about your partner?"

Delray watched as Hoffman shifted in his seat.

"Why don't we see if we can talk this one through, Lance? Maybe we won't need the paperwork?"

Hoffman nodded and was about to continue, but Delray cut in again.

"I could hear most of the conversation from this office. From what I've heard, it appears Detective Casseldhorf worked through until around two a.m. and was twenty minutes late this morning?"

Hoffman replied, "That's correct, Chief."

Delray added, "And she was working on the Travers' case, but not on the surveillance video like you directed?"

Hoffman nodded again.

Delray looked at Bridgette.

"You didn't seem to be getting much of a word in out there, Detective, so you mind telling me your side of the story?"

Bridgette paused for a moment to collect her thoughts.

"First of all, Detective Hoffman is right. I was late for work and this is a murder case, so... I'm sorry—it won't happen again."

Delray nodded and looked at Hoffman as he said, "Apology noted."

Bridgette continued, "I worked through the first three days of the security footage of the florist shop where Monica Travers worked until after seven p.m. Detective Hoffman called in and we had a brief discussion at which point he told me to stop working on it and go home."

Delray looked across at Hoffman who nodded slightly confirming what Bridgette had said was correct. Delray looked back at Bridgette.

"Okay, go on."

"I got Chinese takeout and thought I would come back here for a while and search NatTrack to see if there were any matches for the word shovel or other similarities between this and other cases. I was able to—"

Delray interrupted, "Other cases? Yesterday we were talking about the killer maybe wanting his work discovered. What are we talking about now?"

Hoffman shook his head, "I'm sorry , Chief. Detective Casseldhorf jumped to a conclusion that if the killer deliberately buried the body so that it would be discovered, we now have a serial killer on our hands. I told her not to waste time on this nonsense because we don't solve murders sitting behind a computer."

Bridgette calmly replied before Delray could respond.

"With all due respect, Detective, what I said was if the killer deliberately orchestrated the burial so that the crime would be discovered, it implies another level of planning and potentially opens up a wider group of suspects."

Hoffman angrily replied, "And as I said yesterday, Detective, you've been on the job five minutes and have no idea what you're talking—"

Delray held up his hand again and said, "Timeout, Lance. We're running short on time here. Bridgette, you've got two minutes before Detective Hoffman and I have to be out of here. Assistant Commissioner Cunningham wants a meeting before the press conference where he's going to announce we've found the body of Monica Travers and that we now officially have a murder investigation."

Unfazed, Bridgette continued. "I need a lot more than two minutes to explain this properly, Chief, but for now, there are five unsolved murders—all committed in cities that match an emerging pattern that started three years ago. Female victims between seventeen and thirty-five, all buried in shallow graves. All victims have been stabbed or bludgeoned to death and all discovered within a few weeks of the murders. The other—"

Hoffman stared Bridgette down as he interrupted again. "That proves nothing, Detective. You and I both know murder victims are commonly buried in shallow graves and statistically, there are more young women murdered every year than any other group."

Bridgette held his stare and replied calmly, "There are several other pieces of information you need to know that are important parts of the pattern. First, I think these murders are occurring in pairs. I'll show you in more detail later, but for now, you need to know there are two murders in the one city—typically within months and sometimes even just weeks of each other. Second, the bodies are always buried in different geographic policing zones—so there's no chance of the same detectives investigating both crimes. Third, the bodies are all buried near public spaces where they are easily discovered. I'd appreciate you both looking at the data, but I'm almost convinced by the pattern that it's the same killer."

Hoffman stared back at Bridgette—his mouth partially open and speechless for the first time since they had been made partners. Delray was also silent for a moment as he contemplated what Bridgette had said.

Finally, he nodded and said, "Okay, Detective—I'm not sure how this fits with Monica Travers, but we'll go over it in more detail when we get back."

Delray got up from his chair and continued, "Right now your partner and I need to be up on the fourth floor for a meeting with the AC."

As he began to put his jacket on, he added, "There's one thing that doesn't make sense. You said the pattern was murders in pairs, but you've only identified five victims that fit the pattern. Shouldn't that be six victims?"

"It should, Chief. I have a theory about it, but it needs some further investigation."

Delray nodded and then motioned Hoffman to leave and added, "The three of us will continue this meeting as soon as we get back from the press conference. For now, don't breathe a word of it to anyone, not even your colleagues in the homicide room. This is the last thing we want the media getting a hold of."

Bridgette watched as Hoffman and Delray left the office. She stood there thinking for a moment about Delray's last question. The single murder victim had occurred in Vancouver three years earlier and had been investigated by none other than Hoffman himself. The case was one of very few that he had investigated that remained open and unsolved. She thought about the pattern again and wondered if she was jumping to the wrong conclusion. She thought about Delray's response to her briefing—he had listened, but his body language suggested he was also skeptical. She decided she would use the time until they returned searching through NatTrack for other information that could help bolster her theory.

Chapter 7

D elray hated press conferences. It wasn't just the overzealous journalists, the cameras, or the crowds. Mostly, he was concerned about what Assistant Commissioner Leon Cunningham would say. Cunningham had a long-established reputation for manipulating the media for personal gain. There were rumors circulating that he was planning a move into politics shortly and was now using every opportunity he could to get in front of a camera to build a profile as a tough, but caring senior law enforcement officer.

Delray had attended press conferences with Cunningham before but was rarely asked to speak. Cunningham would get all the facts in a meeting beforehand and then embellish and twist them to suit his own agenda in front of the cameras. Delray sometimes found it difficult being on the same podium when Cunningham manipulated the truth as much as he did. He preferred police officers to simply tell the truth or answer 'no comment'.

Today was no exception and Delray was glad when Cunningham finally stopped taking questions and the press conference was over. He was keen to get back to the homicide room and continue the discussion with Casseldhorf and Hoffman, but

Cunningham had other ideas and wanted a 'quick meeting' in his office.

Delray wasn't interested in hanging out with the media after the press conference and found himself waiting outside the AC's office while Cunningham finished pressing the flesh with a few remaining journalists in the Media Liaison Room.

Cunningham's secretary offered him coffee while he sat and waited in one of the plush leather armchairs in the reception area, but Delray politely declined. He had tried the secretary's bitter brew once before and decided it wasn't worth risking a second time.

He used the time while he waited to think about his meeting with Hoffman and Casseldhorf. It was clear Lance Hoffman felt threatened by the young detective's intellect. He would leave them together for now, but he didn't want any repeats of the scene Hoffman had created earlier that morning. He was confident Casseldhorf would take it in her stride, but with less than three months to go before he retired, he didn't want to see Hoffman embarrass himself any further or permanently sully his good reputation.

He shook his head in amazement as he thought about what Casseldhorf may have uncovered through NatTrack in such a short amount of time. Hoffman had mumbled something about 'maybe she got lucky' in reference to the pattern she had discovered with the five murder victims when they rode up in the elevator to the fourth floor. Delray hadn't said anything to Hoffman then, but he knew that wasn't the case. Casseldhorf had been put through a rigorous series of physical, physiological and intellectual assessments as part of the recruitment process and he had read the reports. She had an IQ of one-fifty-one, which put her in the MENSA league as a certified genius. She could have been anything she wanted but had chosen a career in law enforcement after a stint in the Navy ended unexpectedly.

His thoughts were interrupted as he saw the tall, slim figure of Assistant Commissioner Leon Cunningham striding up the wide corridor towards his office in full-service uniform, complete with medals. Cunningham had a preference for wearing business suits to work most days, but always kept the formal uniform in a cupboard in his private bathroom for media appearances. Still only in his early fifties, he kept his full head of silver hair at regulation police officer length and looked every bit the model police officer, but Delray knew better. More than one good colleague had been forced out of Vancouver's police force early because they had crossed Cunningham. Delray's strategy had always been to stay at arm's length and never let the man do him any favors. He had seen two colleagues put into compromising situations when Cunningham had asked for something in return later.

Cunningham ignored Delray as he walked past, and after pausing briefly to whisper something to his secretary, disappeared into his office. Minutes later the secretary's phone rang. She didn't bother to pick it up, but looked up at Delray instead and said, "You can go in now."

Delray thanked her and walked through to Cunningham's office. The fourth floor of the Vancouver Metro building had recently been refurbished and the entire east wing of the floor was now dedicated to the police executive. Cunningham's office was now twice the size it had been previously and included a plush range of timber and glass furnishings. It was almost the size of his team's homicide room which currently housed twelve detectives. Delray was glad none of his team ever got to see inside this office—there was no way to explain away the contrast in working conditions between the hardworking police officers and the senior executives who he considered nothing more than bureaucrats.

Now dressed in a normal business suit, Cunningham looked up from a newspaper he was reading and motioned Delray to sit down on the opposite side of a highly polished wooden desk that was twice the size of most family dining room tables.

"I won't keep you long, Chief Inspector, you've got a killer to catch."

After Delray was seated, Cunningham held up the morning newspaper. The front page showed a picture of Monica Travers with a headline that indicated the woman's disappearance was going to be upgraded to a murder investigation.

"Right now, the Monica Travers' murder is headline news and probably will stay that way for the foreseeable future. You can't pick up a newspaper or go onto any Vancouver news website or TV program without it being front and center news. You're bright enough to know the public is watching what we are doing and expecting results quickly."

Delray nodded but didn't say anything. He'd found from experience that it was best to let Cunningham do the talking.

"We need a team on this. I want this killer caught and caught soon. As of now, this is your top priority. I want six of your most experienced officers assigned to this immediately. Hoffman can lead the team, but I want you to stay close to everyone and everything that happens. You've got seventy-two hours, but I want you up here each morning for a short briefing, and if you get any sort of significant breakthrough, I'm to be informed immediately. Are we clear?"

Delray knew the 'breakthroughs' that Cunningham was

referring to were anything he could use to hold an impromptu press conference to further raise his profile.

Delray kept his response brief and nodded as he answered, "Perfectly clear, Sir."

Cunningham's face creased into a frown. Delray had seen this look before and knew trouble was coming.

"I was given a briefing on Friday about the placements for the new graduates—six in total. The one which is currently assigned to the homicide team caught my eye."

"She's very smart, Sir. I think with time she is—"

"It's not her results that caught my eye, Detective. It's her last name..."

Delray instantly knew where this was going. He was not about to say anything he didn't need to and waited for Cunningham to continue.

Cunningham almost spat out the name, "Casseldhorf?"

Delray nodded, "That's correct, Sir. Bridgette Casseldhorf in fact."

"Tell me she's not related... tell me we've done our due diligence here?"

"I wasn't involved in the selection process, Sir, but from what I gather, she is, in fact, the daughter of Peter Casseldhorf."

Cunningham leaned back in his chair and shook his head slightly.

"How is it, that Vancouver Metropolitan Police—with all its recruitment security checks and balances, winds up hiring the daughter of a murderer—one of our own no less?"

Delray had no answer for this but knew from experience that answers like 'I don't know,' or 'that has nothing to do with me' were not tolerated by the AC. He considered the question for a moment before he replied.

"Sir, I guess recruitment were just following the Commissioners' guidelines. The opportunity is there for everyone to apply as long as you don't personally have a criminal record and meet all the mandatory education requirements."

Cunningham frowned and replied, "If I didn't know better, I'd say you're starting to believe all that politically correct crap on our website. You've been around here longer than I have and know that this place only works when cops respect and trust one another. How is that going to happen when we have a trainee running around whose father, a former cop no less, is still wanted for fraud and a murder he committed twenty years ago?"

Delray had no answer but was not about to sell Bridgette out.

"Sir, with all due respect, Detective Casseldhorf is extremely intelligent—MENSA level in fact. She hasn't seen her father since he disappeared and has grown up under difficult circumstances with her aunt, which—"

Cunningham interrupted. "You forget I used to be part of internal affairs. I know all about Bridgette Casseldhorf. I personally supervised putting her and her aunt into witness protection following the murder of her mother. We all presume her father is dead, but until I see the body of Peter Casseldhorf up close and personal, I'm not presuming anything, and I certainly don't want his daughter running around here and being open to compromise."

Delray knew there was no way he would win the argument and sat fuming but said nothing further. Somehow, Bridgette would need to prove her worth to Vancouver Metro before her probationary review came up, otherwise, Cunningham would have his way.

Cunningham said, "We're done for now. I want Casseldhorf's access to all computing systems suspended immediately. I'll be writing to the Commissioner later this morning
recommending her probation be terminated. We can't have
Vancouver Metro open to such compromise. Until you hear
more from me, she is to be closely watched."

Cunningham waited for a response, but Delray said nothing.

"Are we in agreement here, Chief Inspector?"

There was a lot running through Delray's mind, most
of which had to do with how he would explain this to his
young detective and what would he need to do to protect her
job. Up until now, he had always played the diplomat with
Cunningham, but today was different.

With no attempt to hide his displeasure, Delray replied, "Sir,
you've made your position very clear. If there's nothing else,
I've got a murderer to catch."

As Delray went to rise from his chair, Cunningham held up
his hand.

He held Delray's stare for several seconds and then said in a
quiet voice, "Be very careful, Chief Inspector, she's not worth
your career."

Delray considered Cunningham's threat for a moment before deciding there was nothing to be gained from getting into
an argument he couldn't win.

He rose from his chair and said, "I'll contact you immediately if we get any significant breakthrough."

Without waiting for a reply, Delray turned and walked out
of the office.

Chapter 8

Delray sat at his desk fuming as he thought about Cunningham and what he had been directed to do. To be targeting Bridgette like this because of her father was close to paranoia. She had much to offer, and he planned to do everything in his power to prevent her dismissal.

He looked down at his phone and knew he should be calling Hoffman and Bridgette back into his office to continue their meeting. Delray let out a long sigh and got up from his desk and walked across to his office window. He thought about how he was going to explain to Bridgette that he had to take away her computer access as he stared out into the car park. There was no way he could hide what was really going on—Bridgette would know immediately if he was not being straight with her.

Delray watched two uniform police officers drive towards the boom gate in a blue and white Vancouver Metro patrol car. He remembered the motto—'Keep our city safe'—that had been drilled into him as a young probationary constable. He increasingly wondered what it meant as policing seemed to be getting more political by the day. He couldn't blame the rank and file for being overly cautious about what they said and did in the line of duty when guys like Cunningham occupied senior positions.

He returned to his desk, and with a few practiced keystrokes on his keyboard, brought up the confidential file of his star recruit on his computer. He wasn't sure if reading her file again would help any, but he knew he needed to know as much as he could about her if he were to have any chance of saving her career.

Vancouver Metro had a policy of only recruiting uniform police. Everyone who rose to the rank of detective or above had started out life as a uniform police officer, serving three years before being considered for promotion. There were exceptions, however, and every year for the past five years they had employed a handful of the brightest university graduates directly into forensic or detective roles. He remembered skim reading Bridgette's file along with the files of the other applicants during this recruitment process. He was time poor and had mainly gone on the recommendation of Vancouver Metro's recruitment section and his gut instincts from the interviews he had sat in on. He remembered reading her assessment grading. She had excelled in all physical, psychological and intellectual aptitude tests and had attained a score of eight hundred and eighty-two out of a possible perfect score of nine hundred. Nobody he could remember had ever scored higher than the low eight hundreds before Bridgette and he had jumped at the opportunity to have someone this capable on his team.

Delray read the summary information again and then clicked on a screen tab that took him to past employment history. He knew Bridgette had left the navy with an honorable discharge, but from her own admission, the circumstances had been less than ideal. He knew Cunningham would be

58

looking for any dirt he could find against Bridgette and figured this would be an area he would target.

He spent the next ten minutes reading her past employment history. It mainly centered around a three-year term in the Navy after graduating with an engineering degree. Delray was impressed by her naval career—she had topped her class in officer training school and had become a Navy and then state champion in martial arts by the age of twenty-two. Delray continued to read through the notes and found that she had been a rising star in the Navy until there had been an incident with a senior naval official which ultimately ended her career. The incident wasn't spelled out in any detail, which Delray found frustrating. Her psychological assessment contained the usual psychobabble that Delray found difficult to understand. He re-read the text several times and was fairly confident the psychologist was using a lot of fancy words to say Bridgette was mentally sane and had the required mental constitution for police work.

Delray took his glasses off and pushed back from his desk. He wasn't normally one to pry into the private lives of his detectives—what they were before they joined Vancouver Metro was of no concern to him, provided they passed all the entry criteria. But the incident bothered him. He knew enough about Cunningham to know that this was potentially something he would use against Bridgette. He decided he needed to go on the front foot if he were to have any chance of saving her career and picked up the phone and dialed her desk extension.

After waiting a moment, the phone was answered.

"Bridgette, it's the Chief. I need to see you in my office right away."

Moments later both Bridgette and Hoffman appeared at his doorway. Delray looked up and shook his head.

"Sorry, Lance, this isn't about the murder. I'll call you in shortly."

Delray watched as Bridgette came through the door on her own.

"Close the door, Bridgette, and have a seat."

Delray waited until Bridgette sat down. Her face was impassive—if she was anxious or curious, he couldn't read it. Clasping his hands together, Delray looked down at his desk for a moment as he tried to figure out how he was going to break the news to her. He decided to go with the direct approach as he looked up.

"Bridgette, we have a situation."

He went on to explain what happened in the press conference and then the private meeting he had been asked to attend with Cunningham. Delray paused for a moment to scratch his head before he continued.

"That's when it turned ugly... The AC started asking questions about why Vancouver Metro recruited you when your father is still wanted for murder. I tried to tell him the recruitment process is impartial and that you're a valuable asset to the department, but he wasn't listening."

Bridgette tried to hide her anger as she replied, "So, I'm being fired?"

Delray let out a breath and said, "Not immediately. Cunningham is going to write to the Commissioner today with a recommendation that you're unsuitable for permanent appointment. He's going to justify it on the grounds that until your father is arrested or confirmed as dead, you're open to unacceptable compromise."

The room was silent for a moment as Bridgette thought through what Delray had just said. Delray could see her struggling to control her anger and felt sorry for her.

"Bridgette, you have every right to be angry—incredibly angry in fact. If you need to blow off some steam, the door's closed and I wouldn't blame you—"

"I don't understand how I got through a recruitment process that took six months, and they now decide I'm unsuitable?"

"It's not the recruitment process, Bridgette. It's just one man who holds a very senior position within the organization."

The room was silent again. Delray looked at Bridgette. She was clearly upset but remained composed with her gaze fixed on Delray.

"All is not lost, Bridgette. Cunningham doesn't always get his way, regardless of his power and position. We need to play this smart and maybe, just maybe, we can win."

Bridgette nodded but didn't look convinced.

"What do you want me to do, Chief?"

Delray thought for a moment.

"I have to take your computer access away, but that's all I've been instructed to do."

He paused for a moment to study Bridgette. She looked to have turned a little pale with the news, but he thought she was holding up well—so far.

"You're still free to come and go and take part in the investigation. We need to work the Travers' case hard over the next couple of days, Bridgette. If we can solve this crime quickly, it will go a long way to seeing my recommendation has enough weight that Cunningham's will be ignored, or at least force a meeting with the Commissioner himself."

Delray scratched his chin and thought again before he continued.

"We can keep your computer access for another twenty-four hours. The computer guy here that looks after my team is on leave today. I'll send the request to formally suspend your access only to him. He won't action it until he returns tomorrow, but if Cunningham asks, I can say the request has been formally made."

Bridgette nodded but didn't say anything.

As if reading her thoughts, Delray continued. "I will get one of the other team members to sit with you from tomorrow onwards. We can use their login credentials to access NatTrack. We won't be breaking any rules unless Cunningham gives me further instructions. I intend to keep as far away from him as I can so that can't happen."

Bridgette nodded.

"Would it be easier if I just resigned, Chief?"

Delray shook his head.

"It wouldn't be right. I've been doing this for over thirty years, and the right way is never easy."

Delray studied Bridgette again for a moment. Her anger had dissipated, and her face looked impassive—he didn't find her easy to read.

"Do you want to fight this, Bridgette?"

"I don't want to get anyone into trouble."

"It's all part of the job, Bridgette. I think for now the best thing we can do is keep going with the investigation. I'm not going to pretend it's going to take your mind off what's happening much, but at least you can be working on things you can influence."

"I'm keen to help for as long as I can, Chief."

Delray grimaced and said, "There's something else we need to talk about."

"Okay..."

Delray pointed at his computer screen and said, "I've been reading your file. Cunningham is going to be looking for any dirt he can find on you. I've gotta say it all looks very impressive... Except for one thing in the psychologist's report."

Bridgette paused for a moment to compose herself and then replied, "The incident when I was in the Navy?"

Delray said, "Yes," and shifted slightly in his chair before continuing.

"Bridgette, between you and me, Cunningham's paranoid, plain and simple. He's the most risk adverse senior officer in Vancouver Metro, and nothing he does surprises me. You don't have to tell me—it's before your time here at Vancouver Metro but having some background might help if it comes up."

In a quiet voice, Bridgette responded, "It's okay, Chief. I have nothing to hide."

Bridgette let out a deep breath and continued. "Just before my eighteenth birthday, my aunt had a heart attack and died in hospital three days later. To cut a long story short, I graduated high school with good grades, but with no family and money, my options were limited. I got a Naval scholarship and completed an engineering degree and then shipped out to sea as a junior officer. I enjoyed life in the Navy until the night of the incident when it all changed..."

Delray was shocked to see tears welling in Bridgette's eyes.

"Bridgette, if this is too personal, we don't have to go on."

Bridgette shook her head as she composed herself.

"I have nothing to be ashamed of—I just don't talk about this very often, and it's hard to relive."

Delray was not sure where this was headed and said, "You can stop at any time, okay?"

Bridgette closed her eyes and tilted her head back slightly.

"My third ship posting was to a smaller vessel which was mainly used for reconnaissance and recovery. It had a crew of eighty..."

She hesitated for a moment and then continued in a quieter voice.

"We'd been at sea for four days. It was about one in the morning, and I was up on the bridge with the commanding officer. His name's not important, but he was one of the few men I'd met in the Navy that I never really trusted. I was piloting the ship when he came up behind me and grabbed my breasts. He asked me how I liked to do it and I turned around and pushed him away and told him he was out of line..."

Delray watched as Bridgette paused for a moment to take a few deep breaths. He began to understand why the psychologist had chosen not to put any of the details on her file. After she regained her composure, she continued, still with her eyes closed.

"He laughed and locked the door to the bridge and said we can do this the easy way or the hard way. I told him to back off, but he pushed me to the ground and tried to reach up under my uniform to rip off my panties."

Bridgette opened her eyes. Delray could see her strong resolve returning as she continued.

"He slapped me hard across the face when I resisted, and I kicked him in the chest. I got to my feet while he caught his breath and I warned him to stay away but he came at me again. I caught him with two spin kicks. The first one dislocated his left elbow and the second broke two of his ribs."

Delray's eyes widened, but he couldn't think of anything suitable to say in response.

Bridgette continued, "I never put out any signals to him or anyone else on the ship that I was remotely interested. I was just there to do my job and learn as much as I could... It's the only time I've ever had to use my martial arts training to actually defend myself."

Delray frowned and shook his head. "Bridgette, I don't know what to say, other than I'm really sorry."

Bridgette shrugged and said, "I put in a formal complaint when we got back to base, but it went nowhere. His word against mine. He told the inquiry I tripped and fell, and I attacked him when he tried to help me up. The fact that I had no physical injuries and he had two broken ribs and an arm in a sling didn't help my cause."

"So what happened?"

"Unofficially, I was told my career in the Navy was over and that I would never be promoted. My lawyer negotiated an honorable discharge, a counselor for as long as I needed and a scholarship to undertake further studies."

Delray nodded but didn't say anything. His respect for Bridgette Casseldhorf was growing by the minute as he listened to her recount her harrowing story with honesty and poise.

"After I left the Navy, I had some counseling for a while. It was good for me in the beginning and helped me work through a lot of my pain and frustration. In the end, I was just left with disappointment."

Bridgette let out a short laugh as tears began to well in her eyes again.

"My counselor was a raging feminist and when it came time to choose my next career path, she tried to get me to join the cause, but it just wasn't for me. I always felt my father's profession was honorable..."

"And that's when you decided on Criminology?"

Bridgette nodded.

"I think I can make a difference, Chief—if I'm given a chance."

"I know you can, Bridgette. We just have to figure out a way to get through this situation with Cunningham."

Delray could see Bridgette looked slightly drained from having to relive the experience.

In a gentle voice, he said, "Bridgette, I know that must have been hard, and I hope you never have to speak of it again. If it ever comes up, I can say I've discussed it with you and have full confidence that it won't impact your work here."

"Thanks, Chief, I appreciate the support."

"Why don't we take a ten-minute break and then reconvene with Detective Hoffman? I'm keen to continue going over what you discovered last night and how it may be related to the Travers' case."

Bridgette got up without another word and headed for the door. Delray knew it was going to be hard for her to stay focused with what she had hanging over her head. He watched her walk out of his office and thought about what she had been through. He admired her resolve and hoped this chapter in her life would turn out better than the last.

He didn't think she had made many friends within Vancouver Metro yet and knew he couldn't rely on Hoffman to give her support—that was something he would need to do as her boss and mentor. As painful as it was, he was glad Bridgette had felt comfortable enough to share the incident with him. He had no doubt that Cunningham would look for ways to twist what happened to suit his own agenda if he ever found out.

He sighed as he picked up the phone to call Hoffman. There was little more they could do right now except get on with the Travers' case and wait and see what unfolded. Hoffman answered after three rings.

"Lance, I need you in here right away. The Travers' case is getting very political and we're going to have to change our approach if we don't want this to blow up in our face."

Chapter 9

Bridgette needed a few minutes before she was ready to return to Delray's office. Going over the attempted rape incident hadn't been easy and had re-surfaced a lot of unpleasant memories she had been hoping to permanently put behind her. She was confident Delray was someone she could trust and hoped the incident wouldn't be twisted and used against her by anyone else.

Still in shock from the news that Cunningham wanted her off the force, she had walked downstairs to the police cafeteria and had spent the next fifteen minutes sitting at a small table in a far corner of the austere, poorly lit facility contemplating what she would do next. The cafeteria was fitted out with cheap metal furniture and hardly the place to come if you needed to lift your spirits. But it was quiet at that time of day and gave her some time on her own to think. As she sat sipping a peppermint tea, she contemplated quitting on the spot, but quickly dismissed the idea. She would fight, just as she had done in the Navy, and only walk away if she was forced to.

By the time she had finished her tea, she realized she had very few options. If Cunningham really wanted her out, it was only a matter of time unless she could prove her worth. As she got up from the table, she decided she would continue to do everything she could to help Delray and Hoffman with the Travers' case. If they could bring the killer to justice quickly, hopefully, that would be enough to persuade the probation board that she was worth keeping.

Bridgette used the short walk back up the flight of stairs to compose herself. She did her best to mentally force what was hanging over her to the back of her mind as she walked into Delray's office.

Hoffman, who was sitting across the desk from Delray, stopped speaking and looked at her with a scowl.

"You're late, Detective Casseldhorf. Do I need to remind you that we've got—"

Delray held up his hand and said, "Slow down, Lance," before looking at Bridgette.

"Bridgette, I haven't mentioned any of our conversation to Detective Hoffman, but I think for the sake of the investigation, I need to explain to him in general terms what happened this morning?"

Bridgette could see Delray was waiting for her reply before he continued.

She nodded and then added, "Sorry, I needed a break," as she sat down.

Delray turned back to Hoffman and said, "We have a problem with Cunningham."

Delray went on to briefly explain Cunningham's concerns and how he wanted Bridgette out of Vancouver Metro as soon as possible. She was thankful Delray didn't mention anything about the incident when she was in the Navy. Hoffman surprised her as he shook his head in disgust.

"How does a guy as incompetent as Cunningham get to be

in a position where he can play God with people's careers?"

Delray replied tactfully, "That's not a question we have time to answer now, Lance," and then looked across at Bridgette.

"Are you ready to continue, Bridgette? If so, I'd like to pick up with where we left off with your discoveries from NatTrack."

Bridgette replied, "I'm ready."

Delray settled back in his chair and said, "Okay, we're all ears."

Bridgette started with a brief recap of what she had said earlier and explained that NatTrack currently showed eleven unsolved murder cases. She emphasized it was only a theory, but she was suspicious about the number of similarities she had found in the murder cases of the young women. Delray and Hoffman both listened without interrupting.

"Around midnight, I'd read through the summaries on all eleven case files. There were nine of them that looked like they were possibly connected and I focused on them for the next two hours. At two a.m., I decided I needed to go home—I wasn't thinking straight anymore, and I didn't want to miss anything. But, by then, I was satisfied I had found an emerging pattern for at least five of the murders."

Delray leaned forward in his chair and said, "The pattern being two women are murdered within months of each other in the one city and buried in shallow graves, but never in the same police jurisdiction?"

Bridgette was impressed with Delray's conciseness.

"Yes, and all victims buried in locations where they would be discovered."

Hoffman still didn't look convinced and asked, "So what happened to the sixth victim? According to your theory, the murders happen in pairs, so aren't we one body short?"

"I haven't had a chance to look any further into what happened here in Vancouver, but—"

Hoffman shot back, "Vancouver?"

Bridgette nodded and said, "There was a murder of a young woman here in Vancouver three years ago that fits the pattern. I haven't found anything to suggest another murder has taken place that matches the pattern, but it's possible the body of the sixth victim is still buried and has never been discovered. Or, it's also entirely possible the sixth murder never took place."

Hoffman fired back, "So, don't we have a rather large hole in your theory, Detective."

Bridgette replied evenly, "If the killer meticulously plans each crime to avoid being caught, he may have aborted an attempt if he thought his risk of discovery was too high. Or, maybe he tried to go through with it and didn't succeed?"

Delray added, "It will be easy enough to go back through our files for any cases of missing persons or assaults that occurred about three years ago."

Bridgette and Delray both watched Hoffman roll his eyes—it was clear Hoffman was not convinced.

Ignoring Hoffman's protest, Delray said to Bridgette, "While you were out of the office, Lance and I explored some options for how we work this case. We're going to cop some heat over the next couple of days and, as you well know, not just from the media. Cunningham wants a team of six on this and made it perfectly clear this has to be our top priority."

Looking across at Hoffman, Delray continued, "He's happy for you to lead the investigation, Lance, so I'm going to assign four of my team to you."

Delray rattled off the names of the detectives to Hoffman

and then looked back at Bridgette. "Cunningham wants you supervised. I can't ignore the request, but this discovery of a possible pattern needs further investigation, so I'm going to assign Bates to work with you."

Bridgette nodded. Charlie Bates was in his late twenties and seemed to be a reasonable guy. He had transferred into Homicide about six months earlier after spending most of his career hunting down computer fraud. He was considered the 'IT Geek' of the homicide room and Bridgette had a feeling there was no coincidence with Delray's selection.

"Bates and you will work NatTrack together. Find out everything you can about these other cases and what their current status is. If there is a definite link to the Travers' case, it's a game changer and Cunningham will want to know all the details before he goes anywhere near the media."

Delray paused for a moment and looked at Hoffman.

"You've been quiet for thirty-seconds, Lance. Are you okay with all of this?"

Hoffman didn't look happy, but responded, "I'll go and get the teams organized, Felix."

Delray held up his hand to stop Hoffman leaving.

"I don't need to remind you both how sensitive this is. I want everyone involved to assemble in the muster room in fifteen minutes to go through the case and what everyone's role and responsibility will be."

Delray paused long enough to eyeball both of his detectives.

"I can't stress how important it is that we don't talk about the serial killer angle out loud to anyone outside the team. Hopefully, there's no connection to the Travers' case and we can put this one to bed within the next forty-eight hours. Any questions?"

Bridgette had a few about how and where she would work with Bates but figured Delray would make that clear in the muster room and shook her head.

Delray continued. "All right, I'll see you both in fifteen. Lance, I'll leave it to you to assemble the troops."

Hoffman nodded and walked out of the office.

Bridgette made a move to follow Hoffman, but Delray motioned her to stay a moment. Bridgette watched as her boss searched for words.

"Bridgette, I'm not sure what else I can say or tell you right now about Cunningham—other than to go about your job as best you can and know that I've got your back. If anything changes, you'll be the first to know."

Bridgette appreciated Delray's concern. She had never worked with anyone who was as supportive and appreciated Delray's confidence in her.

She wasn't sure how she should respond and simply said, "Thanks," and then headed for the door.

Once outside, she was surprised to see Hoffman waiting for her. She steeled herself for another rude tirade from the man she was beginning to dislike intensely, but it never came.

Hoffman looked up and down the corridor to make sure he wasn't being overheard and said, "Detective, I have no idea what this thing with Cunningham is, and frankly it's none of my business."

Bridgette nodded as Hoffman continued.

"You don't need me to tell you you're on shaky ground right now, but here's one piece of free advice."

Hoffman paused and pointed back at Delray's office before he continued, "Over the years, Felix Delray has saved the careers of more than one detective here—me included. I suggest you do exactly as he says if you want to stay on here—he's your best and only hope."

Before Bridgette had a chance to respond, Hoffman turned on his heel and walked off. Bridgette watched the large burly detective walk to the end of the corridor, not entirely sure what to make of the conversation. His tone was still a long way from friendly, but the sentiment suggested despite his crustiness, in a strange way he was looking out for her.

Bridgette sighed and walked back into the homicide room. As she walked through the drab room with its antiquated metal office furniture toward her desk, she wondered whether she would still be working there at the end of the week.

Chapter 10

I t was well after six p.m. and Bridgette needed a break. She leaned back in her chair and rolled her head slightly to release the tension in her neck muscles before looking across at Charlie Bates. Delray had given them control of a small meeting room next to the homicide office and they had spent the last five hours using their laptops to review the five unsolved murder cases in NatTrack.

Bridgette got up from her chair and walked across to the meeting room's whiteboard. They had written up everything they had found of significance with each case in the hope of finding more points in common that would help them identify the killer. Bridgette continued to massage her neck muscles as she studied the board.

They had used the left-hand side of the board to record everything they had found in common about each murder. Other than everything she had learned the night before; they had only added another two other points. All women had dark shoulder length hair and were Caucasian. She knew every clue helped to strengthen the pattern, but they were still a long way from discovering anything that would help lead them to the killer.

She focused on all the cryptic notes that they had written on the right-hand side from their case reviews. All but one of the women were single and they had a range of professions from student to lawyer. Bates had written the heights of each woman on the board a few minutes ago. Bridgette noticed the height of each woman was slightly above average, not particularly tall like a basketball player, but still taller than average. She thought it might be meaningful and circled the heights with a marker and then looked down at Bates, who continued to pound away at his keyboard, totally oblivious to her presence.

Even though he was almost thirty, Bates could easily pass for someone ten years younger. His thick, dark-rimmed glasses, disheveled light mousy hair and a bad case of dandruff all helped reinforce the stereotype that the tall and gangly detective was a computer nerd just out of college. If his rumpled suit, that was at least one size too big for him, was anything to go by, Bridgette suspected dandruff control, like the rest of his appearance, was not a priority.

She had barely spoken more than a handful of words to him prior to today and still didn't know much about him, other than he was highly intelligent and seemed more at ease in front of a computer screen than with people.

Bridgette stopped massaging her neck and said, "Are you ready for a break, Charlie?"

Bates absently replied, "Yes," without looking up.

He stopped what he was doing to read his screen for a moment before getting up from his chair to come over to the whiteboard. Bridgette handed him the whiteboard marker and watched as he wrote the words 'single' and 'tickets' on the right-hand side of the board. She studied the two words as

Bates handed back the marker.

Bates stepped back from the board and said, "I've been reading through the Michelle Wilson file—the second victim in Rochford. She was the airline clerk."

Bridgette nodded.

"She was the only one who was married."

Bates shook his head as he replied, "Technically she was still married, but according to the police statement taken from her husband, they had separated some months before she was murdered. The husband called the police and reported her as a missing person when she failed to turn up to pick up their daughter from a parenting visit on the Sunday she disappeared. So, although she was married, she had no partner at the time of her murder."

Bridgette nodded and underlined the word 'single' on the whiteboard as she asked, "And tickets?"

Bates shrugged and replied, "I was reading through the statements from her friends. One of the last people to talk to her by phone before she went missing said she was going to pick up free tickets for a concert and promised she would call back later—but the call never came."

Bridgette frowned.

Bates asked, "Problem?"

Bridgette replied, "Maybe," as she sat down at her laptop again.

Using a few quick keystrokes, Bridgette brought up the file for one of the other murder victims and began explaining what she was doing as she skim read the witness statements.

"Bonita Sargent was one of the victims who lived in Bolton. She was the school teacher—aged twenty-three when she was..."

Bridgette stopped talking as she continued to read. Bates watched without interrupting.

After a few moments, Bridgette stopped reading and said, "I think we might have found something, Charlie. Bonita Sargent was due to attend the ballet with a fellow teacher on the night she disappeared. When she didn't show up, it was her friend who raised the alarm."

Bridgette pointed to her laptop and continued.

"This is the friend's witness statement. Bonita had won some sort of competition... the tickets were free."

* * *

Delray called out to Hoffman, who was currently talking with two of his detectives, as he followed Bridgette through the homicide room.

"Lance, Bridgette may be onto something. I think you need to hear this."

Hoffman frowned and then followed Bridgette and Delray back into the small meeting room. Bridgette waited until they were all seated around the meeting table before closing the door.

"Charlie and I have made some progress with the murder pattern of the five victims. We're both now positive that at least some, if not all of these women, were killed by the same man."

Bridgette went on to provide a brief summary of what they had written on the left-hand side of the whiteboard and focused on the additional information they had uncovered about all the women being Caucasian with shoulder length dark brown hair and all being slightly taller than average.

Hoffman didn't look convinced and said as much.

"Detective, most women in this country are Caucasian and have brown hair. This really doesn't—"

Bridgette held up her hand and politely said, "Excuse me, Detective, it would be better if you hear me out before you pass judgment."

Delray smiled to himself as he quickly glanced sideways at Hoffman who was now fuming. He was beginning to think Hoffman had finally met his match.

Bridgette picked up the whiteboard marker and underlined the word 'tickets' on the board.

"The last person to talk to Michelle Wilson before she disappeared said she was on her way to get free tickets to something—exactly what we don't know. Bonita Sargent was due to attend the ballet with a fellow teacher when she disappeared. She had won a competition... the tickets were free."

Bridgette expected Hoffman to fire back with another volley of insults, but the aging detective sat motionless, staring at the whiteboard.

Delray had also expected Hoffman to come back with an argument and turned to him and said, "Lance?"

Hoffman let out a long breath and said, "I interviewed Monica's parents earlier today. We went through everything they could remember about her movements over the last week. On the day she disappeared, she had rung her mother earlier in the day to say she was going to be a few minutes late getting home."

Hoffman looked directly at Delray and continued, "She'd won free tickets to a concert and was going to pick them up after work."

Chapter 11

The small workroom fell quiet for a moment as Bridgette, Delray, and Bates contemplated what Hoffman had just shared.

Delray broke the silence and said, "There are too many similarities to ignore. Two victims getting free tickets might be a coincidence, but not three."

Delray looked at Hoffman and said, "Lance?"

Hoffman responded, "We can't ignore the patterns in the evidence Bridgette has uncovered."

Bridgette took note of Hoffman's use of her first name. It was the first time she could recall him referring to her as anything other than 'Detective'. She wondered if Hoffman was finally starting to respect her as the room fell silent again.

Delray got to his feet and said, "Okay, I think we're all in agreement that until we discover evidence to the contrary, Monica Travers' murder could very well be the work of a serial killer."

Delray paused to looked at his watch and said, "I have to call Cunningham on this straight away. He's not going to like it because the media's going to have a field day with it, but—"

Hoffman interrupted, "Shouldn't we spend a bit more time

on this, Felix? To make absolutely sure first?"

Delray shook his head as he answered, "If Cunningham finds out we've left him in the dark, even for a short period, our careers will all be in the toilet. We can't sit on this—Cunningham needs to know so that he can brief the Commissioner. They're going to have to figure out if and when they tell the media."

Delray looked at each of them in turn and said, "We could lose control of this very quickly if we're not careful. If this is the work of some sort of serial killer and he's operating in multiple states, it's going to attract the attention of the Feds whether we like it or not. The best hope we have of solving this ourselves is to move quickly with the new evidence. I think we can buy the team a couple of days at most, but after that, we're most likely going to wind up working as part of a national task force."

Hoffman added, "In other words, we become the local grunts, while the federal boys and girls get all the glory."

Delray ignored the gripe—he knew Hoffman was right, but it was out of his control.

"I need to go and make some calls. Cunningham will have left for the day already, so it might take me a while to track him down."

Delray paused for a moment to look at Bates.

"Charlie, you're across the five cases, so I want you to go and start writing a briefing report. Cunningham will want something to put on the Commissioner's desk when he gets in at seven o'clock in the morning."

Delray headed for the door and as an afterthought turned and looked back at Bridgette and Hoffman.

Raising his eyebrows slightly, he said, "Obviously, you two

are going to have to figure out a way to work together on this...
"

Bridgette and Hoffman watched Delray and Bates leave the meeting room. An awkward silence descended on the room. Bridgette decided it would be wise to let Hoffman speak first and waited.

Hoffman continued to stare at the mass of notes written on the whiteboard and said, "I've only ever worked with the Feds twice. Both cases were straightforward and should have been solved in weeks, but they turned into train wrecks because of the politics."

Hoffman turned and faced Bridgette. "By comparison, working with you, Detective, is a pleasant experience."

Bridgette replied, "I'm not sure how to take that?"

Hoffman leaned back slightly in his chair and replied, "I'd take it as a compliment. For what it's worth, I think you're an opinionated pain in the ass. You don't accept anything that anyone tells you at face value and you have this extremely annoying habit of wanting to follow your gut instincts... It makes you almost perfect for the job."

Bridgette nodded as Hoffman continued, "Good detectives have to push the boundaries. It's not how you get promotions, but it is how we get justice for people like Monica Travers."

Hoffman clasped his hands behind his head as he returned his gaze to the whiteboard. "I'm not looking forward to the Feds coming in on this. If the Chief can buy us another two days, we need to do everything we can to make them count."

Bridgette replied, "How can I help?"

Hoffman let out a deep sigh and then grimaced.

"We've got a team of seven—until we're told otherwise, I think you and Bates need to continue your research in

NatTrack. Find out everything you can about the witnesses in each case and the friends that were close to the victims. I'll get the guys to start making contact with each of them—even fly them to Bolton and Rochford to personally interview them if necessary.

Before today, nobody knew anything about the tickets thing. We find out whether any of the other victims also got free tickets and we might learn something else about the killer."

Hoffman turned and looked at Bridgette again. He held her gaze, almost as if he was studying her before he spoke again. "You don't need me to tell you you're very intelligent, Detective. A team of ten men could have spent a month on this and probably still wouldn't be this far along in the investigation."

Bridgette was slightly taken aback by the compliment, but recovered quickly. "Thank you—coming from you, that means something."

Hoffman replied, "Don't be telling anyone outside that I said that because I'll deny it."

Bridgette nodded but didn't respond. Hoffman got up and walked over to the whiteboard.

He studied it for a few moments. "They're all white and slightly above average height. You can't help but think that's important to him..."

While still looking at the whiteboard Hoffman continued, "You do any profiling subjects in your degree?"

"Three."

Without taking his eyes off the whiteboard, Hoffman asked, "What does all this tell you about the killer then?"

Bridgette looked at the whiteboard, somewhat surprised that Hoffman was seeking her opinion.

"He's obviously very intelligent—that much is clear if you can plan and carry out this many murders without being caught. The fact that all the women are similar looking is telling."

"Meaning?"

Bridgette massaged her neck muscles again and said, "It's hard to be certain, but it looks like he's either got very specific tastes, or they are symbolic."

"Symbolic?"

"Some serial killers act out a fantasy every time they kill someone. The victim is sometimes picked on looks alone to make the fantasy as real as possible."

"Like he's killing the same person over and over again?"

"Yes."

Hoffman scratched his chin. "It's like looking for a needle in a haystack if the killer picks his victims purely on looks."

"Maybe..."

Hoffman turned to look at Bridgette. "Maybe?"

"If we can figure out how he selects his victims and how he dupes them with free tickets, maybe the haystack isn't quite so large?"

Chapter 12

Bridgette felt slightly guilty as she withdrew the printed copy of her mother's murder file from the large manila envelope. Delray had called her into his office at around seven p.m. as he was getting ready to leave and told her she needed to go home and get a decent night's sleep. They had talked a little about the Monica Travers' case on the way down to the basement parking lot and Delray had surprised her by handing over the envelope as they had walked to their cars.

She had been touched by his words, "You're going to lose your computer access tomorrow Bridgette, so I printed you a copy of everything on the computer from your mother's murder file. It's not much, but at least it's a start."

She had resisted the temptation to open the file before she got home and had gone straight to the gym for an overdue workout. She liked to train three or four times a week to keep in shape and had deliberately pushed herself tonight in the hope it would help her sleep. After returning home to her small, inner-city, one-bedroom apartment, she had pulled leftovers from the freezer and defrosted them in the microwave while she took a shower. After her meal, she made herself a cup of peppermint tea and decided to read the file in bed. The time she spent reading before she went to sleep was her favorite time of the day.

Bridgette knew she wasn't supposed to take any classified information away from the Vancouver Metro office without written approval, but she didn't think it was likely to be a hanging offense if Delray had chosen to give her the file. The front page of the file caused her to stiffen slightly as she read her mother's name. She put the file down and sipped her tea for a moment while she composed herself. She was surprised at how much her mother's murder still affected her even though it had happened twenty years ago.

When she felt ready to go on, she picked up the file again. She flipped through the pages briefly and estimated there were about forty in total before she returned to the front page. She looked through the summary artifacts list on page two. It contained a list of all the cataloged information on her mother's murder including a summary of what had been copied to computer record and what was still only available in hard copy format from the records department.

She began by reading the coroner's report. The report went into lengthy medical detail but was consistent with the explanation her aunt had given to her when she was just a young teenager—her mother had been shot in the head by a small caliber pistol and had died almost immediately from the gunshot wound. Bridgette had to stop several times to compose herself as she made her way through the report. When she finished reading the coroner's final summation, she paused for a moment. Even though she had only been seven when her mother had died, she still had strong memories of both her mother and father and their happy life as a family.

She looked across at the small framed photo on her bedside table of her as a four-year-old with her parents. She would be forever grateful to her aunt for the precious reminder that at one time she had a family who loved her.

Bridgette decided to read the crime scene report next. The report was in two sections, the first written by Paul Ferringa who had been assigned as the lead homicide detective for the case. There was always a second section prepared by internal affairs whenever the crime involved a police officer or family member. She flipped over several pages and was not surprised to find LeonCunningham's name listed as the author.

Memories of the house she had spent her early childhood in came flooding back as she read the opening paragraphs of Cunningham's report which clinically described the layout of her family's small semi-detached two-story house.

She closed her eyes and was instantly seven again, sitting on the couch and playing with her favorite doll. She remembered listening to her mother and father talking in the kitchen in low voices.

She remembered calling out to ask if everything was all right and her mother responding in her calm and gentle voice, 'We're just talking about Daddy's work honey—no need to worry.'

Keeping her eyes closed, Bridgette let out a deep breath as she allowed herself to relive more of that day.

She remembered the knock on the door—three knocks in quick succession, firm but not loud and then turning with surprise to see her mother, now standing beside the couch, whispering, "We need to go upstairs, Bridgette."

She wanted to ask her mother a question, but her mother gestured for her to be silent.

She remembered the worried look on her father's face as he waited by the front door until they had gone up the stairs before he opened it. She remembered sitting on her mother's bed holding her hand. She remembered her mother whispering words of comfort as they heard men's voices coming from downstairs growing louder as they began to argue. She thought she heard her father's voice but couldn't be sure. She flinched as she relived the unmistakable sound of a gun discharging.

What happened next was a blur. She thought she heard their front door open and men shouting and running, but she could not be sure. She remembered tears streaming down her mother's face as she quickly led Bridgette across to the wardrobe. She was confused as her mother pushed her inside and into a corner behind a suitcase before pleading with her in a whispered voice not to come out until she said so. Bridgette remembered crying as she sat alone in the dark, scared for her mother and father. She remembered the smell of the camphor as she drifted off to sleep and then the second gunshot that woke her as it rang in her ears. It was still dark, and she was not sure how long she had been asleep for. She could still smell the camphor as the door to the wardrobe briefly opened before shutting again. The second gunshot had sounded close, but perhaps she had dreamed it? She sat alone in the darkness for a long time and felt her bladder getting full. Would her mother be upset if she came out? The camphor was making her feel sick and she began to cry again.

She remembered the door of the wardrobe opening again.

And then the flashlight and then the man's voice. "I've found her. She's here in the wardrobe..."

Bridgette opened her eyes. The next memory was too hard

to relive with her eyes closed. As tears welled in her eyes, she remembered looking back as she was led firmly out of the bedroom by a policewoman. The image of her mother laying on the bed at an odd angle and covered in a blood-stained sheet would haunt her for the rest of her life. She bit down on her bottom lip for a moment to get her emotions under control before looking across at her bedside clock. It was already well after ten thirty p.m. and she knew she needed a decent night's sleep. She debated leaving the rest of the file to the following day, but there were still so many questions she knew sleep would be impossible now until she found some answers.

She continued reading Cunningham's report but stopped at the end of page two. Frowning, she re-read the last paragraph. It wasn't the cold and clinical description of the murder scene which had once been her home or the grisly details of her mother's fatal bullet wound that troubled her, but the words of the last sentence.

She re-read the words again.

The victim appears to have been killed by a single gunshot to the left temple, consistent with the reports of what nearby neighbors heard.

Bridgette stopped reading for a moment and thought about what this meant. It almost sounded like the witnesses had only heard one gunshot. She made a mental note to carefully read each witness statement before she jumped to any conclusions, but the assumption by the investigators bothered her. The rest of the report focused on evidence collected from the crime scene and Cunningham's own observations. Suicide or accidental death were ruled out immediately as a cause of death because no gun was found at the crime scene.

Bridgette had gleaned enough information from the internet and old press clippings over the years to know that her father had been accused of being a dirty cop by some of his peers and remained on a wanted list in connection with her mother's murder. She wasn't surprised to read that sentiment in Cunningham's closing assessment.

The husband of the deceased, Detective Peter Casseldhorf, has been under investigation by Internal affairs for approximately 3 months in relation to allegations of accepting bribes from high profile criminals. During this time, his behavior has been noted as becoming increasingly erratic. The resulting murder investigation will, therefore, focus on Detective Casseldhorf as the prime suspect. His whereabouts are unknown at the time of writing of this report.

She thought back to the last time she had seen her father as he had watched her climb the stairs and wondered if he was still alive? Bridgette knew she should stop reading. She flipped over to the last page of Cunningham's report which provided a list of witnesses who had been interviewed. As she scanned the list, she knew by the addresses that most of them were neighbors. There were several names at the bottom of the list that gave Vancouver Metro south-central as the address and she knew they were clearly police officers. Her eye was drawn to the second last name on the list. She stared in disbelief as she read the name, Lance Hoffman.

Chapter 13

Bridgette pressed the enter key and watched as an error message displayed on her computer screen.

She sighed and then turned to Charlie Bates and said, "Looks like they've taken away my access."

Bates replied, "No big deal, we can read the case files together."

Bridgette thanked Bates for the gesture but didn't think two cops reading the same information off one laptop was going to be a good use of their time and decided to review the notes on the whiteboard again. As she got up from her chair, she was thankful the early morning muster was over and that they now had the meeting room to themselves for the day. Standing in front of the whiteboard, she began to review the information they had written down. Even though she had committed it all to memory, she found the close proximity to what she had written helped her think through the endless possibilities of what it all meant.

She heard Bates ask, "Do you want me to start on the Hannah Mason case?"

Bridgette found it odd that Bates, who technically outranked her, was deferring to her as the lead research investigator. She knew from her conversations with Hoffman and several others that Bates preferred office work to being out in the field and was happiest when he was sitting in front of a computer.

She turned around and was about to answer his question when Hoffman appeared in the doorway and said, "What are you doing, Detective?"

Bridgette replied, "We're just about to start reviewing the Hannah Mason case in detail. She's the second victim in Rochford. According to one of the witness statements, she was due to attend a new play called Chess Games. There might be a similar link to the Wilson and Sargent cases, with free tickets."

Hoffman nodded and asked, "Did you lose your computer access yet?"

"Yes."

Hoffman looked at Bates.

"Can you do without Detective Casseldhorf for a couple of hours, Detective?"

Bates looked slightly confused as he replied, "Sure."

Hoffman looked back at Bridgette and said, "I want to show you some video."

Hoffman said no more and turned and walked back toward his cubicle. Bridgette shrugged at Bates and then followed Hoffman. As he gestured her to sit in a vacant chair next to him, she noticed Hoffman had set up a laptop computer on his desk.

Pointing to the laptop screen, Hoffman said, "I got this video from Delaney in missing persons late yesterday. The day after Monica Travers disappeared, they started collecting all available footage from security cameras in the surrounding streets to try and figure out her last known movements. They spliced together this sequence."

Hoffman pressed the space bar on the laptop. Instantly a video came to life and showed a grainy image of the florist shop where Monica Travers had worked.

"The first feed comes from a camera out front of a jewelry shop on the opposite side of the street."

Bridgette watched as the door to the florist shop opened and a young woman with dark hair emerged and began walking up the street.

Hoffman pointed to a digital clock in the top left-hand corner of the video.

"She left the shop at six forty-seven p.m.—that's around her normal finish time. As usual, she headed west along Edward Street. According to her co-workers, she normally parked on the top story of a car park about three blocks down."

They watched in silence as the young woman walked off screen. Instantly, the video changed to another security camera and showed the same woman again, this time walking towards the camera and talking on a mobile phone.

Hoffman hit the space bar again and the video froze.

"This video came from a delicatessen half a block further down. It's six forty-nine p.m. now, and she's talking on her mobile phone."

"Was the phone ever recovered?"

"No. She never made it to her car and the phone and shoulder bag you can see in the video were never found."

"Did you—"

"The last two weeks of her mobile phone records were subpoenaed from the telephone company. Every number checks out with a family or friend except for two calls she made to an untraceable mobile number. You're watching one of those calls now."

"Untraceable?"

"A dead end. One of those prepaid numbers you get from a convenience store. Bought with cash and registered with a bogus name and address."

Hoffman hit the space bar and the video image changed to another camera further down the street. Monica Travers was no longer on the phone and walking with purpose as she passed by a street lamp.

Hoffman pointed to the screen again and said, "She takes a left turn at the next intersection and heads up Creek Street."

Bridgette watched as the video cut to another camera angle as Monica Travers rounded the corner and entered Creek Street. There were very few pedestrians on the street and Bridgette watched as Monica walked under the camera and out of sight.

Hoffman added, "This next video is the last footage we have of Monica Travers alive."

Bridgette watched as the camera captured the young woman continuing to walk down Creek Street before she stopped at an entry way to an underground parking lot. She looked up momentarily at the signage before heading down a ramp. Hoffman hit the space bar and paused the video again.

"That's it. The team looked at the video from this camera for the next two hours. She never came back out."

"What about cars exiting from here?"

Hoffman shook his head and said, "It's an entry only, but the footage was fully checked. Nobody walked or drove out of the parking lot through that entrance."

"What about other exits?

"There are two other exits. The main exit is further down

Creek Street. We checked all the security footage and nobody matching her description left from there either. We checked all the cars that left there in the following two hours, but none of them have stolen plates or anything else about them that makes them look suspicious. Missing persons have compiled a list of vehicle owners and have been interviewing them, but so far they all check out."

Hoffman swiftly made some keystrokes on his computer and brought up another video screen.

"The second exit's the one I really want to show you. It runs under the Garrick Brothers department store and out onto Wellington Street."

Hoffman hit the space bar again and the second video began to play.

"This camera is located across the street from Garrick Brothers. It's got the best view of the Wellington Street exit. I got Delaney's team to edit this video down to the half-hour immediately following Monica's disappearance. There was no late-night shopping on the night she disappeared, so it was relatively quiet—just seven vehicles exiting during that time-frame."

Bridgette nodded and said, "That will make it easier to check."

Hoffman nodded and hit the space bar to freeze the video.

"They all check out with one exception that I want to show you."

Hoffman hit the space bar again and the video continued to play. Bridgette watched as a large black van drove slowly up the ramp before indicating and turning left onto Wellington Street. Hoffman hit the space bar again to freeze the video. They now had a side-on image of the van and Bridgette was just able to make out the grainy image of a man with a full dark beard and wearing a baseball cap behind the wheel.

Hoffman pointed to the image and said, "I think that's him. The beard's probably false, but at least it's a start. The plates on the van belong to a Honda Civic owned by a grandma who lives in an apartment block in Weston, about twenty minutes out of the city. She parks her car in a carport at the back of the complex. When I called her early this morning, she was adamant the plates were on her car and hadn't been stolen. It looks like they were borrowed and then returned to avoid raising suspicion. I've sent two detectives out there to interview her and look around, but I don't think they're going to find much."

Hoffman pressed the space bar again and Bridgette wondered if Monica Travers was in the back of the van as she watched it disappear off the screen.

She thought for a moment and then responded, "If this is him, he's very careful. Borrowing plates and having more than one exit strategy shows he likes to carefully plan everything."

Hoffman nodded and then grabbed his coat off the back of his chair.

"I've got Jones ringing all the car rental companies across the city that hire out vans. It shouldn't be too hard to track it down if it's a rental."

"What are you doing now?"

"I'm taking you to the florist shop to interview a fellow worker of Monica's. She's been on an overseas holiday for three weeks and just got back yesterday. She was friends with Monica outside of work and according to the owner, they were reasonably close. She may not open up to me, but someone younger like you may be less threatening."

Bridgette nodded and said, "I'll grab my coat."

As she followed Hoffman out of the homicide room towards the elevator, her thoughts returned to her mother's murder file and she wondered again why Hoffman's name was on the witness list. She decided the car ride would be a good opportunity to ask him what he knew.

Chapter 14

Hoffman turned onto the Iron bridge and headed across the Vancouver river towards the city's CBD. Traffic was heavy and Bridgette figured they still had fifteen minutes of travel time before they would arrive at the florist shop. Hoffman had used most of the car trip to bring her up to date on the results of the Travers autopsy which had been completed late yesterday. Travers had been stabbed thirteen times and, according to Ray Warner, the third or fourth stab wound had been the fatal one.

Hoffman paused his update to change lanes, and Bridgette used the opportunity to ask a question.

"Was Monica raped or sexually molested?"

Hoffman answered while he adjusted his rear-view mirror.

"Ray wouldn't give an iron clad guarantee one way or another. He's running some more tests, but he believes it's highly unlikely."

Bridgette nodded and said, "It fits the pattern. None of the other victims had been raped either."

"It strikes me as unusual that a serial killer who kills lots of women doesn't attempt to rape any of them?"

Bridgette looked down and watched several boats moving

slowly down the river below as she thought about the question.

"The need to kill can become such an obsession that it suppresses every other urge. If the killer is that single-minded—killing is all he's thinking about."

They were silent for a moment and then Bridgette added, "The killer might also be sexually dysfunctional, but it's hard to say without more evidence."

Hoffman frowned. "Dysfunctional?"

"There have been many recorded cases where serial killers are not capable of normal sexual function. The dysfunction can sometimes be the reason why they begin to kill."

"As in a power thing over women?"

"Sometimes, but not always. I studied one case where the killer was so shy, he only ever felt comfortable around dead people. The guy worked in a morgue, and when he was on his own, he would get bodies out of the freezer just to talk to them. Unfortunately, he took that a step further and started to kill women that he liked so that he could talk to them as well."

Hoffman frowned and then replied, "They caught him then?"

"No. This was back in the nineteen-twenties. They found him hanging on the end of a rope one morning in the morgue where he worked. He'd left a note with a full confession."

Hoffman shook his head and said, "I've been doing this job a long time, and the things people do never cease to amaze me."

The car went quiet again as Hoffman concentrated on the traffic. Bridgette decided it was time to ask her question.

"Chief Delray gave me a printout of my mother's murder file yesterday."

Hoffman nodded but didn't say anything.

"It lists you as a witness interviewed by Cunningham as part of his investigation."

Hoffman glanced across at her briefly and then stared out the front at the traffic again. No one spoke for over a minute. Bridgette decided not to push him. It was Hoffman who broke the silence.

"Your father and I were friends. My late wife and I actually came to your house for dinner several times when you were very young."

Bridgette raised her eyebrows slightly—this was certainly news to her.

"I made Cunningham take my statement. It was more of a character reference than anything. Even though I didn't work directly with your father, we talked a lot. He worked narcotics and told me a lot of things in confidence. Things, we as police officers should never have needed to discuss."

"What things?"

Hoffman sighed and replied, "A lot of his work was collecting evidence through surveillance. I got a call from him two weeks before your mother was murdered. He told me he had observed two police officers taking money from a man connected to a drug syndicate. He wouldn't tell me who they were at the time, but we talked about what he should do."

"What did you tell him?"

"He wanted to go to internal affairs—to Cunningham, but I told him to wait. He needed video evidence or a tape recording at the very least. One cop's word against another gets you nowhere, and it's an easy way to wind up a corpse if you get in the way of organized crime."

"So what happened?"

"I offered to help him gather evidence, but he said it was too risky. He didn't know who he could trust and decided dragging me in would only raise suspicions. I'm not sure he ever went to Cunningham, but someone definitely found out."

Hoffman looked across at Bridgette for a moment and then returned his gaze to the river.

"I don't know who killed your mother, but it wasn't your father. I said as much in the statement I gave Cunningham. I spilled my guts on the little I knew about two police officers on the take, but Cunningham refused to buy it. The next thing I know, it's your father who's accused of corruption and the prime murder suspect."

Bridgette was quiet for a moment while she processed what Hoffman had told her. She was surprised by the news that her father and Hoffman had been friends. Her aunt had never mentioned it. Perhaps she didn't know? She thought back to the day of the murder.

"I was seven years old when it happened. I still remember a lot about that day."

Bridgette recounted everything she could remember and then asked a question.

"The two men who came to visit my father—do you think they were police officers?"

"If you and your mother were sent upstairs, it sounds like your father was expecting visitors. I can't imagine he'd meet anyone connected to organized crime in his house, so it's highly likely he thought it was someone he could trust."

"That's what I figured."

"If you read through the eyewitness reports, you'll find they all say the same thing. One gunshot and a man seen running from the building—your father."

"There were definitely two gunshots. I'm not sure how far

apart they were because I fell asleep."

"I know your father. If someone pulled a gun on him in your house, he would have done his best to draw them away. I think they lost him and came back to..."

Bridgette thought about what Hoffman had just said. She wondered again if she would have been killed if her mother hadn't hidden her in the wardrobe? Very likely, she thought. She found herself saying out loud what she had never said to anyone, not even her aunt.

"I hated my father for years after that."

"You blame him for your mother's death?"

"I blamed him for abandoning us. When we needed him most he wasn't there."

Hoffman didn't respond. Instead, he pulled off the freeway and drove down an exit road that ran parallel to the river. They drove in silence for three blocks before Hoffman turned right into a small picnic area next to the river. Hoffman parked the car under the shade of a tree at the far end of the parking lot and switched off the engine.

They sat in silence and watched an ancient wooden power boat as it cruised down the river. When the boat rounded a bend and was out of sight, Hoffman finally spoke.

"Your father was a good man. He would have never knowingly put you or your mother in danger. He doted on you both and was extremely proud of his daughter."

Bridgette closed her eyes tightly to stop herself from crying. Her aunt had said similar things, but it was nice to hear somebody else say it as well.

After regaining her composure, she asked, "What do you think happened to him?"

"I've thought about that off and on ever since it happened.

He was running from corrupt cops, a murder indictment and most likely a drug cartel as well. And then there was you to consider."

"Me? He abandoned me."

Hoffman watched as a charter boat came cruising down the river. He could see people on the upper deck laughing and joking as if they didn't have a care in the world. He was growing increasingly tired of living in a world that was so different.

"I don't think your father ever abandoned you. Peter Casseldhorf was never a quitter. You want my opinion; I don't think he had any choice."

"Why?"

Hoffman shifted in his seat before he responded. "There's one part of your story I don't agree with."

Slightly confused, she asked, "Which part?"

"You said the second gunshot woke you up and then the door of the wardrobe opened and quickly closed again?"

"Yes."

"If it was a couple of cops, corrupt or not, do you think they would have given up searching for you that easily?"

Bridgette wanted to argue that they may have been in a hurry to leave, but deep down she knew Hoffman had a point.

She replayed what had happened over in her mind. The gunshot, waking up and rubbing her eyes as the door to the wardrobe opened and then quickly closed again.

Finally, she replied, "They didn't give up at all, did they?"

Hoffman replied softly, "Your father may have escaped, but while you were alive, they held all the cards. Your father knew he couldn't come forward to clear his name or set the record straight because it would very likely cost him his daughter's life."

Bridgette shook her head. She had been over everything that had happened a thousand times and had never thought about the possibility that maybe she had been seen when she was hidden in the wardrobe.

As if reading her mind, Hoffman added, "Don't beat yourself up over this, Detective. You remember this as a traumatized seven-year-old, not as a police officer."

Hoffman started the car. He looked all business again as he mumbled, "We need to keep going," and then put the car into reverse.

It was going to take her time to make sense of everything Hoffman had told her. Perhaps her opinion of her father had been wrong? Bridgette decided she needed to ask one final question before they left the car park.

"Do you think my father is still alive?"

Chapter 15

The rest of the car trip into the city was quiet, which gave Bridgette time to think. She knew she should be focused on the Travers' case, but she found it hard to take her mind off her mother's murder. She was surprised that Hoffman had been friends with her father and even more surprised that he knew her as a young girl.

She replayed the conversation from the car park over in her mind as they slowed to almost walking pace in heavy city traffic. She had long ago realized it was wrong to hold on to feelings of hatred towards her father but was surprised that she had shared as much as she had with Hoffman. She had hoped that as the anger subsided she would be left with peace, but as she let go, the hole it left had simply turned into a restless void that yearned for the truth.

She stole a quick look at Hoffman as he focused on looking for a car park. His explanation that her father had severed all contact to protect her gave her comfort, but it made her question again if he was still alive? For years she had assumed he was dead, but maybe she had been wrong about that too? Bridgette wondered if he was still protecting her father.

She recalled his brutal response to her question as they had left the parking lot—'Nobody stays hidden for that long unless they're a corpse,' and wondered if he knew more than he was letting on?

Her thoughts were interrupted as Hoffman pulled up in a loading zone out front of a small shop on Edward Street called 'Dino's Flowers'.

Hoffman placed an official police business sign on the dashboard and then said, "The lady we're here to interview is Sally Longmire. She got back into town yesterday and according to Dino, she is still pretty upset. Normally, I would take the lead, but today you get that job. Even though she wasn't here at the time of Monica's disappearance, she was close to Monica. If we can dig enough into Monica's background and her personal life, we might find something useful."

Bridgette nodded and asked, "How do you want me to play it?"

"Just be yourself. One concerned young woman talking to another. Like you already know each other."

Before Bridgette could respond, Hoffman was out of the car and walking towards the front door of the florist's shop. The shop looked small and had a large range of flowers setup for sale in buckets on the footpath. Bridgette walked in behind Hoffman who waved to a slim looking man in his early forties who stood behind the counter arranging a bunch of carnations.

"Morning, Dino."

Dino nodded at Hoffman and with his face set grim, replied, "Sally's out back in the storeroom. You want me to go get her?"

Eager to talk to Sally in a more private setting, Bridgette answered, "We're happy to talk to her out back if that's okay?"

Dino pointed to a service door behind the counter and said, "Through there. She's currently unpacking this morning's delivery."

After saying thanks to Dino, Hoffman motioned Bridgette to go first as he mumbled, "Like I said, you take the lead, Detective."

Bridgette pushed through the heavy swing door and walked into a long, narrow storeroom. She saw a young woman standing behind a wooden table at the other end of the room. Sally Longmire was twenty-two, but with her slim build and white blonde hair pulled back in a ponytail, Bridgette thought she looked barely old enough to be a senior in high school. She looked up from a small arrangement of roses she was currently packing into a gift box when she heard the door open.

Bridgette could see sadness in her eyes and knew the interview wouldn't be easy for either of them.

"Good morning, Sally. I'm Detective Casseldhorf and this is my partner, Detective Hoffman."

Sally put the roses down and said, "You're here about Monica, aren't you?" as she took off her gloves.

Bridgette nodded and said, "Yes," as she walked across the storage room.

She stood on the other side of the table that Sally was working on and added, "I understand you and Monica were quite close. I'm very sorry for your loss."

Sally's lower lip quivered, and she said something in a soft voice that Bridgette couldn't understand. Hoffman walked forward and stood next to Bridgette but didn't say anything.

"I know this must be very hard for you, Sally. We really want to catch whoever did this, and we were hoping we might be able to ask you some questions?"

Sally sat down on a stool and stared off into vacant space for a moment.

"I've been away on an overseas holiday. I wasn't here when it... happened."

In a gentle voice, Bridgette responded, "Dino told us you and Monica were close. We thought finding out a bit more about what she did after work might help."

Sally looked up at Bridgette and said, "She didn't deserve this. Why would anyone want to harm her?"

Bridgette sat down on a stool and said, "That's what we're trying to find out, Sally. Dino tells me you and Monica used to hang out socially after work?"

Sally nodded and said, "We'd go to movies after work at least once a week and also the odd party."

Bridgette decided to tactfully steer the conversation.

"We've checked all the police records. It doesn't appear as if she was ever in trouble with the law?"

Sally replied in a firm voice, "No, she wasn't like that. She didn't do drugs or sleep around and was very careful about what she drank at parties."

Bridgette watched Sally's body language while she answered. She held Bridgette's gaze and spoke firmly without wavering. Bridgette was happy enough with Sally's answer. It fitted with everything else they had already learned about Monica Travers.

"Apart from law school and working here, what did Monica like to do?"

Sally thought for a moment before she responded.

"She was like most other young women, I guess. She was keen to finish her degree and build a career. She dated a few guys, but wasn't interested in anything too serious."

Bridgette nodded. She wanted to encourage Sally to keep talking and said, "She didn't want a serious relationship?"

Sally shook her head and replied, "Not until she finished her degree. She was very busy. Between working at the florist shop, and taking on a full-time study load, she had very little free time. It was all I could do to get her to take one night off a week for a movie or a play."

"Play?"

"We both liked going to musical theater and plays. If we could get cheap tickets, we would go and see whatever was on."

Bridgette looked at Hoffman who nodded. He had clearly heard the word 'tickets' as well. This line of questioning was worth pursuing, she thought.

"I know you were overseas when Monica was abducted, Sally, but did she ever mention if she was planning anything on the night she was abducted?"

Sally shook her head. "I didn't have my phone set up for international calling, so we only communicated a few times by Facebook before she went missing. She never mentioned anything."

Bridgette nodded and thought about other ways to keep the conversation going. Missing persons had been through Monica Travers' Facebook account and personal email and found nothing that could help them.

"I know this is hard for you to talk about, Sally, but Detective Hoffman and I have seen video footage from security cameras in the streets of Monica leaving here on the night she disappeared. It looks like she was planning to meet someone after work. She'd phoned her parents earlier in the day to say she'd won some free tickets?"

Sally thought for a moment before responding.

"We were close, but I don't know all her friends. I'm not sure who else was interviewed here, but she was also friendly with Tessa and Katie who work here part-time. They might know if she was planning on meeting up with someone."

Hoffman spoke for the first time. "Everyone else has been interviewed, Detective Casseldhorf. Nothing specific was mentioned by anyone."

Without breaking eye contact with Sally, Bridgette answered, "It might be worthwhile playing Tessa and Katie the security video, Sally? Maybe it will jog their memory?"

Sally nodded but didn't seem convinced.

"Maybe?"

Hoffman said, "I'll go and get a roster from Dino. Everyone who was working here that day should see it."

Sally pointed to an old computer that sat on a small desk in the corner of the storeroom and said, "I can look up the roster on my work email if you like?"

Bridgette asked, "You have work email?"

"We all do. Dino uses it to send us the work timetable mainly, and we occasionally use it for leaving messages for one another about work stuff. Dino didn't like us messaging each other or using Facebook for anything that's work related."

Bridgette turned to look at Hoffman. The scowl on his face suggested this was the first he had heard of this. In a shop with less than ten employees it was reasonable to assume work email was unnecessary, but still, someone should have checked. She had no doubt Hoffman would be on the phone as soon as the interview was over, berating someone in his team for the oversight.

Bridgette looked back at Sally and asked, "So it's safe to

assume Monica had an email account too?"

"Of course."

"Do you think Dino would have deleted it yet?"

"I doubt it. Dino barely knows how to turn a computer on. Flowers are his thing, not computers."

"Is there any way we can find out what Monica's password was?"

Sally went and sat on an old wooden chair in front of the computer. As she started typing on the keyboard, she said, "Unless she's changed it, we were all setup with 'flowers' as the password. There's only eight of us working here and nobody worried too much about security..."

Bridgette and Hoffman watched as the computer went through a login routine. Sally clicked on several icons on the screen and brought up an email account. She turned to Bridgette and said, "I've logged in as Monica—you can look at her email if you like?"

Bridgette looked at Hoffman who said, "You're far better with the computers than I am, Detective."

Sally got up and stepped back to allow Bridgette to move around and sit at the computer.

Bridgette quickly scanned the emails in the inbox. Most of them were from Dino and appeared to be work-related. She checked the date on the top four emails which had not yet been opened. They had all arrived after Monica's murder. It reminded her how final death was and that Monica was not coming back. She spent a couple of minutes checking the emails before she said anything to Hoffman.

"I've done a quick check. Thirty-six emails in total and as Sally said, they're mostly work related. Obviously, they will need to be read in greater detail, but there's nothing here that

I can see that provides any clue as to who she was meeting or why."

Hoffman nodded and said, "I'll get Rogers to come back. He was compiling everything from the other employees, so this is his job."

Bridgette looked across at Sally who looked disappointed that they hadn't found anything and said, "This has been helpful, Sally. It's all pieces of a puzzle that we have to put together."

Sally nodded but didn't look convinced.

"Sally, are there any other computer programs that you use here at work other than email?"

"Just the program for ordering flowers from the whole-salers."

Bridgette nodded and started tapping at the keyboard again.

"Are you allowed to browse the internet from here?"

Sally briefly glanced at the door that led to the shop area and replied, "Dino didn't like us using it. He said it cost him money and we wasted time... but I guess we all occasionally used it."

Bridgette didn't respond and was now totally focused on the computer screen.

Hoffman stepped up behind Bridgette and asked, "You find something, Detective?"

"I'm just looking through Monica's internet browsing history. She has used the computer quite a lot over the last month..."

Bridgette's voice trailed away as she concentrated on the screen again and began rapidly typing on the keyboard. Sensing she was onto something, Hoffman found it difficult to stand back and watch. He had no idea what she was doing and only interrupted after she pushed back from the computer.

"Detective?"

Bridgette pointed to the screen, which currently showed a 'Page not found' error message.

"We may have something here. This website that Monica visited is some sort of promotions website."

"Promotions?"

"As in competitions and giveaways. Kind of like Facebook. You go in and set up a page for a short period of time to promote your product or event. The actual page Monica visited has been deleted."

"Can we get it back?"

"We may not need to." Bridgette clicked the mouse button and brought up a new page on the computer screen. Hoffman moved forward and began to read the contents.

"It looks like another competition."

Bridgette nodded and said, "Free tickets to the play 'A Cold Summer' right here at the Vancouver Playhouse Theater. It looks like it's been set up by the same identity that set up the page Monica visited."

"You think this is him?"

"Only one way to find out."

Bridgette pointed to a date at the bottom of the web page and continued, "And we don't have much time. The competition closes tomorrow at five p.m."

Chapter 16

The call came over the police radio before they had even made it three blocks from Dino's florist shop. Hoffman was keen to get back to the South Precinct to brief Delray on the breakthrough from the interview with Sally Longmire and cursed as he listened to the dispatcher's urgent plea for any cars in the vicinity of Wharf Street to respond immediately to a robbery in progress at a jewelry store.

Hoffman muttered, "It's less than two blocks from here," as he pulled a U-turn in heavy traffic.

Bridgette had no field experience with Hoffman beyond the Monica Travers' murder investigation.

She began to think through the possibilities if the robber was armed and asked, "What would you like me to do, Detective?"

Hoffman replied absently as he weaved through traffic, "Let me take the lead and just give me backup".

Bridgette hadn't been involved in any confrontations with armed criminals and wasn't entirely sure what to expect. She assumed they would go in with guns drawn but was surprised when Hoffman pulled into a loading zone several shops short of the jewelry store.

Hoffman got out of the car and said quietly, "We move in

from here on foot. I don't hear any sirens, so no squad cars are close yet. If they have a getaway vehicle parked out front this gives us a better chance of identifying it."

As they closed in on the jewelry store, a slim man in his late twenties emerged from the store clutching a small black felt bag. Bridgette could see the man putting something that looked like a knife in his pocket as he turned and walked quickly in the opposite direction to their approach.

"That's him," replied Hoffman as he picked up speed.

As they reached the front of the jewelry store, both Hoffman and Bridgette peered in briefly through the front window and saw a man with the left sleeve of his shirt soaked in blood anxiously dialing from a desk phone.

Hoffman muttered, "Go and check he's okay," as he quickened his pace in pursuit of the thief.

Bridgette walked in through the front door and flashed her badge at the man who looked to be alone in the small, upmarket store.

"Detective Casseldhorf from Vancouver Metro, Sir. Would you like me to call you an ambulance?"

The man, who was in his early sixties stopped dialing and clutched at his bleeding arm. His face was a mixture of pain and anger, but Bridgette thought mostly anger.

"Just catch the bastard. He cut me even after I gave him thirty-thousand in diamonds."

Bridgette replied, "You should sit down, Sir. General policing has been notified and squad cars are on their way," and then headed back out onto the street.

She could just make out Hoffman, now jogging about half a block ahead. She figured if Hoffman was jogging it probably didn't matter if she drew attention to herself and set off after

Hoffman at a sprint. She closed to within a few paces of Hoffman just as he turned left and headed into an alley.

Bridgette slowed back to a walk and debated whether to draw her gun before entering the alleyway. She heard a cry of anguish and had no doubt it had come from Hoffman. Drawing her Glock service pistol, she sprinted the remaining few steps to the alleyway and looked down the narrow corridor that separated the buildings. The alleyway was short and barely wide enough to allow car access and finished in a dead end. It smelt faintly of rotting food and other garbage. She could see Hoffman lying on the ground, about half way down in front of a large dumpster. He was holding his stomach and writhing in pain. Above him stood the jewelry store thief with what looked to Bridgette like a steel bar raised above his head ready to hit Hoffman again.

As the man went to swing the bar again, Bridgette raised her gun at the man and yelled, "Stop!"

The man pivoted slightly but kept the bar raised. He seemed surprised by her presence and said, "What the—"

For the first time in her career, Bridgette yelled the words, "Police officer!" and demanded the man drop the bar and step away.

The man laughed but made no move to obey the command. She strained to hear the sound of any approaching police cars above the drum of the traffic but heard nothing. Keeping her gun pointed at the man's chest, she walked several steps forward, analyzing the man for any sign of weakness before she responded.

The man's eyes were dilated, and his muscle movements seem erratic. She was reasonably sure he was high on something and that his spatial judgment would be impaired—probably, but not certainly. Her years of competing in martial arts tournaments had taught her winning was as much about understanding and exploiting your opponent's weaknesses as it was about anything else.

The man tightened his grip on the steel bar and in an almost mocking voice said, "So what're you gonna do—shoot me?"

More than anything else, Bridgette feared Hoffman would recover enough to try and stand up and would almost certainly be hit again.

She knew she needed to quickly draw the man away from Hoffman and answered, "No. That won't be necessary."

Without taking her eyes off the man, she bent down and placed her pistol on the ground and then slowly stood up again. The man stood almost transfixed as he watched her every move but made no sign of lowering the bar or moving away from Hoffman.

Bridgette kicked the pistol into a shallow concrete gutter that ran down the left-hand side of the alley and stepped back two paces.

"There's no way out of this alley. You know it's a dead end otherwise you'd still be running, and my partner wouldn't be lying on the ground."

The man laughed again and said, "So what do you have in mind now you don't have a gun, police lady."

Bridgette replied in as even a voice as she could muster.

"It's simple. I step back and let you walk out of here. I don't think you'll get far, but it gives you a chance to get away and my partner gets to stay alive."

"And what if I club your partner before I leave?"

Bridgette could still see her gun and was confident she could step across and pick it up before the man got to her. She was tempted to answer, 'I'll shoot you dead,' but didn't want to risk inflaming the situation anymore. Right now, all she wanted was for the man to move away from Hoffman.

She calmly replied, "I'm giving you a choice. Right now, you're just another criminal wanted for robbery and assaulting a police officer. You kill my partner and every police officer in the state will be looking for you."

Bridgette could now hear a police siren faintly in the distance. The man cocked his head slightly and she knew he'd heard it too. Hoffman groaned again and tried to get up. Bridgette tensed as she watched the man take a step back from Hoffman, unsure if he was leaving or just giving himself more room for a final swing.

To her relief, the man lowered the bar and began walking towards her to as if the sirens had been his cue to leave. Bridgette debated lunging for her gun but decided to let the man pass. Hoffman was now groaning and trying to get to his feet and looked to be in complete agony. She stepped sideways to allow the man to pass but tensed again with the man's approach as he was still holding the bar.

She sensed the man swinging the bar towards her before she actually saw the blur of the weapon as it hummed through the air towards her head. Her martial arts training had helped hone her reflexes and improve her decision making, but this was no tournament. The winner today wouldn't get a ribbon and the loser didn't get to pick themselves up off the canvas to fight another day. Most people's instincts in her situation would be to sway sideways or rock backward on their heels. She knew neither move would get her head out of the way quick enough and she would be dead before she hit the pavement.

She bent forward and dropped her knees in the one motion,

hoping she could get her head down low enough to avoid contact. The hum of the bar seemed incredibly loud to Bridgette, almost as if it had a voice of its own as it screamed towards her. She felt a rush of air against her scalp as the bar swung past her in its deadly arc barely missing her. Looking up, she realized the man had swung the bar too hard and the momentum had put him off balance.

Before he had time to recover, Bridgette quickly rose to her full height and pivoted on her right foot in one motion. As the man started to swing the bar back in her general direction, she delivered a left foot round house kick to the man's rib-cage. She had executed thousands of round house kicks in practice and competition and they were as natural to her as walking was to most other people.

She heard the whoosh of air being expelled from the man's lungs almost before she heard the unmistakable sound of bones breaking as her kick found its mark. The man dropped the bar and collapsed in a heap at her feet and began to writhe in agony. She looked up and saw Hoffman, now standing unsteady on his feet, holding his stomach and staring at her.

She gave him a moment and then asked, "Do I need to call you an ambulance?"

Hoffman stared in disbelief at the thief who lay groaning in a heap on the ground and said, "I think he needs one more than I do."

Chapter 17

Lance Hoffman glared at Bridgette as she stepped up into the rear of the ambulance and said, "Do you mind, I'm still getting dressed here."

Bridgette ignored the fact that her partner was still shirtless as she sat down next to him and replied, "Sorry, there are two news crews with cameras just pulling up. I'm not real keen on having my face plastered all over the evening news, so I'm going to hang out here until you're ready to go."

Hoffman mumbled inaudible words of complaint that Bridgette ignored. She was concerned about the two patched up wounds on his head but waited until he had his shirt on and was reaching for his tie before she asked any more questions.

"Should you be going to the hospital?"

Hoffman shook his head as he began to deftly knot his tie and said, "I don't have concussion and the ambulance guy doesn't think I've cracked any ribs, so hospital is a waste of time."

"What about pain killers? You're going to be in a lot of pain when all that bruising comes through?"

"I'll manage."

Bridgette shrugged and was about to ask Hoffman if he

should at least take the rest of the day off when her partner reached out and pulled the rear ambulance door closed.

"We've got at least one camera crew coming this way and I don't want to be on TV either."

"So, what do we do, just sit and wait?"

Hoffman nodded and leaned his head back on the side bulkhead of the ambulance and closed his eyes. Bridgette could see that he was clearly in pain and wondered whether she should just let him be.

After getting comfortable, Hoffman said, "I've always thought martial arts was a bit of a gimmick. You know, fine for gymnasium workouts, but not much use out on the streets."

"I mainly do it for fitness now. But you're right in a way. If the other guy has a gun or hits you with an iron bar, it's pretty much game over, no matter how good your skills are."

Hoffman opened one eye and asked, "You ever break anyone's ribs before?"

Bridgette tried to suppress a smile as she replied, "No, but I was angry."

After another moment's silence, Hoffman said, "Thanks again for what you did, Detective. If you hadn't shown up when you did, I think I'd be on my way to the morgue right now."

Bridgette nodded and replied, "Just doing my job."

Hoffman opened the other eye and held her gaze.

"I've worked with a lot of police officers in my time and not all of them would have done what you did today. That was a lot more than just doing your job."

Bridgette wasn't sure how to respond. She felt slightly awkward about his blunt praise and mumbled, "I've still got a lot to learn."

Hoffman closed his eyes again and as he leaned back on the bulkhead, he replied, "We're all learning, Bridgette. I'm sixty-one and I learn something new every day."

"What have you learned today?"

Hoffman opened one eye again and with half a wry smile, shot back, "Don't make you angry."

Hoffman winced as they both laughed.

Bridgette became serious again and said, "I was lucky. If I was a fraction of a second slower, it could have been me getting a free ride to the morgue."

"It was a good outcome, Bridgette—everybody, including the criminal is still alive. I've worked with enough police officers to know a lot of them would have panicked and just started firing. The body count could have easily been two."

Bridgette nodded and eager to get the focus off her said, "I'm getting hungry. You think we could get a pizza delivery in here?"

With an amused look, Hoffman responded, "Forgive me, Detective, but you don't strike me as the kind who would eat pizza."

"I get cravings every now and then. This is one of those times."

Hoffman nodded, "A double meat lovers with extra onion and cheese would be very nice right now."

"I was thinking more a vegetarian supreme on a thin crust."

Hoffman rolled his eyes and said, "I should have known you were a vegetarian."

"Not quite. I do eat fish and chicken, only not on pizza."

Before Hoffman had a chance to respond, the rear door of the ambulance opened and the officer who had patched up Hoffman said, "Sorry to break up the party folks, but I've got to get to my next job."

Hoffman held a hand up in a show of apology and said, "Sorry, officer. We were just hiding here to keep away from the news crews."

After taking a quick look back at the crowd behind him, the ambulance officer replied, "Sit tight and I'll drive you around the corner and let you out where it's quiet."

Before they had a chance to say thank you, the door closed, and they were left looking at one another again.

Hoffman said, "I think you better drive when we get back to the car. I can barely move my left arm."

"Okay."

"We'll have to file a report on this incident, but as soon as we get that out of the way, it will be back to work on the Travers' case, starting with figuring out what to do about that competition."

Bridgette nodded thoughtfully. She shared Hoffman's concern about catching the killer, but right now she was far more concerned about stopping the next killing. As the ambulance's engine started, she began to formulate a plan. She knew it was a long shot, but at least it was something. She figured they had forty-eight hours to make the breakthrough before another young woman from Vancouver became the next victim.

Chapter 18

Delray looked up from his computer screen when he saw the large frame of Lance Hoffman appear in the doorway to his office. Hoffman had played down the extent of his injuries when he had phoned his boss while on the drive back to the South Metro complex. Delray was in no doubt his lead detective was in enormous pain as he watched him shuffle into his office clutching an incident report.

Delray stared at the two large gauze patches taped to Hoffman's forehead as he sat down and bluntly declared, "You look awful, Lance."

Hoffman replied, "Looks have never been my strong suit, Felix," and winced as he tried to get comfortable in the chair,

Delray frowned and said, "Seriously, Lance, you look a mess. You must be in a lot of pain."

Hoffman pushed the incident report across the desk towards Delray and said, "I'll be fine, just a few bumps and bruises."

Delray wasn't buying it and got up and closed the door to his office to give them privacy. He frowned again as he returned to his desk and said, "Have you been checked by a doctor yet?"

Hoffman shook his head. "The ambulance guy checked me at the jewelry store. No broken bones, but I'm gonna look like crap for a few days once the bruising kicks in."

Delray knew it was pointless arguing with Hoffman and picked up the incident report. As he began reading, he said, "I got a call from Sargent Ben Hanley not long after your call. He was the first uniform guy on the scene and from what he says, you're lucky to be alive. He also said the thief was on his way to the hospital with broken ribs after losing in one round to Detective Casseldhorf?"

Hoffman nodded.

"That pretty much sums it up," and then went on to explain in detail what he could remember.

Delray listened without interrupting and then shook his head. "Unbelievable."

Hoffman added, "I've worked with a lot of experienced detectives in my time, Felix, but what she did, putting her gun down like that and backing away to diffuse the situation..."

Hoffman paused a moment and then said, "For a rookie, her judgment was flawless."

Both men were silent for a moment. Delray didn't know whether to be impressed that Bridgette had managed to disarm the thief without a shot being fired, or angry that she had voluntarily put down her own weapon and put herself in a vulnerable position.

As if reading his thoughts, Hoffman added, "Bottom line is, Chief, if Bridgette hadn't shown up and did what she did, the bastard would have caved my skull in."

"Hanley wants to put her up for a bravery award."

Hoffman groaned slightly as he shifted in the chair to get comfortable and then said, "Well, she deserves it. The guy looked to be high on crack or something. Whatever it was, he wasn't in a state to be reasoned with, but she managed to get him to walk away."

"So, let me get this straight. The guy walks away from you towards the exit and then decides to attack Bridgette?"

"It all happened so fast. He makes like he's accepting Bridgette's offer to leave the alley and the next thing he's swinging a steel bar at her head."

"Is she okay?"

"Not a scratch on her. The guy missed with his swing and Bridgette caught him with one of those martial arts kicks. I heard the guy's ribs break. It was all over in just a couple of seconds."

Hoffman straightened up in his chair and tried to get comfortable again before he continued. "I've worked with a lot of cops over the years—tough cops used to brawling in the streets. I'm not sure anyone of them would have survived that attack as well as what Bridgette did."

Delray nodded and tried to think about what this said about his new recruit.

Hoffman continued, "There's one other thing you need to know."

"And what's that?"

"A TV crew showed up while I was being looked over by the ambulance officer. We gave a no comment, but the guy who owned the jewelry store was far more talkative. He remembered Bridgette's name and went into great detail about what happened."

Delray raised his eyebrows. "So, this is going to make the news then?"

"Unless world war three starts between now and six o'clock, I'd say it's a fair bet Detective Casseldhorf will be a lead story."

Delray took his glasses off and then leaned back in his chair and clasped his hands behind his head. It was one of his favored positions when he needed to think about something in detail. "Ordinarily, I don't like our detectives getting media coverage. I prefer they keep a low public profile and we reward them in private with our—"

Hoffman interrupted, "In her defense, Chief, Detective Casseldhorf didn't give any interviews and did her best to keep away from the cameras."

"That doesn't surprise me, but as I was saying, normally I don't like media coverage, but today we might be able to use it to our advantage."

Hoffman frowned as he replied, "How so?"

Delray leaned forward and said, "I've been summoned to the Commissioner's office at three p.m. It's supposedly a review of the risk exposure Vancouver Metro is facing if it continues to employ Bridgette while her father is still wanted for murder."

Hoffman shook his head and spat out, "How can they still think Peter Casseldhorf is alive? Nobody survives that long off the grid without being caught."

"Be that as it may, Cunningham's not letting this rest. I've seen these kinds of memos before and this is just a formality. They plan to fire Bridgette today and will cite risk exposure or some other nonsense about the recruitment process to justify their decision. But ..."

"But what?"

Delray raised his eyebrows slightly and answered softly, "I would find it hard if I were the Commissioner to dismiss someone who's just saved a fellow police officer's life and is the subject of a positive story on the evening news for Vancouver Metro."

Hoffman smiled. "That would be a public relations' disaster."

"For now, don't say anything to Bridgette. This development won't make this go away entirely, but hopefully; I can buy us enough time to get the Travers murder case solved. If we can get Bridgette through to the official board review like the other rookies with some runs on the board, it might be enough to make sure Cunningham doesn't get his way."

"I don't plan on saying anything more about it, Felix—this has been a distraction we don't need. I thanked her for her bravery and we're both keen to focus on the Travers' case again."

Delray leaned back and said, "Okay, bring me up to date on what happened with the interview with Sally Longmire."

Hoffman gave Delray a full briefing on their visit to Dino's Flowers and what they had learned from interviewing Sally Longmire. Delray noted how much credit Hoffman was giving Bridgette for making the breakthrough with the information they had gleaned from the computer Monica Travers used at the shop. It was clear the crusty detective's respect for Bridgette was growing.

When Hoffman had finished his summary, Delray asked, "So what's Bridgette doing now?"

"She's currently working with Bates. They're analyzing the website she found to see what more they can learn about the killer. We're almost certain he's using the website and the lure of free tickets to somehow find his next victim."

"And the next competition closes tomorrow?"

"Wednesday at 5 p.m. according to the web page, so we don't have much time."

Delray looked at his watch and said, "I have to be upstairs

in two minutes for the meeting with Cunningham and the Commissioner. When I get back, let's call a meeting of the team to review what they've found and figure out what we do next."

Hoffman began to rise slowly from his seat.

Delray shook his head and said, "Lance, you really need to see a doctor."

Hoffman ignored the plea and wished Delray good luck with his meeting as he shuffled towards the door.

After opening the door, Hoffman looked back and said, "Maybe I should come with you?"

"To the Commissioner's meeting?"

"Yeah. I could wait outside and if the media angle isn't working so well for saving Bridgette's career you could call me in. I could give them a firsthand account of why I'm still alive and not lying in a morgue."

Delray knew Hoffman wouldn't find it easy telling the top brass that another police officer, particularly a woman and a rookie, had saved his life. Everybody, including the Commissioner, knew of Hoffman's reputation as a proud, self-sufficient cop who preferred to work alone. Any positive testimony coming from him couldn't be easily ignored.

"It can't hurt, Lance. I can use all the help I can get."

Both men left the office in silence and headed for the elevator. Delray reflected on the few meetings he'd been asked to attend in the Commissioner's office. Cunningham had been present for most of them and usually got his way by manipulating the truth to suit his own agenda. He had no doubt Cunningham would have heard about the incident at the jewelry store and would do his best to discredit Bridgette as a reckless cop who got lucky. Bridgette deserved the best defense he could muster, and he wished he had more time to prepare.

The doors to the elevator opened and as they stepped inside, Delray said, "I don't win many of these when Cunningham's involved."

Hoffman pushed the button for the fourth floor and said flatly, "Today has to be different."

Chapter 19

Bridgette watched Delray and Hoffman through the glass window as they walked back through the homicide room. It was after five p.m. and their body language suggested the two-hour meeting with the Commissioner and Cunningham hadn't gone well.

She pretended not to notice their demeanor as they walked into the small meeting room, but inwardly she started to tense as she braced to hear about her future.

Bates, ever impatient for an answer, asked bluntly, "How did the meeting go?"

Delray grumbled, "You really don't want to know, Charlie," as he looked around the room.

Holding his arms out wide, Hoffman looked at Bridgette and said, "Where is everybody? Nobody's out in the homicide room. I thought we were trying to solve a murder here?"

She replied evenly, "We think we've tracked down the hiring company for the black van with the stolen plates which was seen leaving Garrick Brothers."

Hoffman's mood changed a little as he pulled up a chair and said, "Okay, don't keep us waiting."

"Jones and Vincent reviewed the video footage and are

confident it's a late model Ford Transit van. There are only two companies in Vancouver that rent these out. The first company has three of these vans, but they're all white in color. The second company has one black van and hired it out nearly four weeks ago. The guy paid cash for six weeks hire in advance. Jones and Vincent have gone to interview the employee who did the paperwork. We talked to him on the phone and he vaguely remembers the guy who hired the van. They've taken the facial composite software to start to put together a likeness and do a more thorough interview."

Hoffman interjected, "And what about Donescu and Smith?"

"We got an address from the hire company for the guy who hired the van. It's north of the city. We looked it up on Google maps and it looks to be a vacant block of land, but Donescu figured we needed to go check to be certain."

Delray nodded and said, "Good work," but his praise was less than convincing.

Bridgette looked across at Hoffman and could tell by his body language that bad news was coming.

Hoffman said, "It doesn't look like we can get the whole team together before tomorrow morning, so they may as well hear it now, Chief..."

Delray paused a moment and then said in a deflated voice, "They're bringing in the Feds. Cunningham has convinced the Commissioner we're out of our depth and don't have the right level of experience with a serial killer case—if that's what this is. They'll be here for a few days collecting background information, and if they think it's legit, then we lose the Travers' case and any other cold case they think is connected... "

The room went quiet as everyone contemplated what Delray had just said. Bridgette expected Delray to tell her she was fired, which she figured might still happen, but no one had expected this development quite so soon. She began to understand Delray and Hoffman's gloomy disposition.

Hoffman finally broke the silence.

"We argued for over an hour to be given more time, seeing as how the serial killer link was made here through this office by Bridgette, but it fell on deaf ears. Cunningham is so risk adverse, he convinced the Commissioner he should play it by the book, which means the Feds have been officially notified. We think they'll be here within forty-eight hours."

Delray sighed and added, "There's nothing more we can do about it—it's a fight we're not going to win. The best we can do is work hard until they show up, which should be Friday. Regardless of the politics, Monica deserves our best."

Everyone nodded in agreement.

Keen to lighten the mood a little, Delray looked at Bridgette and Bates and continued, "I meant what I said before. You've made some great progress today. We know a lot more now than we did at the start of the day."

Taking this as her cue, Bridgette swiveled a laptop around to show Delray and Hoffman what she and Bates had been working on.

"We've got something else to show you, Chief."

Pointing to the laptop screen she said, "This is the website we believe the killer is using to lure his victims. As we said earlier, we think he's creating bogus competitions where you can win free tickets to events by registering online."

Delray looked at the screen and said, "It all looks very professional."

Bridgette knew professional looking websites could now be created by a twelve-year-old in their bedrooms but decided pointing this out might seem insulting and took a more tactful approach.

"If he's smart enough to get away with multiple murders, nothing about him should surprise us."

"So, have you found anything that can lead us to the guy?"

Bates, keen not to be sidelined, jumped in and said, "He covers his tracks pretty well, Chief. All his work is done using proxy servers and through a variety of ISPs, so we're finding it difficult to trace. This website is hosted by a small ISP company who don't keep very good records. I talked to them this afternoon and they're sending me a log file to work through, but—"

Bridgette could see Delray's eyes glazing over as he did his best to follow Bates' technical explanation and decided to interrupt with a plain English explanation.

"What Charlie is saying, Chief, is that whoever is behind this is going to great lengths to keep their identity anonymous."

She looked at Bates as she said, "We don't think we're going to find him by tracking him through the internet..."

Bates reluctantly nodded his agreement and then added, "Bridgette's come up with a plan B."

Delray looked skeptical as he asked, "And what's that?"

"We're reasonably confident he's tricking women into entering a competition to get personal information, which he uses to choose his next victim. The competitions seem to be launched a day or two before a local event and mainly offer free tickets to shows that would be popular with young women. This one is for a play called A Cold Summer. The competition closes tomorrow night at 5 p.m."

Delray kept his focus on the computer screen and frowned as Bridgette clicked another button which brought up her Facebook profile. He instantly knew where this was heading and didn't like it.

Undeterred by his body language, she pressed on and said, "All seven women have been under thirty-five, Caucasian and have dark shoulder length hair. We think he's using the competition to get a list of potential victim's names, which he then profiles through social media to select a target."

Delray shook his head in disgust and said, "So, what you're saying is he's using a bogus competition to get a bunch of names, which he then looks up on Facebook until he finds someone he likes?"

Bridgette nodded and said, "That's what we think."

There was a short silence while Delray and Hoffman processed the information. She was not convinced Delray would entertain plan B and waited for him to make the next move.

When he was ready, Delray asked, "Okay, so tell me about plan B."

"Charlie doesn't believe we will ever get enough information to be able to track this guy down through the internet. So, if we can't track him, we have to find a way to get him to come to us..."

Delray shook his head, "Hence why I'm now looking at your Facebook page?"

Bridgette could see the word 'No' forming on Delray's lips before she answered and decided to change her approach.

"This is an old Facebook profile I don't use anymore, Chief. I started it seven years ago when I was still in the navy but didn't continue with it when I left. There's no personal information there other than my first and middle names and a little about my navy training and a few pictures of me in my early twenties."

Delray looked less than impressed. "What about your police career and criminology degree?"

"No, as I said, I haven't used it in years. It doesn't include my last name and anyone looking at it would think I was still in the navy. If you think it's worthwhile, I'll put a couple of fake posts and some current pictures up to show it's still active."

Delray looked across at Hoffman and raised his eyebrows as a cue for his opinion.

Hoffman shrugged. "We're going to lose this investigation completely within the next day or two, Felix. I vote for anything we can do to flush this asshole out before that happens."

Delray still didn't look convinced.

Bridgette decided to pare back what he was committing to and said, "The first step is to see if we can establish communication with him, Chief, and nothing more. My guess is nothing will come of this anyway, but if it does, we can figure out how we want to respond then."

Hoffman added, "It might help keep us more in the loop if the Feds arrive earlier than expected."

Delray thought for a moment and then asked, "Okay, so what do we need to do, Bridgette?"

Bridgette clicked on the screen again and brought up a form. "I've filled in the details—which isn't much. Just my Facebook name, email and why I want to go to the concert... the only thing left to do is click the submit button."

Delray took one last look at the screen. Hoffman was now leaning over his shoulder also reading the competition details. She waited until both men looked satisfied and then said, "Are we ready?"

Delray nodded and replied, "Ready."

Bridgette moved the laptop's mouse until it was directly over the submit button. Even though she was a good likeness to many of the victims, she knew what they were doing was a long shot at best.

She took a deep breath and clicked the button. The screen refreshed and a message appeared confirming she had entered the competition.

Chapter 20

Delray flipped the light off to his office and walked out into the homicide room. It was just after seven p.m., and he was looking forward to heading home for a hot meal and a long bath, but not necessarily in that order. As he put his jacket on, he could see Bridgette sitting alone in the meeting room still working on a laptop.

He stopped in the doorway and said, "I thought you'd be watching the news? Apparently, you're one of tonight's lead stories."

Bridgette looked up from the laptop and half smiled, "I don't watch much TV, Chief."

"You should pack it in for today, Bridgette. We've made some good progress, and you never know; we may just get lucky with that competition thing tomorrow."

Bridgette leaned back to stretch and said, "That's probably a good idea."

Delray made no move to leave and after a short pause in the conversation he added, "I'm really not keen on standing here all night..."

Holding her hands up in a sign of surrender, Bridgette smiled and said, "Okay, I can take a hint."

Bridgette shut down the laptop and walked back out to her desk to retrieve her gym bag.

She decided to make the most of the opportunity she had to talk to Delray alone as they walked to the elevator and said, "Did the subject of my future come up with the Commissioner today?"

Delray nodded and said, "It did."

She tensed as she waited for Delray to continue.

"I'm not going to lie to you, Bridgette—there are still people at a senior level that don't want you here. I don't think it's as simple as this operational risk nonsense on account of your father... I think it has more to do with the fact he embarrassed senior members of the force and they resent you for it."

Bridgette tried to hide her frustration. While it made sense, it didn't make it any easier.

Delray pushed the elevator button and continued, "What you did at the jewelry store changed things. They can't come after you now that you've made the news for saving a fellow police officer's life, so you at least get to see out your probation."

"And then?"

Delray motioned her to step into the elevator first as the doors opened.

"We worry about that when it happens. You've got a lot of support here in the homicide room. You just need time to prove yourself."

Eager to change the subject, Delray pushed the B1 button for the basement parking lot and asked, "Did you have a chance to look at the printed file I gave you on your mother's murder."

"I did. It was very interesting, but it probably raised as many questions as it answered."

"What kind of questions?"

"A lot of the evidence wasn't included in the report. It's still only available on the physical record."

Delray nodded and replied, "Have you met Don Raisin yet?"

"No."

"Don runs our archives down in B2. He's going to retire as soon as all the physical records have been digitized, so he's currently working most nights until around eight p.m."

The elevator door opened to the parking lot on basement level one. Delray pushed a button to hold the elevator doors open and said, "We can take an extra five, and I can take you down and introduce you if he's there. He'll be able to pull the physical file for you tomorrow if you like?"

"That would be great, Chief, but you really don't have to go out—"

Delray pushed the button for B2 and said, "It will help give you closure, Bridgette—and that's important. I'll only get the best out of you when you're not distracted, so there's something in this for me as well."

The elevator hummed for a moment and then the door silently slid open at basement level two. They stepped out into a small foyer area that was fully enclosed by steel mesh. The furnishings consisted of a heavily scarred wooden desk pushed hard up against the left side of the cage and two plastic chairs with steel legs. Bridgette guessed the desk might have once been used by a senior executive within Vancouver Metro, but the plastic chairs looked like they had come straight from the canteen. A mesh door framed by heavy steel was set into the rear wall of the enclosure and boasted a sign that read, 'Authorized Personnel Only'.

Delray pressed a buzzer on the wall next to the elevator and then pointed at a security camera that sat above the mesh door.

"If Don's still here we should—"

Before he had a chance to finish, they both heard the distinct soft metallic click of an electronic lock releasing. Delray walked across and pushed on the metal door, which released and swung inward.

He motioned Bridgette to follow him and said, "They're very particular about who they let in beyond this point. If Don Raisin doesn't like you, you get to wait in the cage while they retrieve your file. I know guys who have worked here for twenty years that have never been past this point."

Bridgette followed Delray into a large cavernous area that was dimly lit and much bigger than she had expected. She looked along the long row of tall racks that stretched back into the darkness and estimated each rack easily held a thousand archive boxes. She'd heard about the physical records storage room from some of the other detectives. Some called it the warehouse and others called it the dungeon, but they all agreed the job would lose some of its charm when all the old records were eventually copied to computer. She wondered about the stories each box contained—information collected by detectives, many of whom had long since retired, and began to understand why some of her colleagues were less than enthusiastic about the digital age.

She breathed in deeply and smelt the smell of old books, like a library, and said, "I hadn't expected it to be this big."

"It's the same size as the parking lot above which holds close to five hundred cars. There's a lot of history down here."

Turning to his left, Delray pointed to a long narrow pre-fabricated three-room office that sat up against the south

141

basement wall. Looking in through one of the windows, Bridgette could see a man in his early sixties with thinning gray hair, sitting at a desk looking at a computer screen in the middle office.

"That's Don, let's go meet him."

Raisin looked up when he heard a knock at his door and waved them in. He had large bags under his eyes and a craggy complexion that made him look permanently sleepy. Bridgette had heard nothing but glowing praise from Delray about the man who had run archives for almost thirty years and knew better than to judge him by his looks.

After introductions, Delray briefed Raisin on the background to the murder of Bridgette's mother and why they were here. Bridgette picked up on Delray's subtle and careful use of words as he tiptoed around the politics of the situation with Cunningham and her access privileges.

Raisin listened politely and then said, "I knew your father, Bridgette. He was a good man and I never believed any of the BS about him being involved in your mother's murder. As far as I'm concerned, they were always looking for the wrong guy."

Bridgette smiled and said, "Thank you, Don. I'm not sure we'll ever catch who did this, but I would like to understand as much as I can about what happened."

Raisin smiled and the sad, craggy face became happy for a moment.

"Well, we have a strict protocol for managing our archive records. Anything that leaves the floor has to be signed for and officially checked out by me or one of my staff. We keep a complete inventory of all our records and know exactly where they are at any given time."

Raisin winked at her and continued, "Of course, if you stay down here and do your reading in this office, you're not really borrowing anything, so I don't need to record your name on the register, do I?"

Bridgette appreciated the gesture. It was clear both men were keen to see her research remain off the record and not turn into something that could be tracked by Cunningham and potentially used against her.

She nodded and said, "Thank you, Don. I appreciate it."

Raisin waved her off and said, "Don't mention it. I'm down here most nights until around eight o'clock, so come down when you like."

He went on to explain how he would be retiring as soon as the digitizing of all the archive records had been completed, which would probably be another three months.

Delray asked, "You can't be too popular at home with Kitty if you're working back till eight o'clock every night?"

Raisin laughed and replied, "First time in my life I actually get paid to work overtime—my wife loves it."

Delray and Bridgette both laughed politely, and Delray then made a move to leave.

"We should let you get back to it, Don. Thanks for your time tonight."

Raising replied, "Don't mention it," and then looked at Bridgette and said, "Ring me tomorrow with the case number and I'll get one of my guys to pull it for you. I'll put it in my office safe and it will be ready for you whenever you want to come down."

She replied, "I've committed it to memory. I can write it down now if you like?"

Raisin replied, "That's a fair memory you have, Bridgette,"

as he slid a piece of paper and a pencil across the table.

Bridgette wrote down the case number and handed the paper back to Raisin.

Raisin studied the case number for a moment and said, "This record is close. Hang on."

Without another word, Raisin shuffled out of his office and over to the archive racks. Bridgette and Delray watched as he walked down six rows before turning left and disappearing. They watched with interest as he emerged moments later carrying an archive box.

As they watched him walk back to the office, Bridgette whispered to Delray, "Do you think that's it?"

"We'll know soon enough."

Raisin walked back in the office and winked at Bridgette as he placed the dusty box on his desk.

"You get to know the case number sequences and their locations pretty well when you've been doing this job for as long as I have. I knew from the number it wasn't going to be much of a walk to find it."

They all stared at the box for a moment before Delray said, "You should take a quick look tonight, Bridgette, otherwise you won't sleep."

Bridgette looked at Raisin as if asking his permission.

Raisin gestured at the box and said in a soft voice, "Be my guest, Bridgette."

She stepped forward and gently gripped the dusty cardboard lid. Pausing for a moment, she read the box's identification label. The words 'Casseldhorf - Murder' jumped out at her. She couldn't explain it, but every now and then random reminders of her mother's murder still caused her to catch her breath. She gently removed the lid and looked inside. She was surprised the box only contained one slim manila file. She gently lifted it from the box and immediately knew something was wrong as she read the case number.

Chapter 21

Bridgette closed the murder file and placed it carefully on the bedside table next to her clock. She looked at the time—it was almost eleven p.m. Frustrated by not being able to make any more progress on her mother's murder, she picked up her mug of peppermint tea and took another sip as she thought back to the meeting earlier that evening with Don Raisin.

Her hopes of being able to read more about her mother's murder had been high when Raisin had walked back into his office with the archive box. Raisin was initially very embarrassed when Bridgette pointed out the file in the box belonged to another case. But his embarrassment quickly turned to anger as he checked the archive register and realized her mother's murder file hadn't been checked out.

She had waited patiently with Delray for almost an hour while Raisin called several of his employees and then made his own search in the hope the correct file had been accidentally misfiled. Raisin finally admitted defeat and while it was too early to call the file officially missing or stolen, everyone found it hard to believe the file had simply been misplaced.

Delray had asked how long it might have been missing and a

red-faced Raisin admitted it could have been years as the file hadn't officially been checked out in more than a decade. They had left a rather somber Don Raisin promising to make the file's recovery a priority the following day. She had spoken briefly with Delray in the car park before they left and he had readily admitted the chances of finding the file were slim.

She recalled his words as she took another sip of tea, "The system's usually very good—we don't lose many files at all. The ones that do seem to permanently disappear generally involve some cop who's afraid he'll wind up going to jail or losing his career if case evidence becomes public."

Troubled by Delray's words, Bridgette had come home and re-read every word in the abbreviated computer record Delray had given her. Nothing stood out to her as being inconsistent with what she remembered except for the two gunshots. Cunningham's summary in the murder record stating that only one gunshot had been heard by neighbors still bothered her. She wondered about the witnesses and whether their testimony had been accurately recorded?

She had no doubt that if the file had been deliberately taken, it contained incriminating evidence that someone never wanted to be made public. She wondered what it was. If her father had been meeting with cops on the day her mother had been murdered, maybe one of the neighbors saw them and provided a description in their testimony? As she took another sip of tea, she decided she would go and visit the townhouses where her family used to live. Maybe some of the neighbors still lived there and knew things that never made it into the official record?

The sound of her phone ringing brought her back to reality. It was after eleven p.m. and highly unusual for anyone to ring at this hour. She didn't recognize the number and debated letting it go through to voice mail, before deciding to answer.

"Hello, this is Bridgette."

Silence followed. She could hear the caller breathing and began to think it was a crank call.

"Hello, who is this?"

When there was no immediate response, Bridgette rolled her eyes and said, "I'm hanging up now."

A slightly raspy male voice replied, "Please don't hang up."

"Who is this?"

More silence followed. Growing frustrated, Bridgette said, "I don't have time for this."

As she went to hang up again, the male voice responded. The voice was familiar to Bridgette and she froze as she listened.

"Bridgette, this is your father... I'm not sure where to begin."

She closed her eyes tight and listened to a voice she had not heard in over twenty years.

"I'm so sorry about your mother... If I had any idea I was putting my family in danger that day, I would never have agreed to the meeting."

Biting down hard on her bottom lip, Bridgette breathed in deeply as the shock began to set in. She began to shake her head in disbelief as she realized her father was still alive.

"There's a lot I need to tell you, but for now, you need to know you're in real danger, Bridgette. These men will stop at nothing to see their reputations protected..."

Bridgette barely heard any of the words. She wasn't interested in any warning, she just wanted answers to questions she had carried around for twenty years.

Doing her best to control her anger, she asked in a tight

voice, "Why? Why leave it until now? Didn't I at least deserve to know if you were still alive or not?"

There was a slight pause before the voice responded.

"Of course you did."

Bridgette didn't respond. She knew the anger she felt towards her father for letting her suffer for twenty years would take time to get over.

"I was set up, Bridgette. I knew too much, and they wanted to buy me off. I'm sure you've heard a lot of stories, but I didn't realize they were involved until it was too late. When one of them pulled a gun, I ran. I just wanted to get them away from you and your mother. When I drew them out of the house, I thought I had succeeded.

I didn't realize until much later that..."

The phone line went quiet for a while. Unsure that she could control her emotions, Bridgette said nothing and waited for him to continue.

"I came back to the house about two hours later. It was close to dark and I used back streets because I knew they would still be looking for me. I planned to pack our bags and for the three of us to leave Vancouver that night and never return. When I saw the police cars and the ambulance out the front of our house, I knew something was terribly wrong. I called the only person I could still trust in Vancouver Metro from a public phone, and he told me your mother had been..."

Bridgette could hear her father's voice faltering as he spoke. Her anger started to give way to sadness as she realized how painful this must be for him.

"He told me I was the prime murder suspect, and every cop in Vancouver was looking for me. I wanted to come back for you, Bridgette, but I left it too late."

More silence followed and then her father said, "I'm so sorry, Bridgette."

"I'm sorry too..."

They were both quiet for a moment, lost in their thoughts as they both relived the horror of that day.

Finally, Bridgette asked, "But why? Why not make some sort of contact? It's been twenty years."

There was more silence before her father replied, "Your mother's murder was incredibly hard for me, but not seeing you was even harder. Even though I desperately wanted to be with you, the only way I could protect you was to stay in hiding. These people have no conscience, no sense of right and wrong and would think nothing of killing you if they thought they could use it to stop me exposing them.

Eventually, you grew up, but they haven't gone away, and I know they'll kill you if you get too close... that's why I called."

Bridgette wasn't sure what to say. Her mind was racing as she tried to process everything her father had told her.

There were still too many unanswered questions and she said, "I want to see you."

Silence followed before her father replied, "I want to see you too, Bridgette, but it's not safe. I'm still wanted by the law and while there are powerful people with secrets to protect, I can't take that risk."

Bridgette found herself shaking her head as she responded, "You can't contact me after twenty years of my not knowing whether you're alive or dead and leave it at a phone call. That's not fair, I just—"

"I can't talk any longer now, Bridgette. I've been on the line too long already."

Bridgette tried desperately to interrupt, but her father

continued, "I love you, Bridgette. I always have and always will. Not a day goes by where I don't think about you."

As tears streamed down her face, Bridgette whispered, "I love you too, Daddy".

"I promise I'll call again soon, Bridgette, but for now, please let this go. I don't want to lose you as well."

The phone line went dead, and Bridgette sat for a long time in a total daze. She felt more confused than ever, but she was glad her father was still alive. She switched off her bedside light and lay down on her pillow. Staring up into the darkness, she knew sleep would be hours away.

Chapter 22

Bridgette watched as Lance Hoffman shuffled in through the front door of the coffee shop. The shop had been styled to look like a classic New York diner and it was one of her favorite places to sit and relax. She had chosen a booth in the back to give them privacy and raised her hand slightly so that Hoffman could see her. Hoffman gave her a nod and then navigated his way through the tables filled with customers who were all busy talking and eating breakfast.

Clearly still in pain from the beating he had taken in the laneway, he winced as he slid into the booth seat opposite her.

Bridgette asked, "Are you taking your painkillers?"

Hoffman snarled as he replied, "What are you—my mother?"

"You'll function better if you're not in so much pain."

"They make me drowsy and I need to be on my game. Besides, the Doc said there's nothing they can give me to speed up the healing process."

Before she had a chance to respond, Hoffman changed the subject.

"I get a phone call from you at six in the morning requesting a meeting. I know it's not my health you want to discuss, so why am I here?"

Bridgette nodded and said, "Firstly, thank you for coming on such short notice."

Hoffman nodded but said nothing.

"I wanted to talk to you away from the office—off the record if that's okay?"

Hoffman rolled his eyes.

"I'm not a fan of off the record meetings. I've been burnt more than once by them."

"I can't give you any guarantee, so if you don't want to listen just say so."

Hoffman fired back, "Let's hear it," and then waited.

Bridgette started with a brief summary of what happened the previous night when Delray had introduced her to Don Raisin. She told him how her mother's murder file couldn't be located and how she thought the file had probably been stolen by someone connected to her mother's murder case.

When she had finished speaking, he said, "I still don't understand why I'm here. You could have told me this at the office."

"So, what do you think of my theory?"

Hoffman replied evenly, "I don't think anything of your theory. You said it yourself, the file could have been missing for a decade. It's hard to jump to any conclusion when a file has been missing that long."

Bridgette nodded. Ordinarily, she would have found it highly unusual for Hoffman not to be offering an opinion—you usually got one whether you wanted it or not.

"My father is still alive."

Hoffman responded evenly, "And how do you draw that

conclusion from a missing file?"

"You don't seem surprised?"

In a slightly irritated tone, he replied, "Again, how do you draw that conclusion from a missing file?"

Bridgette held his gaze and said, "Not from the missing file. He called me late last night. It was definitely him—I remembered his voice."

Silence followed. Hoffman stared at her but said nothing. Bridgette was prepared to wait him out and an awkward silence followed.

A middle-aged man wearing a black apron diffused the standoff when he approached them to take their order. Bridgette ordered peppermint tea and waited while Hoffman ordered coffee with bacon and eggs.

After waiting until she was sure they couldn't be overheard again, she continued, eager to press Hoffman for a response.

"We didn't talk for long. He called to warn me to stop trying to find out more about my mother's murder case. He believes the people that were after him back then are still after him now, and that's why he's still in hiding."

Hoffman couldn't hold her stare any longer and looked away.

Bridgette continued, "My father said a lot of things last night that I'm still trying to make sense of. He told me how he returned to our house about two hours after being confronted by the men, only to find it surrounded by police tape."

She paused for a moment, but Hoffman still wouldn't make eye contact.

"He told me how he quietly slipped away without being spotted and called a colleague at Vancouver Metro to find out what had happened... he described this colleague as the one person he could trust."

Bridgette paused again. She didn't expect Hoffman to respond—they both knew what was coming.

"I tossed and turned for hours. I was happy that he was still alive but also angry that he had left it so long to make contact. The question I kept asking myself was, how did he know I was looking into my mother's murder? Was it a guess, or maybe he just assumed that's what I'd do?"

She paused again as the waiter returned with their coffee and tea and a promise that Hoffman's breakfast would be arriving soon.

When the waiter left, she continued, "He said I was in danger, like he knew exactly what I was doing. It dawned on me then that someone had contacted him. The three people that came to mind were Don Raisin, Chief Delray and... you."

Hoffman looked back at her and held her stare, but still said nothing.

"You and my father were friends. You said it yourself. You came to our house with your wife for social visits—cops only do that with people they trust."

She paused to take a sip of her tea. In a voice barely above a whisper, she said, "It was you he called on the day of my mother's murder, wasn't it? When he needed someone on the inside to tell him what was going on, he turned to the one guy he knew wouldn't give him up."

Bridgette took another sip of tea and continued in a more conversational tone.

"It all makes sense. You've had his back ever since. You knew about my investigation and contacted him because you were nervous too."

Hoffman picked up his coffee and took a long sip before

replying.

"Peter Casseldhorf was one of the best detectives Vancouver Metro ever had. When he told me about the two detectives on the take with the drug kings, no one had any idea it would end like this. The day before the meeting at your house, he got a call from a Vancouver Metro lawyer connected to internal affairs. The guy wanted to come and see him to discuss what he knew. Peter agreed, but only if it was off the record and away from the office because he didn't want anyone seeing him talking to internal affairs."

Hoffman put his coffee down and continued, "The lawyer then suggested they meet at Peter's house so that they weren't seen in public together. When he showed up at your house, he had a friend with him. They offered Peter a lot of money for his silence. When he refused, all hell broke loose..."

"Why would my father trust someone he didn't know to come to his house?"

"I asked him the same question. According to your father, the call came in on an internal line while he was in the office. After the call, he looked up the guy's name on the staff phone list and got a match, so he thought it was legit. It turns out the real lawyer was away on leave at the time, so Peter had no idea who it was who called him. Back then the phone system was a lot less sophisticated than it is now, so it's possible someone hacked in from outside."

"My father didn't recognize either man who turned up pretending to be lawyers?"

Hoffman shook his head, "No. He thinks they were hired guns from out of town. Peter knew most of the men capable of something like this that were residents of Vancouver."

Bridgette nodded. Some of it was at least starting to make

sense. She had wondered for a long time how her father could have made such a fatal mistake as to let someone that dangerous get so close to his family.

"So, if they were just hired hit-men, does my father know who they were working for?"

Hoffman shifted uncomfortably in his chair. She noticed he had a habit of fidgeting when he didn't want to answer a question.

"We both have our suspicions, but you can't go around making accusations without hard evidence. Whoever it is, they've gone to considerable lengths to keep themselves separate from the dirty work."

"Someone high up in Vancouver Metro?"

"Maybe."

Hoffman sighed and then continued, "I don't talk with your father very often and I have no idea where he's living. I've tried to get him to come out of hiding, but he refuses. He says he would be arrested and after twenty years on the run, no jury is going to believe he's innocent of your mother's murder unless we can prove who did this. He's probably right."

"So in twenty years, no one else has come forward? Surely somebody must know something?"

Hoffman picked up his coffee again and took another long sip. "The two cops who Peter saw on the take were arrested about two years after your mother's murder on a separate corruption matter. They were never the smartest tools in the shed and eventually got caught. They did jail time and I followed the case pretty closely. Neither of them gave up anything that remotely connected them to your mother's murder."

"They were investigated for involvement in my mother's

murder?"

"No. Almost everyone at Vancouver Metro is convinced your father went off the rails and killed your mother."

"Do you think one of them could have taken my mother's murder file?"

Hoffman shook his head.

"They were long gone from Vancouver Metro when the file went missing. They were just grunts who got caught and did their time. Whoever was behind stealing the file hasn't been caught and wants to keep it that way."

Hoffman paused as the waiter returned with his bacon and eggs. When he was out of earshot, he continued.

"Whoever was behind your mother's murder has a lot to protect and is very careful. Your father eventually tracked down the two men who were at your house that day, but that turned out to be a dead end literally. One guy was found floating in the river with a bullet hole in his head not long after your mother's murder and the other guy, the one posing as the lawyer, was killed in a hit and run."

"How convenient."

"Your father hasn't given up trying to find out who's ultimately behind this, but he's never been able to find concrete evidence that will stand up in a court of law, and frankly, he probably never will."

After stabbing a large piece of bacon with his fork, he continued. "When they couldn't find your father after he escaped, I'm sure the two trigger men were told to come back and kill your mother as a warning."

Bridgette sat for a moment trying to absorb everything Hoffman had just told her. The last twelve hours of her life had turned her world upside down. She knew there was no way she could stop what she was doing. She craved order and understanding and would continue to investigate until she found the answers.

As if reading her thoughts, Hoffman added, "He's incredibly proud of you, Bridgette, but also very scared. Take my advice, don't push this. If you do, who knows where it will end."

"So what do you suggest I do, just sit back and do nothing? That's not how I'm wired."

Hoffman put his fork down and leaned in a little and said, "You're investigating shadows. Whoever ordered your mother's execution was never caught. Twenty years is a long time, but not long enough. He might be dead by now, but who knows?"

"If I keep investigating, we might flush him out?"

Hoffman hissed back, "And you might also get yourself killed. Your father wouldn't have contacted you unless he thought that was a real possibility."

She shook her head and replied, "I'm not letting it go. This is my mother, and her killer needs to be caught and prosecuted."

Hoffman stared back at her angrily as he slid out of the booth.

As he stood up, he poked a finger in her direction and said, "You're too damn stubborn for your own good."

Bridgette watched as he turned and stormed out of the diner. She had learned more from the short meeting than she dared hope for. She wondered for a moment whether Hoffman and her father were overreacting? Only time would tell. She looked down at Hoffman's bacon and eggs now going cold and picked up her peppermint tea again. As she took a sip, she was confident she could find the truth if she kept at it long enough. Her mother deserved justice, and her father the chance to live again as a free man.

She wondered again about who was behind this? Perhaps it was someone within Vancouver Metro she had already met? Assistant Commissioner Cunningham kept coming to mind—perhaps that was why he was so keen to see her removed from the force?

She checked her watch and decided there was nothing to be gained from sitting here any longer. She did her best to switch her attention back to the Monica Travers' case as she slipped a twenty-dollar bill under her tea cup. She wondered about the serial killer again and whether he had seen her entry for the competition yet? A shiver ran down her spine as she realized two men may now be hunting her with totally different motives.

Chapter 23

The day dragged for Bridgette. Hoffman had barely spoken to her, and she knew he was still mad at her after storming out of the coffee shop that morning. He had sidelined her from much of the real investigative work that the murder team had been tasked with for the day. Jones and Vincent had been sent back to re-interview the attendant from the van hire company in the hope they would learn more about the killer, while the rest of the team had been tasked with re-interviewing all the business owners and shop keepers in the block surrounding the Garrick Brothers department store. Now that they had a vehicle description, Hoffman hoped someone may have seen the black van on the night Monica Travers had disappeared and be able to give them more information about the killer's identity.

Hoffman had directed Bridgette to stay in the office to build a profile of the killer from the sketchy information they had learned so far. She was thankful he had given her free reign to research and investigate whatever she thought might be relevant to the case. Her computer access had still not been reinstated, and she had spent another eight hours in the homicide meeting room, sharing a computer screen with

Charlie Bates. They were now being referred to as the Siamese Twins by some of the other detectives. It didn't seem to bother Bates, but it was a nickname she was keen to move on from as soon as possible.

Looking up from the computer screen to give her eyes a break, she gazed out through the large window that separated the meeting room from the homicide office. Hoffman was hunched over at his desk, deep in conversation on his phone. She wondered whether he was simply punishing her because she had refused to follow his advice, or if he was trying to protect her by keeping her where she was easy to supervise.

Her thought process was interrupted by Bates, who leaned back in his chair and said, "It's after five and we're not making much progress here Bridgette. I think I'm going to pack it in for the day."

They had spent much of the day continuing their research on the five other linked murder cases that Bridgette had discovered in NatTrack. She believed they had made good progress and Bates was just using this an excuse to get out of working late.

Too tired to start a debate, she said, "Okay," and watched the gangly detective as he stood up and put on his jacket.

"You got plans for tonight, Bridgette?"

Don Raisin had called her earlier in the day to say that there was a chance her mothers' missing murder file may have also been copied to microfilm, an archival process they had abandoned years ago. She was planning on heading down to see Raisin shortly, but after the call from her father last night, she decided it was wise not to broadcast what she was doing too widely.

"I'm planning on a good night's sleep, Charlie. The case has been all consuming, and I haven't been sleeping much—hopefully that changes tonight."

Bates shook his head and said, "You work too hard, Bridgette. If you're not careful, you'll burn out before you're thirty."

Bridgette knew that wasn't about to happen to Bates. Unless pushed by Delray or Hoffman to work longer hours, he was strictly a nine-to-fiver.

Ignoring his comment, she replied, "Thanks for your help today, Charlie, I'll see you tomorrow."

Bates mumbled something to her about not staying late as he walked out of the room and headed for the elevator. She was thankful he had shared his password with her so that she could continue her research, even though it was strictly against police policy. She got up from behind the laptop and walked across to the whiteboard to review the information they had added that day.

Her thoughts were interrupted by Delray's voice behind her.

"Has Bates left already?"

Bridgette turned around to see disappointment written all over Chief Delray's face as he stood in the doorway to the meeting room. Everyone but Bates was putting in long hours on the Travers' case, particularly as it looked certain they would be playing second fiddle to a federal task force from tomorrow onward.

"Just a minute ago, Chief."

Delray nodded but said no more. She could see the Chief seething inside and decided there wasn't anything she could add that would improve his mood.

Delray walked a couple of paces into the room and stood with his hands on his hips studying the large whiteboard. His mood seemed to improve almost immediately as he could see the progress they were making.

Nodding at the board he said, "This is getting busy."

Bridgette nodded. "We made some progress today."

Delray walked back to the doorway and called out to Hoffman to join them. When they were both seated, Delray said, "Okay, walk us through it, Bridgette."

Bridgette wasn't sure where to start. The whiteboard was now a mind map of ideas and observations that she had worked up with Bates' help over the last two days. She thought she should start with some of the basics.

"Charlie and I spent some hours in NatTrack this morning looking for other murder cases in the system that match the pattern we've identified, but we haven't found anything else that's even close."

Delray frowned and said, "So no other unsolved cases like this anywhere else?"

Bridgette shook her head. "Not that closely match the shallow grave pattern or the victim profile."

Hoffman asked, "So what do you make of that? Are there only five previous victims before Monica Travers?"

"I don't pretend to be an expert, but most serial killers seem to have a geographic zone that they operate inside of. From what I've studied, it's rare that the same killer will have victims spread right across the country. They seem to prefer to operate in environments they are familiar with."

Hoffman shot back, "Then why three cities and not just one?"

"That's one of the questions we hope to answer in time. For now, I would guess the killer is familiar with all three cities. Perhaps he's lived in all three? Rochford has a population of over a million people and is only a five hour drive south of Vancouver. In a city of that size, it would be easy to come and go without leaving a paper trail if you drove a car."

Delray nodded and added, "Bolton is a similar size to Rochford and only three hours north by car. What are the odds he lives right here in Vancouver?"

Bridgette replied, "It's too soon to tell, but it's a logical choice."

Delray looked at Hoffman who didn't look convinced.

Pointing to a section of the board called profile, she continued. "Serial killers are usually male, but beyond that, there are no distinct patterns in their behavior or motive. They are not always intelligent and have a variety of motives—sometimes it's about power and the thrill of killing another human being, other times its paranoia, or fantasy, or sexual dysfunction that drives them, but there are no rules. I took three subjects on serial killers as part of my degree and, to be honest, I don't think I really know a whole lot more now than before I started."

She paused for a moment and looked at Hoffman and Delray in turn.

"I know the Feds will be here tomorrow and will bring in a specialist profiler, but profiling is far from an exact science. Most killers are caught because they make a mistake or want to be caught."

Hoffman pointed at the board and asked, "So all of this is a waste of time then?"

Bridgette looked back at the board as she continued.

"Profiling will never give you a description of a person of interest like a witness can, but it can help you narrow down your more likely suspect groups. We've learned a few things already. From what we can gather from each case, it looks like all victims have been lured to him with the promise of something for free. It's hard to see anyone being able to pull that off multiple times without being very intelligent. This is reinforced by the fact that each victim has been carefully selected by race, height, age, weight and hair color.

Also, we know the graves were carefully chosen so that the bodies would be discovered within several weeks of each murder. None of this is possible without meticulous planning. Some serial killers will choose their victims at random, or wait for an opportunity to present itself, but not this guy. He carefully chooses his victim and maps out every detail of what he's going to do and well before each crime."

Delray replied, "Okay, so he's highly intelligent and very organized. What else?"

"I think he's acting out a fantasy. Maybe somewhere in his past, he's been involved with a tall, dark-haired young woman. Perhaps she was even his first victim? Whatever his reasoning, I think he acts out the same fantasy over and over again with each murder."

Hoffman looked far from convinced and asked, "And how do you arrive at that conclusion?"

Bridgette looked at the board for a moment and then replied, "It's only a theory. But he sure is going to a lot of trouble to profile his victims. If you look at the photos of all five victims, they all have an uncanny resemblance. Either, he has very specific tastes or like I said, he's acting out the same fantasy each time and it's important to him that the victims all look the same."

Hoffman asked, "So he's insane?"

Bridgette thought for a moment before responding.

"I'm not sure anyone committing murder is really sane, but in a court of law, acting out your fantasies doesn't make you insane. Lots of people deliberately dress and have their hair styled to look like someone famous. It may be a fantasy on one level, but it's also part of our human nature."

They were all quiet for a moment before Hoffman pointed to the board and said, "You've written more about the murder weapons, but I'm not following?"

"I had a conference call with the detective who was in charge of the Michelle Wilson murder case in Rochford. He said Rochford Police never considered one person being responsible for both murders. As you recall, Mason, the other Rochford victim, was bludgeoned to death, but Wilson was stabbed multiple times like Monica. They never made the connection because the murder weapons were so different. It got me thinking about the Bolton killings..."

Delray leaned forward and said, "Don't keep us hanging, Bridgette."

"It's the same pattern—Bonita Sargent was stabbed multiple times, while Paige Ramsay was bludgeoned to death."

Hoffman looked slightly confused, "Okay so what does that tell us—he likes to mix it up a little?"

"Yes, but for what reason? I thought about it for a while after I got off the phone. The only thing that makes sense is he uses different methods to help further obfuscate what he's doing."

With a look of exasperation, Hoffman said, "Plain English please, Detective."

"Two young women stabbed within weeks of one another in the one city will make it a lot more likely for police to suspect the one culprit—the Rochford Detective said as much. But when you get two violent murders within weeks of each other where one victim has been stabbed and the other has been beaten to a pulp, you're more inclined to think society is simply getting more violent."

Delray asked, "So the way he kills his victims isn't important?"

Bridgette looked back at the whiteboard and underlined the word fantasy. "Perhaps not? Killing is a means to an end, but somehow I don't see it as his prime motivator."

Hoffman shook his head and said, "Do you hear what you're saying? If killing isn't the prime motivator, then why the hell do we now have six murder victims?"

Delray looked at Bridgette and nodded as if he thought this was a good question. Bridgette paused for a moment to collect her thoughts. Hoffman's question was a good one and right now she didn't have all the answers.

"All I can tell you is what I've learned so far. Like I said in the car yesterday, I studied one case from last century, where the killer was so shy, he killed women just so that he could talk to them. The murders allowed him to act out his fantasy and weren't the real motive."

Delray shook his head and said, "We'll probably never really know what makes someone like that do what they do."

Bridgette nodded, "This is why I don't put too much stock in profiling. It can help to a degree, but at the end of the day, it's not going to give you a physical description or the killer's address."

She looked at Hoffman and half smiled as she continued, "To paraphrase Detective Hoffman, you don't catch the bad guys with a whiteboard or computer."

Hoffman didn't return her smile as he replied, "You make

me incredibly nervous whenever you start agreeing with me."

Delray, clearly amused, smiled and said, "It doesn't seem to happen very often, Lance, so I don't think you've got too much to worry about."

Bridgette picked up her smartphone from the table and looked at the screen before putting it down again.

Delray raised his eyebrow and said, "The competition?"

"It closed twenty minutes ago. If he was contacting the winner and his next victim straight away, he's targeting someone other than me."

Delray nodded and said reflectively, "It was a long shot at best..."

Bridgette sat back down at the table in front of her laptop.

"There's one other thing I want to show you. It's been bothering me that we only have five murder victims and not six if you exclude Monica Travers, who it would appear, is the start of the pattern all over again.

The Jenny Sommers killing occurred here in Vancouver almost three years ago. She was stabbed to death four days after starting an apprenticeship as a hairdresser and found three weeks later in a shallow grave. I'm almost positive she was his first victim."

Hoffman replied, "Haven't we had this conversation? I thought we agreed he failed to pull off the second murder?"

Bridgette could see Hoffman was getting irritated. Even though he wasn't the lead investigator on the Sommer's case, he had been involved in an advisory capacity and maybe this was touching on a raw nerve. She pressed on knowing he wasn't going to like what she had to say next.

"We've learned a lot about the killer over the last two days. As I said, he's intelligent, calculating and meticulous in his planning. So far, he hasn't made any mistakes that we know of. It got me thinking—what if he had committed the second murder as planned, but the body was never discovered?"

Bridgette twisted her laptop around so that the screen now faced Delray and Hoffman.

As she pushed it across the table towards them, she continued, "This is an old newspaper clipping about a seventeen-year-old girl by the name of Haley Green. She disappeared one month to the day after Jenny Sommers. Because she was young and had been in trouble with her parents a lot, the investigation focused on her as a missing person. It was assumed that she would re-surface somewhere like most runaways do. But that never happened. Her missing person's file now has her listed as presumed dead... Her body has never been recovered."

Bridgette paused to allow Hoffman and Delray the opportunity to finish reading the newspaper article.

"Delray pointed at the photo of Jenny Sommers in the article and said, "See the resemblance? She could pass for Monica Travers' sister."

When they had both finished reading the article, Bridgette continued.

"I kept thinking, what if he had committed the murder, but something happened that prevented the body being discovered?"

Still clearly irritated, Hoffman replied, "Like what?"

Bridgette reached across and grabbed the laptop and dragged it back to her side of the table.

"I started browsing newspaper articles from the Vancouver Times archives. I worked my way forward day by day from the date of her disappearance, looking for anything that might make sense."

She paused for a moment to make a couple of keystrokes, then twisted the laptop around and slid it across the table again.

"I found this article and it made me wonder. Three days after Haley Green disappeared, we had torrential rain for thirty-six hours. There was some minor flooding around Vancouver, but what intrigued me was the rain triggered several landslides, one of which closed a walking trail at the edge of Catalin Mountain and the other did severe damage to several horse riding trails on a ranch in the hills beyond the northern side of the city."

Hoffman looked unconvinced as he replied, "What, the body got buried under a landslide?"

"I called State Parks about the walking trail and talked to a senior ranger. The landslide wasn't large, but it required heavy machinery to clear the trail. According to the ranger, the trail was out of action for about six months."

Delray looked at Hoffman and asked, "If a body was buried somewhere close to a trail, what are the odds it would still smell after six months?"

Hoffman shrugged, "It depends. If it's not disturbed and you've got undergrowth growing over the top of the grave and no animals have got to the body, then it might go undetected."

Delray nodded and turned to Bridgette for her opinion.

"I think we're better off directing that question to Doctor Warner."

Delray looked at his watch and said, "We'll call him tomorrow."

"I also called the owner of the ranch. He said the landslide occurred in the steeper hill section of his property and closed one of his most popular riding trails. He got contractors in to clear the rock and debris off the path, but it was going to be too costly, so he simply carved out another trail further around the hillside and away from the landslide. I asked him what happened to the old trail and he said it's almost unrecognizable, with large areas of it now overgrown."

Delray leaned forward again and said, "So the trail's been shut ever since the landslide—as in no one's used it since?"

Bridgette nodded and replied, "It might be nothing, but if the killer did bury the body near one of these trails, it may explain why it was never discovered."

Delray looked at Hoffman who nodded and said, "Like Bridgette said, it might be nothing, but these are loose ends that need investigating."

Hoffman's phone buzzed. He picked it up off the table, checked the number and then mumbled he needed to take the call as he left the meeting room.

While they waited for Hoffman to return, Bridgette said, "I browsed all the other major news stories for the next three weeks, but nothing else stood out."

"This is great work, Bridgette. You're thinking way outside the square and that's getting us results."

Bridgette blushed a little. She was enjoying working with Delray and felt the feeling was mutual.

"Thanks, Chief."

"You get a call from Don Raisin today?"

Bridgette nodded. She felt she could trust Delray and told him about the possibility her mother's murder file had been copied to microfilm.

Delray replied gently, "Don't get your hopes up too high, Bridgette. The microfilm system wasn't managed by Don—he just inherited it, and it was a mess. A lot of files got lost in the move and Vancouver Metro abandoned the program in favor of computerized archiving."

Bridgette tried to hide her disappointment, which Delray picked up on.

"The answers will come, Bridgette. We just need to be patient and figure out—"

Hoffman burst back into the room and said, "That was Jones. The guy who hired out the black van has just rung the rental company. He wants to return the van a week early and get some of his money back."

Delray leaned forward and said, "When?"

"Sometime tomorrow."

Delray scratched his chin and said, "Well, that's a curve-ball I didn't see coming."

Bridgette looked up at Hoffman and said, "If he's bringing the van back tomorrow, that means he no longer has a need for it..."

Delray let out a long breath and said, "The bastard has his next victim lined up."

Bridgette picked up her phone again. There was no text message. She felt sick in the stomach as she wondered if some unsuspecting young woman had already gotten a message congratulating them on winning the competition.

She had a sinking feeling that someone else was about to die, and there was not a thing they could do about it.

Chapter 24

Bridgette stepped out of the elevator into the small mesh caged foyer area on basement level two. Before she had a chance to reach for the button to notify Don Raisin that she had arrived, she heard the soft metallic click of the electronic lock on the security door releasing. Somewhere above her head, she could hear Raisin's voice echoing through a tinny speaker, "Come on through, Bridgette, I've got you all set up."

She pushed the steel mesh door open and walked past the racks of archive boxes towards Raisin's pre-fab three-room office. She could see Raisin through a glass window in the third office sitting at a machine that looked like a cross between an old photocopier and a microfilm reader.

After knocking politely on the closed door, she heard Raisin call out in a friendly voice, "It's open, Bridgette."

Bridgette could tell immediately that Raisin was in considerably better spirits than when she and Delray had left him the previous evening.

He motioned to her to sit in a chair next to him and said with a smile, "We may not have the physical file yet, Bridgette, but I got a full microfilm copy of it right here."

Raisin went on to explain he had searched for over two hours that morning through dozens of boxes of microfilm records before he finally found the murder file for her mother.

"I've never had much luck with locating anything on microfilm because it was never properly filed, but today, I got lucky."

"Thank you, Don, this means a lot to me."

Raisin raised a hand and replied, "Before we get into this, what's happening upstairs, Bridgette? I hear all hell's broken loose?"

Bridgette explained the phone call Hoffman had with Jones and how the black van they suspected of being involved in the Monica Travers' murder was being returned to the hire company tomorrow.

"So it's all hands on deck up there now?"

"Yes, everyone's been called back in to set up for surveillance around the hire company's warehouse."

Raisin cocked his head to one side and said, "Then why are you here and not up there helping?"

Bridgette shrugged and said, "It was the Chief's call. We have the federal task force arriving tomorrow, and he wants me to assist him with the briefing we have to provide on the Monica Travers' case and the other murders we think are related. Assistant Commissioner Cunningham will probably be involved as well, and the Chief thought the less I knew about this operation the better."

Raisin smiled knowingly and for a brief moment, the bags under his eyes almost disappeared.

"Good strategy. You can't be grilled about things you know nothing about. There's nothing like solving a crime and making an arrest right under their noses. The Feds don't like that."

"I'm not sure what to make of tomorrow... it almost seems staged. Why would the killer announce he was returning the van early? Why not simply dump the van and save yourself any additional risk?"

Raisin nodded and replied, "Good questions. Although if you're in Delray's position, you have to play it out. Second guessing criminals can invariably backfire."

Bridgette replied, "Yes, the Chief has no choice, but it does make you wonder."

They were silent for a moment while Bridgette stared at the strange back-lit reader. She had heard about microfilm but had never actually used the technology.

Sensing Bridgette's eagerness to look at the file, Raisin smiled at her and said, "These things were invented long before you were born, Bridgette. Microfilm was going to change the world, or at least how we stored things."

"But then computers took over?"

"Sort of. Microfilm was messy to manage, particularly when you wanted to add more information to an existing archive. When Vancouver Metro killed it off for good, I inherited it. A lot of files got messed up in the transfer and I never had the budget or need to fix it. We were lucky—your mother's case was one of the last batches of files that were copied to microfilm, so it wasn't too hard to locate."

Bridgette studied the machine. The microfilm was attached to a spool on the left-hand side of the machine and threaded through a back-lit lens that projected the magnified image up onto the screen.

Raisin pointed to a green button and said, "It works very similar to a standard movie projector, except you go one frame at a time. I've set it up so that you can start reading straight away. This is the advance button. Every time you press that, it moves the film forward to the next copied page from the paper file. You press the red button to go in reverse."

Bridgette pointed to a print button and said, "Can we print?"

Raisin shook his head. "Not yet. I can't find the paper tray and the one from the photocopier doesn't fit."

Bridgette smiled and said, "This is fine Don, I really appreciate it."

Raisin encouraged her to advance and rewind the film until she was comfortable with the process.

Satisfied that he had taught her all she needed to know, he looked at his watch and said, "I'm going to leave you with it, Bridgette. My wife has the flu, so I'm going to head home early."

"Do you want me to come back—"

Raisin shook his head and patted her on the arm.

"I make the rules down here, and you have a legitimate reason to be here, and I know my archives are safe. Just lock the office door behind you when you leave. The rest of the place is self-locking and alarming, so don't leave your keys behind when you go, otherwise, I'll have to come back in."

Bridgette thanked Raisin again and watched as he left the office and went to turn out the lights that lit the cavernous storage area. Bridgette shivered slightly as Raisin waved a final goodbye and then disappeared into the darkness towards the elevator.

Now alone, she pressed the green button to advance the film by a frame. The back-lit screen displayed a new page from the murder file. While the image wasn't as sharp as those from modern computer archives, the copy was in focus and easy enough to read. Deciding she should start at the beginning, Bridgette held down the red button to rewind the film.

She looked at her watch. It was well after seven and she hadn't eaten anything for almost six hours and was starting to feel hungry. She decided she would read for two hours tonight and then grab takeout from Ming's on her way home. She quickly became absorbed in the file as she re-read Cunningham's opening summary.

Chapter 25

After almost an hour, Bridgette couldn't take anymore and pushed back from the microfilm reader. Reading the full transcript of the autopsy had been hard enough, but the photographs of her mother's body lying on a slab in the morgue were proving too much. She turned her face away from the screen to avoid looking at a close up of the bloody bullet that had killed her mother and then shook her head to clear the image from her mind.

She sat for a moment trying to compose herself as it dawned on her that this was going to be much harder than she had ever imagined. After taking a deep breath, she got up and opened the office door to let in some fresh air. As she stood in the doorway peering out into the darkness, she closed her eyes and thought about her father. She wondered what he was doing and what he would think of her continuing the investigation despite his plea. Was he being overly paranoid? Could there still be a real threat twenty years after her mother's murder?

Her thoughts were interrupted by a noise and she opened her eyes. Frowning, she listened intently for close to a minute but heard nothing further. She replayed the sound over in her mind—soft and distant, like something metal rolling on the ground. Had she imagined it? She peered out into the blackness of the cavernous storage area but saw nothing beyond the dark silhouettes of the closest archive racks. She found the black void unsettling and stepped back into the office and closed the door behind her. As she peered out into the darkness through the large office window, she wondered if it was just rats or mice that she had heard?

Unable to see anything that would suggest she wasn't alone, she returned to the microfilm reader and whispered to herself, "You're just tired," as she pressed the green button to advance the microfilm past the horrible image of the bullet.

The microfilm display now showed a witness list. As she sat down, she counted off the number of witnesses and frowned. She was positive the computer record Delray had given her listed twenty-six witnesses, but the original typewritten list she was now looking at showed twenty-eight. She wondered whether two statements had been duplicated in the paper file and quickly re-checked the list of names. Unable to find any duplicates, she propped her elbows on the desk in front of the reader and cradled her chin in her hands.

Loose ends had always bothered her. She had been called an obsessive compulsive by more than one of her criminology professors and readily acknowledged it as a character flaw. She knew the list would nag at her until she had the answer and pulled her smartphone from her jacket pocket and took a picture of the screen. She would cross check the physical list with the computer list in NatTrack tomorrow to figure out why they didn't match. For now, she would content herself with reading the witness statements and pressed the green button to advance the microfilm.

The next image was almost completely black. Bridgette

leaned forward to try and distinguish letters or words from the dark background and wondered if the camera flash had failed when the page had been photographed. Realizing there wasn't enough contrast to see anything legible, she pressed the green button again and was relieved when the next page appeared as normal. She paused for a moment and then pressed the red button to return to the black image. She studied the screen for a moment and wondered whether the image could be copied from the microfilm to a computer? She had seen some of the miracles the lab technicians had performed with digital enhancement of grainy images and poor-quality photos. Perhaps they could do something with this image as well? She made a mental note to discuss this with Charlie Bates tomorrow—if anyone knew what was possible, it would be him.

With her finger resting on the green button, Bridgette stared uneasily at the dark screen. She was now totally focused on the reflected image she could see of the office behind her. She wasn't sure what exactly bothered her, but she moved her head forward just slightly to cut out the glare and now had almost perfect mirror view out of the office window and into the archives storage area behind her. She tried her best to remain calm as she watched the screen for twenty and then thirty seconds. Just as she began to relax again, she stiffened as she saw a faint movement in the reflected shadows on the screen.

She was now almost certain something or someone was moving around outside. Her mind raced through the possibilities. She quickly discounted Raisin or one of his staff returning to the office. If one of them had come back, they would have turned the lights on and announced their presence. As she watched the image inching forward in the shadows of one of the closest archive racks, her heart began to pound.

She looked at the phone that sat on the desk beside the microfilm reader and debated picking it up and dialing Hoffman or Delray's extension. What would she say to them? If they came down and failed to find anyone in a search, what would they think of her?

She thought for a moment longer and decided the best thing to do was to pretend she hadn't seen anything and casually pack up and leave. If she could get safely to the elevator, she felt confident she would be okay.

Taking a deep breath, she looked down at her bag lying on the floor at her feet. Her police issue Glock 19 was safely tucked away in an internal side pocket. She knew she would feel better about walking out if she was holding the gun rather than simply carrying it in her bag. As she bent down to retrieve the weapon, Bridgette was momentarily dazed by the sound of shattering glass and the stings of something like hot needles striking her in the back of her neck. Looking up, she saw half the glass screen of the microfilm had been shattered and ducked down again as a second muffled bang rang out and exploded the remainder of the screen.

She reached frantically into her bag and pulled out her Glock as she heard heavy footsteps walking quickly towards the office. Instinctively, she raised the gun and blindly fired two shots out through the broken glass window. She didn't expect to hit anyone but hoped the shots would scare off her attacker. Crawling quickly across the office floor through shattered glass, Bridgette reached up one hand and flicked off the light switch. As the office was plunged into darkness, she was thankful Raisin had switched off the lights to the other two connecting offices before he left.

Bridgette knew she needed to keep moving and crawled across the broken glass and through the connecting door to the middle office. With no real plan for what she should do next, she hoped putting as much distance as she could between her and her attacker would give her time to think. She heard the door to the third office open and saw the silhouette of a man standing in the doorway holding a gun. As the man scanned left and right looking for any sign of his quarry, she huddled against a desk in the darkness as best she could. Barely daring to breathe, she watched the man through the open doorway as he took two steps into the office before stopping again.

As her eyes adjusted to the darkness, she could see the figure of the man in the eerie darkness, barely illuminated by the tiny power lights of the office photocopier and fax machine. The man looked tall in the shadows, but it was too dark to make out any facial features. Bridgette felt very exposed and knew she had to remain perfectly still if she was going to avoid alerting the man to her position. The man took another step forward and stopped to listen again. He turned his head slowly and focused on the open doorway that led into the office where she was now hiding.

Bridgette's heart went into her mouth as the man brought his gun up into the firing position and started walking forward. He stopped just short of the doorway and Bridgette went rigid as she heard the angry muffled spit of his gun firing two shots over her head. As the man lowered the gun slightly and fired a third shot, Bridgette returned fire. It was difficult to tell exactly where the man was in the darkness, but she knew the bullet had found its mark as the man let out an audible groan and slumped backward against the microfilm reader and grabbed at his left shoulder.

Unsure what to do, Bridgette kept her Glock trained on the man as he quickly recovered and fled out of the office and into the darkness. Shaking almost uncontrollably, she got to her feet and debated following the man. It took her less than a second to decide that was a bad idea. She had no idea if he was on his own or not and she knew she was lucky to still be alive.

She walked back into the third office and stood in the darkness trying to compose herself and waited for any sign that the man might be returning. After two minutes, she lowered the Glock and flicked on the light switch. As her eyes readjusted to the bright light of the office, she steadied her blood covered hand and picked up the phone.

She dialed Delray's extension from memory and wondered if he was still in his office as she listened to the ring tone. She relaxed a little as Delray answered her call.

"Hey Don, you working late again?"

"Chief, it's Bridgette. Don went home an hour ago. I've been down here on my own. The place has been shot up... someone's just tried to kill me."

In an urgent voice, Delray asked, "Are you still taking fire?"

"No, he's gone. I'm pretty sure I wounded him."

Bridgette barely heard Delray's instructions for her to stay calm and not move as shock began to set in. She slumped to the floor and leaned up against a desk, her Glock in one hand and the phone in the other.

She vaguely heard Delray promising that he and Hoffman would be down there within two minutes but heard nothing else as she stared at the broken microfilm reader. It wasn't the bullet holes or the shattered screen that held her attention, but the empty microfilm spool, which was now hanging off

the machine at an acute angle. A hollow, empty feeling began
to settle over her as she realized the microfilm was gone.

Chapter 26

The next half hour was little more than a daze for Bridgette. She remembered Delray and Hoffman arriving shortly after she put the phone down, but not much after that. Now seated in Don Raisin's office with a bloody towel pressed up against the left-hand side of her head, she did her best to compose herself as Delray walked back into the office followed closely by a diminutive, well-dressed woman in her early fifties.

The woman hung back near the door while Delray went and sat down next to Bridgette.

In a gentle voice he said, "Bridgette, this lady is Doctor Carol Sanders. She's one of the female doctors who work for Vancouver Metro. You okay if she takes a look at you?"

Bridgette nodded and said, "Okay."

Delray looked back at Sanders and nodded as he got up from the chair. The two switched places and as Sanders sat down, she introduced herself to Bridgette and then gently explained that the examination she was about to do would form part of the official evidence collected for the internal affairs investigation.

After Bridgette gave her consent, Sanders smiled at her and

said, "You've been hit by a lot of broken glass. If anything looks serious, we'll get you to a hospital—okay?"

Bridgette nodded and allowed Sanders to reach up and take the towel that she had been holding against the side of her head.

Sanders briefly examined her left ear and said, "Well... it looks like the bleeding has stopped," and then proceeded to do a meticulous examination of her scalp and neck. Satisfied that nothing was too serious, she returned her attention to Bridgette's left ear. After several minutes, she sat back in her chair and asked Bridgette if she hurt anywhere else.

Bridgette held up her hands and said, "A few small cuts on my hands from crawling across broken glass, but other than that I'm fine."

"How does your left ear feel?"

"It throbs a bit."

Sanders frowned and said, "You're very lucky to be alive, Bridgette."

She turned and motioned to Delray to come forward and then gently pulled back the bloody mattered hair from Bridgette's ear again. Delray's eyes widened and he let out a low whistle.

Slightly irritated, Bridgette said, "What?"

Sanders said, "You've lost the outside half of your left earlobe. Given what's happened down here, I'd say you've been hit by a bullet. Fortunately, it's stopped bleeding, but it will require some surgical dressing and a course of antibiotics."

Bridgette was momentarily shocked as it began to dawn on her what had happened. She recalled the stinging sensation on her left ear after the first bullet had been fired but hadn't given it much thought as she went into survival mode. She realized if she had been sitting any further to her left, the doctor examining her would have been in a morgue rather than Raisin's office.

As she felt the color draining from her face, Delray asked, "Do you need to lie down, Bridgette?"

She shook her head and said, "No, I'll be fine. I guess it's just a shock when you realize how close you've come..."

There was an awkward silence that followed while everyone reflected on Bridgette's words.

Finally, Sanders turned to Delray and said, "I'd like to take Bridgette upstairs to our examination room on level two to dress the wound. Do you need her down here anymore?"

Delray shook his head and said, "Not for now. We have to make a statement to internal affairs, but that can be done later."

As they got up to walk out of the office, Bridgette realized she hadn't said anything to Delray about the microfilm projector.

She turned to Sanders and said, "Doctor, can you give me a moment with Chief Delray? There's something I need to show him."

Sanders looked at Delray and then back to Bridgette and said, "I'll wait outside."

Bridgette thanked Sanders and motioned Delray to follow her back into the third office.

They only got as far as the door when an internal investigations detective, who was currently dusting everything in the office for fingerprints, put his hand up and said firmly, "You can't come in here. Until we've cleared it, it's officially off-limits."

As Delray rolled his eyes in frustration, Bridgette said, "We don't need to go into the room, Chief, I can show you from here."

Pointing to the microfilm reader she said, "That's what nearly got me killed."

Delray nodded and said, "Lance and I suspected as much. Lance phoned Don Raisin while I was getting you settled in his office. When he told us he had set you up to look at your mother's murder file, we weren't surprised when the reader was empty. Don's on his way back in here now."

Delray studied Bridgette for a moment and said, "You know, Bridgette, I have no idea what's on that file, but someone sure is desperate to see it never sees the light of day."

Delray looked outside the office at Sanders who was doing her best to look like she was waiting patiently and said, "You better get going with the Doc. Give me a call as soon as you're finished. All hell's going to break loose over this, and we need to make sure there's no blow back on you."

Bridgette turned to leave, but then looked back and asked, "How did he get in?"

"It looks like he or they used bolt cutters on the mesh cage. The cage door was still locked. In fact, we used the opening they made to get in ourselves."

Bridgette nodded and said, "Trouble seems to follow me around, Chief. I'm really sorry."

"It's not your fault, Bridgette. In fact, this is a good thing. We've got corruption here somewhere—corruption that's been here for a long time it would seem, and we need to weed it out. One way or another this is bringing it to a head."

Just as she was about to reply, Hoffman appeared at the door and said, "There's no sign of anyone out in the archives. Whoever did this is long gone."

189

Hoffman turned and looked at Bridgette who still looked pale and said, "You okay?"

Bridgette nodded and said, "Apart from needing clip-on earrings from now on, I'm fine."

She left a slightly confused looking Hoffman to ponder her answer and said to Delray, "I shouldn't keep the Doctor waiting. I'll call you when I'm done, Chief."

Delray and Hoffman watched Bridgette and Sanders walk towards the elevator.

When he was sure they were out of earshot, Hoffman said, "I just got through speaking to Crowley. He's taking the lead for internal investigations on this. Apparently, Cunningham's already been on the phone to him, and he's totally pissed."

"Why does that not surprise me?"

"He asked me what I knew about Bridgette. So I told him straight—headstrong, but smart and with training will make a great cop. I even told him about how she saved my life in the alley."

"So, let me guess, Crowley wasn't buying it."

Hoffman shook his head. "No, he certainly wasn't. If I didn't know better, I'd say they're looking at painting Bridgette as some sort of guilty party, rather than a victim."

"If Cunningham has his way, that's exactly what they'll be doing."

"So, what do we do, Felix?"

"We do what we always do. We close ranks, and ride it out. This is going to get ugly and I've no doubt there will be some casualties. We've just got to make sure it's not us... and that includes Bridgette."

Chapter 27

The man winced as he put the first Tramadol tablet in his mouth. He raised a glass of water to his mouth, took a large sip and then repeated the same process with another three tablets. He was surprised he had managed to get back to his apartment without passing out. Right now, all he wanted was sleep, but there were things he needed to do first.

He limped into his tiny bathroom and switched on the light above the mirror. Naked from the waist up, he looked at his body in the mirror's reflection and moved in closer to examine his left shoulder again. He had only been home ten minutes, but the bruising already looked darker. He tried to lift his left arm again but could barely get it to shoulder height without feeling excruciating pain. He wondered how he was going to hide his injury from his colleagues—painkillers could only do so much.

He walked back into his living room and contemplated what he should do next. He looked around his small apartment with its drab, second-hand furniture and consoled himself that even though tonight had turned ugly, the money he was accumulating would shortly change his life forever.

He heard the cheap and unmistakable pitch of the disposable phone as it began to ring on the coffee table. He knew the caller would be angry and would demand to know why he hadn't reported in as instructed. He wasn't in the mood to talk to anyone and debated leaving the call to go through to voicemail, but he knew that would only make the situation worse.

He swore softly as he picked up the phone and pressed the answer button. As usual, the voice was heavily masked by computer software and he had to listen closely to understand the caller's words.

"You were supposed to call as soon as you got out of the complex."

"I ran into some problems, which I'm sure you've already heard about."

"My sources tell me she's still alive?"

The injured man shook his head. He had no interest in becoming a cop killer and firmly responded, "The brief was getting the microfilm, not killing a police officer. I got you what you wanted."

"My sources also tell me you were shot."

"And which sources are they?"

He heard a short laugh on the other end of the phone before the reply came back, "That's information you don't need to know. How bad is it?"

The man decided to play down his response and said, "I got hit by a ricochet. Some bruising but nothing too serious."

"Did you bleed?"

The man knew the caller was worried about DNA being left behind and decided he needed to steer the conversation away from the current interrogation.

"The bullet hit a steel door frame before it struck me in

the shoulder. It was badly fragmented and got caught in my overcoat. I left nothing behind that can be traced back to me. The gun was disposed of as we agreed, and my overcoat is now in a dumpster six blocks from here."

There was silence on the other end of the phone for a moment before the voice came back and asked, "Did she recognize you?"

The man shook his head in frustration. It was a stupid question, but he decided to be tactful with his answer. "It was dark, and I wore a ski mask as planned. After the shots were fired, I stayed just long enough to get the microfilm."

More silence followed. The injured man was used to dealing with the caller and knew better than to interrupt his train of thought.

"Did anyone see you leave the complex?"

"No. I left through a service gate at the rear. It's not manned after six at night and—"

"That's not what we planned."

"No, but I didn't plan on getting shot at either. I couldn't risk being identified and when all hell broke loose, I had to think quickly."

"I thought the rear gates are kept locked?"

"They are, but I used the bolt cutters I had for the wire cage in the basement."

More silence followed.

The man became impatient and said to the caller, "Bottom line is I recovered what you wanted. It will be in your delivery box tomorrow as planned—you can pick it up from there."

"How do I know you haven't been followed?"

"Because I'm cautious and very good at what I do. I've never failed you before and this is no different. Nobody is any closer to making a connection to you."

"While she's alive, there's always a chance."

The man thought about his response. He wasn't being paid enough to take any more risks and needed to make this clear to the caller.

"You need to understand two things. Firstly, she's unlikely to survive as a police officer. Word is, she's not popular with the top brass and they're setting her up to fail."

"And the second?"

"We both underestimated her tonight, and I'm lucky to be alive. I get you information, but if you want more than that, you'll need to hire someone else."

"I want you to continue to watch her. I'll call you tomorrow night after I've checked the microfilm. If I'm satisfied I've got what I want, I'll pay you your fee as arranged."

The caller disconnected and the man stood for a moment thinking about the conversation. He hoped his advice would be taken. Bridgette Casseldhorf was turning out to be much more of a complication than they imagined, and they would need to be very careful about their next steps.

The pain started to ease slightly in his shoulder as the painkillers kicked in. His body longed for sleep, but he was uneasy about what had happened tonight. He had told the caller he'd left nothing behind, but he couldn't be absolutely certain. He picked up the roll of microfilm and studied it as he began to develop a plan. If things turned ugly, he needed to make sure he didn't become the fall guy. The first thing he needed to do was find out who was hiring him. He'd never felt the need to know before now, but after what happened tonight, he knew it could be critical to his survival.

The man gingerly sat down at a small, wooden table that

doubled as both a place to eat and work and opened a laptop computer. After keying in a complex alpha-numeric password, he brought up a list from an encrypted file and began to study it. He'd worked for the caller for almost eighteen months, but they had never communicated through anything other than phone calls. Without an email address, voice file or permanent phone number, he knew finding the identity of his employer would be a challenge.

The caller had never said he was a cop or an ex-cop, but it became evident after the first few jobs that he was mostly interested in monitoring progress on very old cases. Out of curiosity, he'd made a list of all senior cops and ex-cops from Vancouver Metro who'd been active on the force between ten and twenty years ago. Until now, he'd never felt the need to take it any further, but that all had changed. Methodically, he worked his way down the list, considering each suspect against each job he'd done and how they might benefit from the intelligence he had collected.

After almost an hour he had narrowed the list down to three names. He stared at the names and was confident he could find out who he was working for if he had enough time. One was now a senator, another a successful businessman in construction and the third was still a senior law enforcement officer.

Satisfied with his list and in desperate need of sleep, he closed the file and shut off his laptop. The pain in his shoulder was still intense, but he decided not to take any more painkillers. He needed to be back in the office in under six hours and would need to be at the top of his game if he was going to avoid raising any suspicion.

Chapter 28

After a long night involving two interviews with internal affairs where she was made to feel like a criminal, Bridgette finally headed home at one a.m. The doctor had given her some strong pain killers to help her sleep, but she had decided not to take them for fear they would make her too drowsy to function properly the next day. She had slept fitfully through until just after six a.m. before heading back into work. She was surprised to find the homicide room empty when she walked in, but then remembered Hoffman and the rest of the team were on the stakeout at the car rental office.

She spent the next hour finalizing the official file to be handed over to the federal task force.

Just as she finished, Delray, looking haggard and in need of sleep, walked into the homicide room and asked, "How are you feeling, Bridgette?"

Bridgette smiled briefly and said, "I'm okay, Chief. I got a couple of hours sleep, so I'm good to go."

Delray mumbled, "What I wouldn't do for a couple of hours sleep right now..."

"Long night?"

Delray nodded and replied, "After we got through with what happened to you in the basement, we went back to planning for the stakeout at the rental company. The team's been out there and in place since four a.m. I got a call from Lance at five thirty a.m. Two of the federal boys showed up and basically wanted to run the show. As you can imagine, he was not impressed, and I've been out there playing referee."

"I thought they weren't arriving until today. How would they know?"

Doing his best to control his anger, Delray said, "I got a call from Charlie Bates last night telling me Cunningham had requested a copy of the file, so I'd bet a week's salary our esteemed AC has informed them."

Bridgette nodded. "So, is the meeting still on?"

"Yes, and I just had another call from Cunningham's secretary. He wants to see us before we meet with the task-force."

"As in now?"

Delray nodded and said, "Grab the handover file, and I'll meet you at the elevator."

Bridgette put on her jacket and picked up the file. As she walked to the elevator, she wondered how Cunningham would react to what happened the previous evening. Delray and Hoffman had both been very supportive, but she figured Cunningham would be a different story altogether.

As they rode up in the elevator, Delray said to her, "My meetings with the AC generally degenerate into arguments. I have no idea what we'll cover before the official meeting with the task-force, but I'm sure what happened last night is going to get plenty of air time."

Bridgette had only met Cunningham once before and that was with all the other new recruits. Cunningham had delivered an address to them as part of their induction. Like all the other recruits, she had been surprised by his demeanor. They had all expected a strong leader who would challenge and inspire them. Instead, they all felt like they were being lectured by a lawyer or bureaucrat.

As the elevator opened on the top floor, Delray whispered, "I know you'll be polite, but don't be intimidated by this guy. If he asks you anything, give it to him straight and if you don't know, just say so."

They waited at the reception desk while an efficient, middle-aged woman called Cunningham's number.

After putting the phone down, she said, "The Assistant Commissioner will see you now. Please knock once before entering."

Bridgette followed Delray to Cunningham's office. Delray knocked once as instructed and the two waited politely for a brief moment until a voice behind the door said, "Enter".

Delray opened the door and motioned Bridgette in. He had warned her earlier that Cunningham never greeted anyone that worked below him with a 'good morning' or 'hello' and encouraged Bridgette to forget the small talk and just answer the questions.

They both stood waiting inside the main door in what was one of the largest offices Bridgette had ever seen. She tried to be discreet as she looked around an office that was almost as big as the homicide room. With its expensive, solid oak furniture that included a conference table for eight and a selection of large original oil paintings, it had nothing in common with the office she shared with twelve other homicide detectives.

Holding a remote control, Cunningham sat behind his large

desk with his gaze fixed on a large flat screen TV that was mounted on the right-hand wall of his office. The sound was barely audible, and Cunningham made them wait through the news highlights before he hit mute and turned to face them.

"So far you're lucky. That debacle you two were involved in last night doesn't seem to have leaked to the press yet, and I'd like to keep it that way."

After pointing to two chairs in front of his desk, Cunningham picked up a document off his desk and said, "I asked Crowley for an interim report. I have to say in all my years of policing, this is one of the sorriest, most bizarre messes I've ever had to clean up."

Cunningham dropped the report back on the table almost as if he might catch something if he held onto it any longer. He leaned back in his chair and stared at Bridgette as he steepled his fingers. Bridgette held his gaze but didn't say anything. It wasn't the first time someone in power had played mind games with her, and she was determined not to blink or look away.

After a prolonged silence, Cunningham leaned forward and said, "You've stated for the record, Detective, that you were attacked—shot at no less? I have to say; I find this deeply troubling. You're still on probation and you're accusing Vancouver Metro police officers of serious corruption and attempted murder."

Bridgette thought Cunningham might be on a fishing expedition and decided not to say anything until he asked her a more direct question.

In a taunting voice, Cunningham continued, "Of course we only have your word that someone else was down there, don't we, Detective? For all we know, you could have shot the place up and made off with the microfilm yourself?"

Delray leaned forward and made no attempt to hide his anger as he said, "Sir, with all due respect to Crowley and his team, there are far less elaborate ways to steal microfilm than to shoot up a basement office and inflict personal injury upon yourself."

Cunningham shot back, "You're not internal affairs, Chief Delray, so your opinions don't count."

In an effort to diffuse the situation, Bridgette stood up and pulled her hair away from her left ear.

"Sir, part of my ear was shot off. The doctor took a swab for gunshot residue to determine if the bullet had been fired at close range. It was negative. She also removed glass from the lacerations on the back of my head and neck and determined they were caused by flying glass, which is consistent with my witness statement that I had been shot at from behind through the office window."

With a look approaching mild amusement, Cunningham responded, "Sit down, Detective. You can save the theatrics for internal affairs. If you're lying—for whatever reason, they'll find out and your career will be over."

Turning to Delray, Cunningham said, "Needless to say, Chief Detective, I have issued a communique to all Vancouver Metro police officers that they are not to say anything about this to the media under any circumstances. We have issued a press statement to the effect that we are investigating an incident in which an office window in a demountable in the basement was broken and nothing more. No mention of guns, shots being fired, or missing microfilm."

Cunningham leaned forward slightly as if to reinforce his point and said, "If anything leaks to the press, you'll be the first officer I call back in here, so I strongly suggest you reinforce this message with everyone on your team. Are we clear, Chief Detective?"

Delray managed to choke out, "Totally," in a voice that was less than civil.

Cunningham said, "I expect we'll all be called to the Commissioner's office very soon. Crowley's giving the Commissioner a private briefing on this and then I think we're going to be asked to explain ourselves."

Delray responded, "Sir, I welcome any opportunity to discuss this with the Commissioner. Right now, I have a staff member who's been shot at by what looks to be a member of our own force and internal investigations want to turn her into the criminal despite the evidence."

Cunningham held Delray's stare for a moment and then said, "This conversation is over for now."

He pointed to the file Bridgette had brought to the meeting and asked, "Is that the handover file for the task force?"

"Yes, Sir."

"Slide it across, Detective."

Bridgette slid the file across and waited patiently with Delray for the next few minutes while Cunningham thumbed through the file. Bridgette now understood why so many of Chief Delray's meetings with Cunningham ended in arguments. The rumors she'd heard about Cunningham's narcissistic behavior and how he threatened and belittled staff at every opportunity were obviously all true. She wondered again how someone so flawed could rise to the second highest position in Vancouver Metro.

Without looking up, Cunningham finally said, "Most of this information is not new. I got Bates to send me an electronic version of what you had on file last night..."

Cunningham quickly scanned a couple more pages and nodded, seemingly satisfied with the content.

After closing the file and putting it to one side, he said, "The federal agent in charge of the task-force is Dean McKellar. He's got over twenty years' experience and will be joining us momentarily. The other three agents in the team are now managing the stakeout at the car rental company. Before we go any further, you two need to know that as of now, McKellar and his team run this investigation. You cooperate with them fully and give them any and all assistance they require. Is that clear?"

Delray and Bridgette both nodded.

"I'll lead the briefing today, and if I want your input, I'll ask for it. If McKellar asks any questions, you defer to me. Is that understood?"

Bridgette could see Chief Delray becoming extremely agitated.

Doing his best to control his temper, Delray asked evenly, "Sir, shouldn't Bridgette be giving the briefing? She's done most of the profiling and if it wasn't for her analysis, we wouldn't be sitting here now and— "

Cunningham cut him off with a short laugh and said, "Detective Casseldhorf is still on probation and as of last night is now under investigation by internal affairs. There's no way I'm letting someone with so little experience and with such an uncertain future in this organization lead a briefing with a federal task force."

Before Delray had a chance to reply, there was a knock at the door.

Cunningham rose from his desk and said, "That will be

McKellar now."

He motioned Delray and Bridgette to sit at the conference table as he went to open the door. Bridgette watched as Cunningham opened the door and shook hands with a man in a dark blue business suit. He was heavyset and his full head of hair was just starting to turn gray at the temples. Bridgette guessed McKellar's age at somewhere close to fifty. After introductions were made and the four started to settle around the table, Cunningham made it obvious who would be leading the briefing.

"Dean, I've asked Chief Detective Delray and his assistant to join us today. They've been investigating the Monica Travers' murder and will be able to answer any questions you have that relate specifically to that investigation.

Without drawing breath, Cunningham launched into a briefing on the five related murder cases. He used phrases like 'team effort' and implied that the discovery of the murder pattern had been his idea. Bridgette stole a sideways glance at Delray. She expected to see frustration or anger, but with his mouth slightly ajar, Bridgette could see Delray was completely stunned by Cunningham's nerve as he passed off leadership of the investigation as his own work.

McKellar said very little throughout Cunningham's briefing. He jotted several notes in his small leather-bound notebook but only asked two general questions. Bridgette wondered if he had worked out that Cunningham wasn't as close to the investigation as he claimed to be and knew that asking him in-depth questions was pointless.

After forty-five minutes, Cunningham finally came up for air and asked, "Well, Dean, you must have some questions?"

McKellar opened up the thick file that Bridgette had prepared and begun quickly scanning the contents.

He didn't seem to be in a hurry to respond and after thumbing through a few pages, he looked up and said, "I'll have more questions after I've read the report, Leon. Right now, all I need is an office for me and my three staff and access to your principal analyst."

Cunningham asked, "Principal analyst?"

McKellar replied, "Yes. The person who figured out that these murders might all be connected and developed the killer's profile?"

Cunningham said, "As I said earlier, it was a team effort, Dean."

McKellar smiled as if he wasn't buying it and said, "But someone had to connect the dots."

Doing his best to recover, Cunningham looked to Delray to bail him out. Delray didn't need any further encouragement as he spoke for the first time.

"Agent McKellar, Detective Casseldhorf has been acting as the principal analyst on this. It was her investigation in NatTrack for similar cases to the Travers' case that led her to believe this was potentially the work of a serial killer."

McKellar nodded and looked at Bridgette and said, "So I'm curious. How does a probationary detective make the leap from a simple homicide case to a serial killer?"

Delray nodded at Bridgette as a cue for her to reply. She looked momentarily across at Cunningham who seemed to be doing his best to look thoughtful while pretending this was playing out as he expected.

"I guess it was the deliberate covering of the grave with leaves that first got my attention."

Bridgette went on to explain her theory that the killer had

deliberately picked the burial spot so that the body would be discovered within weeks of the murder.

McKellar nodded and then said, "That's still quite a leap to a serial killer?"

Trying to avoid any eye contact with Cunningham who was now giving her an ice-cold stare, she said, "I guess it just didn't make sense. Most killers try and hide their crime for good if they have the opportunity. It made me wonder if he'd done it before."

McKellar responded, "And that's when you started your research in NatTrack?"

"Yes."

Eager to gain control of the meeting again, Cunningham said, "Again, Dean, I must emphasize it's taken a team effort to get to this point in our investigation, but we would be happy to make Detective Casseldhorf available to you and your team if you have further questions."

McKellar thanked Cunningham for the offer and the two talked about accommodations for his team and how McKellar and his team would be reporting progress back to Vancouver Metro.

Never one to miss an opportunity, Cunningham said, "Speaking of reporting, this could become quite a big media story here in Vancouver. If an arrest is made today as a result of the stakeout, I'd be hoping we could come to some arrangement where we hold a joint press conference?"

Bridgette watched McKellar's body language closely. She had no experience with federal task forces, but she didn't think they would be keen to share the media spotlight.

With a deadpan expression, McKellar politely replied, "I don't manage media liaison, Leon. We solve the cases and then my superiors decide when and how we report to the media."

Not easily dissuaded, Cunningham responded, "If news gets out that we have a serial killer running around, the media's not going to accept a no comment until someone's behind bars. I've built up a very good relationship for Vancouver Metro with the media—I'm sure I'd be able to help ensure the coverage is favorable."

"We'll cross that bridge if and when we come to it. As I said, those decisions are made back at head office."

Cunningham nodded and said, "And I'm sure we can all work together cooperatively through this."

Eager to change the subject, McKellar turned to Delray and Bridgette and said, "Is there anything else my team needs to know that's not in the brief?"

Delray looked at Bridgette and said, "Detective, you should tell Agent McKellar about your new theory about the sixth victim?"

With no attempt to hide his anger, Cunningham glared at Delray and said, "Are you telling me, Chief, that this brief is incomplete?"

"No, Sir, but according to Detective Casseldhorf's theory, there should be a sixth body. Late yesterday, Detective Casseldhorf started working on some possible explanations as to why the body was never found. With the preparations required for the stakeout, we haven't had a chance to fully explore it, let alone add it to the report."

McKellar looked at Bridgette and said, "Don't keep me waiting, Detective."

Bridgette spent a few minutes explaining her theory about the significant rainstorm and landslides six weeks after the first Vancouver murder and how this may have prevented the victim being discovered. McKellar interrupted her several times with questions and wrote a few notes in his notebook.

When she had finished, McKellar said to Cunningham, "I think this bears further investigation. I'd like to ask that you make some of your uniform staff available to assist us with a search."

Cunningham nodded and said, "Of course. We can also make some of Chief Delray's team of investigators available as well. They will be able to keep me—"

McKellar cut him off, "That won't be necessary. I've got my own team of investigators, and we will only be looking for general policing assistance to keep the public out of the search areas."

The room went quiet for a moment before Cunningham replied, "As you wish."

Unperturbed by Cunningham's body language, McKellar added, "Also, it's usual in these investigations for local staff associated with these investigations to report directly to me on any matters related to the case."

Without waiting for a reply, McKellar turned to Delray and said, "As of now, you report directly to me on any and all matters connected with the investigation. You can provide briefings to your local superiors as you see fit, but any information you learn that's related to this case comes to me first."

Before Delray had a chance to respond, Cunningham shot back, "We have very formal reporting lines here, Dean. Any change to them would have to be cleared by the Commissioner himself."

Unfazed, McKellar replied, "Then I suggest you set up an urgent meeting with your boss."

Cunningham looked across at Delray and Bridgette and said, "You two can leave now. My secretary will contact you if we need anything further."

Chapter 29

Bridgette and Delray quickly vacated Cunningham's office and walked to the elevator. Only after the elevator doors were shut and they knew they couldn't be overheard, did Delray speak.

"Well, that went well."

Bridgette nodded and said, "Thanks for your support, Chief, I didn't expect a sympathetic ear."

Delray responded, "We've got lots of evidence you were shot at, and I'm looking forward to our meeting with the Commissioner. He's a straight up guy, and he'll be far more concerned about one of his own almost being murdered than how it looks in the media."

Delray paused as the elevator door opened and motioned her to follow him to his office.

As they walked, Delray said, "Lance and I discussed your safety last night. We think the microfilm was the main target and you're probably not in any more immediate danger, but I wanted to get your thoughts before we see the Commissioner. As you saw for yourself, we'll get no support from Cunningham, but the Commissioner will listen and act if necessary."

Bridgette let out a long sigh and replied, "I had the whole

office to myself for over an hour this morning. I must confess I looked over my shoulder more than once. I guess I'm a little spooked by all this..."

Delray nodded and said, "I haven't known you for long, Bridgette, but you strike me as one of the most mentally strong women I've ever met. But nobody's bulletproof. I'd like you to see one of our counselors—just to talk this through. You wouldn't be normal if you weren't feeling some anxiety over this."

Bridgette's first reaction was to say no. She'd had enough of shrinks after her time in the Navy, but the genuine look of concern in Delray's eyes made her think he was right.

She nodded and said, "Thanks, Chief, it's probably a good idea."

Delray nodded and then frowned as he looked down at his smartphone that had just started vibrating on his desk.

"I'd better take this, it's Lance."

Bridgette went to get up and leave the office to give Delray some privacy, but Delray motioned her to stay seated as he answered the phone. He talked in hushed tones for several minutes, but only said a few words—not unusual she thought for any conversation involving Hoffman.

Finally, he disconnected and said, "Well, that was interesting. The guy with the black van showed up fifteen minutes ago."

"They've arrested him?"

Delray nodded, "The federal boys have him in handcuffs and have taken him away in one of their vehicles. They've impounded the van and have their own people on their way to do a forensic examination. According to Lance, apart from providing perimeter backup, they've been totally shut out of the arrest."

"That's not surprising after our conversation with McKellar."

"No, but it gets better."

"Better?"

"Donescu recognized the guy from his time with the drug squad. Hoffman put his name through the computer in his car and it made for some interesting reading. He's spent most of the last two years in jail after being caught in another drug bust. He's been out of jail for less than three weeks, so there's no way he could have killed Monica Travers."

Bridgette leaned her elbows on Delray's desk and said, "Well, that is interesting."

"He's probably just earning a few bucks returning the van and has no idea what this is all about."

"It makes you wonder about the killer's motive, doesn't it?"

"Motive?"

"Why he bothered to go to the trouble of paying someone to return the van. It would have been far easier to simply dump the van and cut his losses."

Delray looked momentarily blank, but then realized where she was going.

"He was watching."

Bridgette nodded. "We don't know for sure, but it's the only thing that makes sense."

Delray scratched his chin and said, "I wonder what his game is?"

Bridgette was distracted by her smartphone vibrating on Delray's desk. She picked it up and frowned and she read the message.

In a stunned voice, she said, "It's him..."

"Him?"

Bridgette slid her phone across the desk. Delray picked it up and read the message to himself.

Congratulations! You've won tickets to Saturday night's performance of A Cold Summer at the Lyric Theater. Please text back your acceptance and one of our ticketing representatives will contact you shortly to arrange collection. Best Regards, JoLo Promotions.

Delray stared at the screen and said softly, "I expected a few curve balls today, but I never saw this one coming."

The room went quiet as Delray got up and closed the door to his office. He returned to his desk and settled into his chair. They sat for a long time, lost in their thoughts as they contemplated what they would do next.

Chapter 30

The silence in Delray's office was broken by a knock at the door.

Stirred from his thoughts, Delray said, "Come in."

Bridgette had seen Lance Hoffman angry on more than one occasion, but this was a whole new level as she watched him burst into Delray's office and launch into a tirade. She estimated he spoke for close to two minutes, seemingly without drawing breath, as he complained bitterly about the federal task force and how they had hijacked his surveillance detail.

Delray let him complete his rant and then said, "Lance, you seem to be forgetting I was out there playing referee. I've spoken with Cunningham and their lead guy McKellar and apart from fighting over who gets the microphone at the press conferences, Cunningham's given them complete control of the case. As of now, we're out."

Not easily deterred, Hoffman shot back, "Chief, if you ask me this is a bad idea. These guys have no idea what they're doing—"

Delray held up his hand and said firmly, "Stop... there's been a development."

Motioning Hoffman to sit in a chair next to Bridgette, Delray said, "Bridgette got a text message from the competition we entered. She's won the tickets."

As she handed her phone to Hoffman, Bridgette said, "It came in about twenty minutes ago."

Hoffman read the message and said softly, "I'll be damned, he's taken the bait."

She said, "We're not so sure."

Hoffman looked across at Delray and frowned as he said, "What am I missing?"

Delray leaned back in his chair and said, "It's all a bit too neat—I'll let Bridgette explain."

"We think the returning of the van was a setup. It would have been far simpler to dump the van and disappear, unless... "

She didn't finish the sentence. She had noticed Hoffman warmed to her ideas much quicker when he was allowed to have input.

Hoffman nodded and said softly, "He was there watching us," as he handed Bridgette back her phone.

Delray added, "Of course we have no proof, but why else would you bother? He gave a false ID and he paid the rental company up front and in cash. It would be far easier to simply leave the van in a parking lot and walk away unless of course, you were watching from a vantage point to see what happened. You wouldn't have needed to hang around for long to figure out we were onto the van."

Hoffman got out of his seat and walked to the window.

As he stared down into the parking lot, he said, "The guy who returned the van is a dead end. It was all organized over the phone—he never met the killer. The task force is

214

interviewing him right now, but they won't get anything more than a number to a throwaway phone..."

Hoffman turned around and leaned back on the windowsill. "So what do we do now?"

Delray replied evenly, "This text message is a development, so we call it in."

Hoffman growled, "You still want to tell the Feds about this after the way they treated us this morning?"

Delray picked up the phone and said, "I have to. It would be my career if I didn't."

Ignoring Hoffman's grumblings as he punched in a number from McKellar's business card, Delray said, "My wife Gloria does crosswords. She got stuck on one-word last weekend that she couldn't figure out. The word was obfuscate—it was the spelling that tripped her up."

Delray waited a moment while the phone connected and then said in a cheery voice, "Good morning again, Agent McKellar, this is Chief Delray again."

Delray paused a moment to listen and then said, "Yes, I appreciate you're very busy, but I wanted to let you know that Detective Casseldhorf and I are exploring another theory about how we can track down the identity of the serial killer. I was—"

Delray paused again and listened intently. A smile began to spread across his face as he ended the call, "Okay, I'll make sure we have a brief ready for you on Monday."

Delray put the phone down and said, "McKellar and his team are too busy to talk to us. Not surprisingly, he also thinks the guy they picked up is a dead end. He's getting searches organized for tomorrow and over the weekend for the two walking trails in the hope of finding a grave. Apparently, he likes your theory, Bridgette."

Hoffman asked, "So what do we do now, Felix?"

"We have until Monday. McKellar has his own profiler flying in on Monday and doesn't want us bothering him before then unless we get something absolutely solid."

Hoffman raised his eyebrows and said, "I'd say Bridgette's text message is fairly solid?"

Delray nodded to Bridgette to answer.

"We're not sure what the killer's motive is with the text message. I'm positive he deliberately called the rental company ahead of time and watched the return of the van to see if we'd made a connection."

Hoffman nodded thoughtfully and said, "Which tells him we've made a connection to the van, but nothing more."

Delray added, "Exactly."

Bridgette continued, "He could simply shut down for six to twelve months and then start up again—but if he wants to know for sure if the police are closing in..."

Bridgette paused again and allowed Hoffman to complete the sentence.

"You set up a pickup for your bogus competition and then watch and see if it's under surveillance or not."

Delray added, "That's why I could be vague with McKellar. All we have are theories. We don't know for sure if he'll show, and even if he does, he could be just watching for signs of surveillance."

Bridgette added, "And if he sees us, he could disappear without a trace and we would never know..."

Hoffman asked, "So what do you have in mind, Chief?"

Delray scratched his chin as he replied, "I've been thinking about this. If Bridgette gets a call to collect the tickets, this could all go down very quickly—we need to be ready for that."

Hoffman replied, "All the detectives from the surveillance detail are back in the homicide room. They're just starting to pick up other cases again, but I'd love to be able to tell them we're not done with this one yet."

"Delray nodded, "That makes ten of us in total including me."

Hoffman shook his head, "Nine. Bates has the flu and we sent him home—remember?"

Delray responded, "Nine will be enough. If I want general duties police as well, I'll need to bring Cunningham in, and that's something I'd rather avoid."

Delray studied Bridgette for a moment and asked, "Are you up for this, Bridgette? There's a good chance the killer will disappear again, but..."

"I'm fine."

Hoffman glared at her and said, "You had part of your ear shot off last night and you're very lucky you're not spending today on a slab in the morgue. Most folks in your position would be a little fragile right now."

She held Hoffman's glare and replied evenly, "I'm not most folks."

Delray continued, "Lance is right, Bridgette. It's been a pretty rough twenty-four hours for you. I'm sure I could arrange for another female police officer to substitute for you?"

Bridgette held Delray's gaze. She'd had very little time to dwell on last night and felt that keeping her mind occupied with things other than the shooting was her best therapy.

She responded, "Thanks for your concern, Chief, but I really am okay."

Delray looked at Hoffman who shrugged and said, "She's almost as stubborn as me, Felix. If she says she's good to go, then we get on with the planning."

Delray studied Bridgette for a moment longer and said, "Any time you feel uncomfortable about any of this, you let me know—okay?"

"Okay."

Satisfied, Delray said, "With Bridgette playing her role as the victim collecting tickets, that gives us four teams of two. A Cold Summer is playing at the Lyric Theater, which is on the southern edge of the CBD. There's lots of side streets and laneways down there and it backs onto the river. It's not going to be easy to cover."

Hoffman said, "I don't like it. We're assuming that's where the pickup will be, but there's no guarantee. He might angle for somewhere else in the CBD that helps him set up for a quick getaway and four teams can't cover the entire CBD."

Bridgette said, "We might be able to skew the odds in our favor."

Delray frowned and said, "I'm not sure I'm following?"

"We know from the Monica Travers security camera footage that he spoke to her by phone. He won't know exactly where I'm coming from, so I should be able to buy us some time by taking longer than I need to get to the pickup location to give everyone a chance to get in position."

Delray scratched his chin and said, "I'm liking it. We'll make sure you're wired so that you can communicate with us at all times. We won't be taking any unnecessary risks."

Hoffman said, "If we're going to do this, Chief, we need to brief my team as soon as possible."

Delray said, "You're right—let's get them together now and

start the planning."

Pointing to her mobile phone, Bridgette said, "There's one thing we should do right now, and that's text him back to say we accept."

Delray nodded and said, "There's always a chance he'll target someone else if we take too long to respond. What do you think, Lance?"

Hoffman replied, "Agreed."

Both men watched as Bridgette picked up the phone and keyed in the response.

Thanks - very excited. Please let me know where and when to pick up the tickets.

Regards B

With her finger hovering over the send key, Bridgette looked up at Delray, who gave a nod and said, "Send it."

She pressed the send key and watched as the screen refreshed to let her know the message had been successfully sent.

Delray rose from his chair and said, "Let's get the team together and start the planning. It may be tomorrow before we hear from him again, but you never know..."

As Bridgette followed Delray and Hoffman out into the hallway, she looked up at the clock on the wall—it was almost midday. She wondered if the killer had read her text message yet and what he was planning next.

Chapter 31

Bridgette frowned as she heard a quiet knock at her door. After waiting patiently until after seven for a response to the text message they had sent to the killer, Delray had sent the homicide team home for some well-earned rest. She had picked up some Ming's takeout on the way home and treated herself to a long bath before settling into bed with a peppermint tea and her mother's murder file. She looked at her bedside clock and wondered who could possibly want to see her after ten p.m.?

She sighed as she put down her tea and slid out of bed. Still tying up her dressing gown as she reached her front door, she looked through the peephole expecting to see the building manager and was surprised to see the face of Lance Hoffman. She immediately knew something was wrong—Hoffman wouldn't hesitate to pick up a phone and call her at this hour, but a personal visit was totally out of the ordinary.

Bridgette removed the security chain and opened the door. Hoffman stood grim-faced in the foyer, as if lost for words.

"I assume this is important if it requires a home visit?"

In a quiet voice, Hoffman said, "You mind if I come in for a minute?"

Bridgette motioned him into her living room and then closed the door.

"Have a seat."

Hoffman sat on the edge of one of her armchairs and looked to have a lot on his mind as he waited for Bridgette to sit down.

"I got a call from Doc Warner. He calls me every time a new murder victim is brought into the morgue, regardless of whether it's in the southern precinct or not. It's something we've done for years. Anyway..."

Hoffman paused a moment and then said, "A man was shot dead out near Catalin Mountain in a place called Tangmere Falls this morning. He was in his early sixties—took one round in the chest at long range. The local police from Stanwyck are in charge of the investigation, but because of their budget cuts, they always bring the bodies into Vancouver for the autopsy."

Bridgette had no idea where Hoffman was going with this but knew from his dark expression this had something to do with her.

She responded, "Okay," and waited for Hoffman to continue.

"He lived in little more than a shack on a small plot of land at the edge of the forest and was shot dead as he stepped out of his front door."

"Why are you telling me this?"

"The man had long hair and a beard, both dyed red. Ray thought it was odd that someone would die their hair red when it was naturally brown. I was a little intrigued, so we talked for a minute. The man was healthy but weathered and aged from working in the sun a lot. He had a long scar on his left rib-cage like someone had branded him with a hot poker."

Hoffman stopped talking and they both sat in silence for a

moment. Bridgette hadn't known Hoffman for long but was already becoming familiar with his body language. She closed her eyes as he started speaking again.

"I said to Ray, I knew someone a long time ago who had a scar like that. I asked Ray to check if the victim had a gold filling in one of his front teeth."

Bridgette let out a long breath and whispered, "My father."

In a gentle voice, Hoffman continued. "We won't know for sure until we get a match on dental records, but both Ray and I think the odds of it being your father are solid."

Bridgette opened her eyes and stared off into space. She felt numb and empty inside. Up until two days ago, she didn't know whether her father was dead or alive. Now, the thought of him being snatched from her before she had a chance to reconnect was incomprehensible.

As she wiped tears from her eyes, she said, "Can we go to the morgue? If it is my father, I want to see him."

"He's in pretty bad shape, Bridgette. Perhaps we should wait?"

Bridgette shook her head and looked at Hoffman through glassy eyes and replied, "I won't sleep until I know... one way or another."

Hoffman nodded and got to his feet.

"Ray and I figured that's what you'd say, so he's agreed to stay on until he gets a call from me."

"Give me two minutes to get dressed."

Chapter 32

They said little on the fifteen-minute car trip to the morgue. Bridgette wanted to know whether it was possibly an accident, but Hoffman thought it unlikely. The theory the Stanwyck police were working with was someone was hiding some distance from the house waiting for the victim to come out through the front door. According to the victim's partner, he was shot as soon he stepped out onto the front porch and dead before she reached his side to give him aid. The Stanwyck police were in no doubt it was a murder and had launched an official investigation.

Bridgette had tried asking Hoffman several more questions, but it was clear he didn't know much more than she did. She hoped Ray Warner would be able to provide a few more answers and prayed they had all made a terrible mistake and it was someone other than her father.

Hoffman drove around the back of the Vancouver General and Emergency hospital complex to a low set two story brick building and parked next to the one vehicle that was still in the morgue's car park.

After switching off the engine he said, "Most people who come here to identify a loved one normally have a close friend or family member for support."

"I was an only child—I don't have any close family here anymore."

Hoffman nodded and said awkwardly, "I might be your supervisor and a pain in the ass, but tonight I'm neither of those things—okay?"

Bridgette bit her bottom lip and nodded but couldn't get any words out. She appreciated Hoffman's sentiment. He was crusty and difficult to work with, but she had started to appreciate his qualities of loyalty and honesty. She followed Hoffman to a side entrance of the building doing her best to control her emotions as she started to feel overwhelmed by the sinking feeling in her stomach. Hoffman knocked once and the door was opened immediately by a grim-faced Ray Warner who was still in his white lab coat. He nodded a quick acknowledgment to them both and then led them inside the building.

Bridgette did her best to control her breathing as they were led down a wide corridor to a door simply marked '3'. She had been in these rooms before and knew they were where the autopsies were performed. Warner whispered something to Hoffman that Bridgette couldn't hear and then disappeared inside the room.

Hoffman said, "He'll call us in shortly."

They waited patiently in the sterile, white corridor that looked no different to any other corridor in a major hospital, except for one thing—the smell of death. No amount of disinfectant and deodorizing could hide the smell that permeated every part of the facility. Bridgette began to picture what she might see when they were led into the examination room when the door swung open and Ray Warner re-appeared.

He said, "You may come in now," and then turned and walked back into the room.

Bridgette had been in this room before as part of a field trip for her criminology degree and was familiar with the cool, sterile room, replete with stainless steel sinks, examination table, cabinets, and fittings. She had prepared herself as best she could, but the site of the body laid out on the examination table and covered with a white sheet made her stiffen and catch her breath. Hoffman and Warner moved around to the far side of the table and waited for Bridgette to get into position opposite them.

When she was ready, Warner gently said, "In a moment I'll lower the sheet and show you the face of the deceased. He's a white male in his early sixties. Distinguishing features include a small heart shape tattoo on his left inner forearm, a scar on his rib-cage and a gold tooth filling in one of his front teeth. His hair has been dyed red and at the time of death, he appeared to be fit and healthy. I'll give you a moment to see if you recognize the victim who has been unofficially identified as Peter Cash, and then I'll replace the cover—okay?"

Warner waited for Bridgette to compose herself and then gently folded back the sheet on her signal.

Bridgette stared down at the man. The gray complexion of death did little to hide his ruddy complexion. In death, he looked peaceful, but the craggy furrowed brow suggested he had lived with worry and burden. It only took her a couple of seconds to look past the man's long hair, heavy beard and weathered complexion to realize she was staring at the face of her father.

Bridgette managed to say, "It's him," as her eyes began to fill with tears.

Warner went to move the sheet to cover his face again, but she reached out her hand to stop him and said, "No. I'll never see him again."

They stood in silence for several moments, before Bridgette softly said, "He came to see me..."

Hoffman looked slightly confused and said gently, "Your father?"

Fighting back tears, she said, "He was there at my high school graduating ceremony, sitting in the second back row with a baseball cap on. I didn't recognize him with the red hair and beard and didn't pay him any attention. I just thought he was the parent of one of my classmates."

She reached out and stroked her father's cheek and continued, "He was there when I graduated from Naval College as well. I never made the connection back to my high school graduation until now..."

They stood in silence for several minutes and then Bridgette gave Warner a subtle nod. No one spoke until after Warner had gently raised the sheet and re-covered the body.

Through glassy eyes, Hoffman said in a faltering voice, "He never stopped loving you, Bridgette."

Unable to find any words to express herself, she was thankful when Hoffman came and put a burly arm around her. She remembered little of him holding her and walking her to the car and then driving her home. In time, she would be thankful that he had insisted on staying the night and sleeping on her couch.

Chapter 33

B ridgette stared at her reflection in the mirror. The pale color of her skin and dark circles under her eyes were tell-tale signs she'd barely slept. After being delivered safely home by Hoffman, she had lain awake staring at her bedroom ceiling for hours, while she tried to make sense of her father's murder.

While listening to the background rumble of traffic, the images of her father lying in the morgue and covered with a sheet continued to haunt her. Her worst fear was that her investigation had been the catalyst for his murder. The timing of his death, so soon after he had contacted her to warn her that she was in danger, couldn't have been coincidental. She wondered how they had found out his location. Had they tapped her phone and traced her father's location from the call? She was not sure how long she had been on the line, but perhaps it had been long enough to complete a trace? Nothing else made sense. She wondered, not for the first time, how sophisticated a group she was up against if they could orchestrate a murder so quickly.

The face in the mirror that stared back at her looked downcast and brokenhearted. She knew makeup could hide the circles and pallid complexion, but her sadness and grief could not be covered up so easily. She watched in the mirror as a single tear welled in her left eye and began to slowly trickle down her cheek.

Conscious that Hoffman was still asleep on her couch in her living room, she whispered, "Pull yourself together. You're no good to anyone like this".

She closed her eyes and took a deep breath and wondered how she would get through the day. Suddenly, she was seven again, holding tightly onto her aunt's hand as her mother's coffin was lowered into the ground. She was confused and wanted her father, but her aunt had told her firmly that he wasn't coming back. A sea of grief surrounded her as relatives and family friends she barely knew hugged her and patted her on the head, promising everything would be okay.

She remembered the lonely months that followed as she adjusted to life without her parents. Her aunt was kind and looked after her, but she missed her parents desperately. She remembered sitting on the armrest of her aunt's couch clutching her favorite doll. She remembered staring out the front window for hours at a time, hoping and praying that her father would pull up in the driveway to take her home.

She opened her eyes and was momentarily taken aback as the reflection of a twenty-seven-year-old woman stared back at her. She studied the reflection, wondering who she really was? People said she was a woman to be admired—attractive, intelligent and capable of anything she set her mind to. Right now, she felt vulnerable and unsure.

Bridgette wondered if taking some time off would help. But she knew from past experience that she would only brood if left on her own while she tried to figure out what had happened.

As she wiped the tear from her cheek, she resolved to keep busy and carry on as normal. Makeup would hide some of her pain, the rest she would have to fake. As she began applying eyeliner, there was a gentle knock at the door.

In a croaky, muffled voice, Hoffman called out, "You going to be much longer, Bridgette?"

Bridgette looked at her watch and realized her shower had taken far longer than she had planned.

"Sorry, Lance, I'm all dressed and just doing my makeup. You need the bathroom now?"

The voice called out again and said, "Yeah, my bladder's not what it used to be."

Bridgette opened the door and mumbled a quick 'good morning' as she vacated the bathroom for Hoffman. She had no appetite but headed to her tiny kitchen to fix herself a cup of coffee before she headed to work. Hoffman emerged from the bathroom moments later and looked almost as bad as she felt. Still dressed in yesterday's clothes, he attempted to stretch his back out.

"Sorry, the couch is a bit firm for sleeping on."

Hoffman yawned and said, "No problem. At my age, I wake up stiff regardless of where I sleep. How are you feeling?"

She shrugged and said, "Not great, but I'll manage."

Hoffman nodded and said, "It's been a shock to everyone. Your dad was one of the best..."

Bridgette nodded and tried not to notice Hoffman's appearance. Unshaven, Hoffman looked a haggard mess as he stood in the rumpled clothes he had slept in.

Sensing her look, he said, "I think I'll head home for a shower and change of clothes. What do you have planned for the day?"

"I'm planning on heading into work."

Hoffman frowned and said, "Do you really think that's wise after what you've been through."

"If I sit at home, I'll just feel sorry for myself. I don't want to wallow in my own self-pity."

"Surely you have friends who can come over and support you?"

"I haven't told anyone yet. I'll reach out to a couple of close friends later today, but right now I'm not ready to talk about it."

Hoffman shook his head and replied, "You know, this operation that's in play with the killer... we need everyone to be at the top of their game. You'll barely be able to function today, and we need everyone—"

"I'll be fine. I haven't seen my father for twenty years and he's played no part in my life since I was seven."

Hoffman came and stood in front of her and gently grabbed her shoulders. "I know you well enough now to know your father was important to you. You need time to grieve."

Bridgette looked up at Hoffman and held his stare.

Doing her best to hold it together, she replied, "We all grieve in different ways, Lance."

Hoffman released his grip. "You need to be taking care of yourself, and this is not how you do it."

"I'll be fine."

Hoffman glared at her and said, "I'm going to call the Chief and recommend you take a few days off to get over this."

Without another word, Hoffman turned and walked back into Bridgette's living room and picked up his coat.

He paused at the front door and looked back at her and

said, "I know when cops are close to the edge, Bridgette. The problem is when they finally fall, they generally take other people with them."

Bridgette watched Hoffman leave and thought about what he'd said. Her respect for the man was growing. Maybe he was right? Her thoughts were interrupted by the ringing of her phone. She checked her watch and frowned—it was just after seven and too early for anyone to be ringing except for Hoffman.

Bridgette picked up her phone and said, "Hello, this is Bridgette."

There was silence on the other end of the line, before a mature woman's voice said, "Hello, Bridgette, my name is Linda ... I was a friend of your father."

Bridgette racked her brain trying to recall anyone from family past with the name of Linda but came up blank.

"I'm sorry, Linda, have I ever met you?"

"No, Bridgette, you haven't."

Bridgette could tell by the pain in her voice that the woman was very upset. In an instant, she knew who she was talking to.

"You were my father's partner."

The phone line went quiet again. Bridgette thought she could hear soft sobbing but couldn't be sure.

Finally, the woman said, "I'd like to meet you if that's possible?"

Chapter 34

Bridgette brought her car to a halt at the end of the laneway. She switched the engine off and sat for a moment looking down a path that led to a small wooden cottage. The cottage was sturdily constructed from rough sawn timber which had turned a mocha gray color from weathering many winters. Although the cottage was largely hidden behind trees, Bridgette had an almost perfect view of the front of the house and sat thinking about her father as she stared at the front porch where he had been gunned down.

Nestled at the foot of the forest about a five-minute drive from the small village of Tangmere Falls, she found it difficult to believe that her father had managed to live only an hour's drive from Vancouver for almost twenty years without ever being discovered. She noticed a small plume of smoke rising slowly from the cottage's stone chimney and thought back to the phone conversation she'd had with her father's partner less than two hours ago.

The call had been brief, but long enough for Bridgette to realize that Linda appeared to have loved her father deeply and had been devastated by his murder. Bridgette asked her if she could tell her more about the circumstances surrounding her father's murder, but Linda wasn't comfortable talking on a phone. They had agreed to meet and while Linda seemed keen to tell her everything she knew; it was her closing words that stayed with Bridgette.

"Your father talked about you constantly, Bridgette. It wouldn't be right if I didn't at least try to explain what you meant to him."

While still hesitant about meeting the woman who had been her father's partner for almost twenty years, she hoped she would be able to get answers to some of her questions. With her father's death still so raw, she had no intention of staying any longer than necessary and let out a deep sigh as she opened the door. She checked the reception on her phone and wasn't surprised that signal was weak in such a secluded location. Delray had phoned her not long after her call with Linda and after offering his sympathy, had insisted she take a few days off. After some negotiation, Delray had agreed to reduce her leave down to one day and had allowed her to keep her phone just in case the killer called.

After checking there were no messages, Bridgette pocketed the phone and walked down the path towards the front door. She tried not to think too much about her father's murder as she stepped up onto the small front porch where he had been gunned down. After knocking on the door, she waited patiently and wondered what the woman she was about to meet would look like as she heard the door unlock from the inside.

The woman who opened the door didn't look anything like she imagined. Linda was a good ten years younger than her father and wore her long ash-blond hair in a pony-tail. The denim jeans and well-worn hand-knitted black sweater she wore accentuated her slim figure. She had smooth skin, blemished only by tiny laughter lines around her mouth.

They both stood and looked at each other for a moment. The pained expression on Linda's face suggested she was struggling as much as Bridgette was with her father's death.

As tears began to well in Linda's eyes, she said softly, "Please come in, Bridgette."

Bridgette followed Linda into the cottage and stood for a moment in the middle of the main living area. The room was an open plan kitchen, dining and living combination. It wasn't large, but the furniture had been neatly arranged to give a feeling of space and openness. She wondered about her father again. The room gave off a warm, homely vibe and she hoped he'd been happy here.

She looked at Linda who had moved over to a rustic leather couch but stayed standing.

"I'm sorry for your loss, Bridgette. I can't really begin to imagine what you're going through. Not having seen your father for so long and to now be standing in the house that had been his home after what's happened must be very hard..."

Bridgette nodded but didn't respond immediately as her eyes were drawn to a small framed picture set on the stone fireplace mantle. She walked across and picked it up.

She studied the photo of a young girl playing on a swing in a park and said, "I remember the day my father took this photo—it was my seventh birthday."

Linda gently replied, "Peter used to carry that picture of you everywhere until it started to get damaged. It's the only picture he's ever had framed in the entire time I've known him."

Bridgette continued to study the photograph as she replied,

"When they brought his body in for the autopsy, they found a picture of me in his wallet from my last graduation ceremony..."

"I hope you don't feel like he was spying on you, Bridgette. He's always been interested in what you were doing and very proud..."

Bridgette put the photograph gently back on the mantle and replied, "When I saw him lying there... at first, I didn't recognize him. The long red hair and beard made him look completely different."

Linda nodded and motioned for Bridgette to come and sit on the leather couch with her.

"He changed his appearance not long after he came here. He knew if he was to have any chance of survival, he had to start a new life as somebody totally different."

Bridgette sat down opposite Linda and said, "As I looked at this man with long red hair and a beard lying on the table, I realized I'd seen him before... He'd been at my high school graduation. I remember him sitting up in one of the back rows near the exit. I remembered wondering briefly at the time whose father he was as we didn't have any redheads in our graduating class. I saw him again in the audience when I graduated with my first degree before joining the Navy, but never made the connection..."

Bridgette looked back at the photo on the mantle and continued, "I didn't realize it was the same man until last night..."

"Your father loved you, Bridgette. He talked about you constantly—you don't feel like a stranger to me."

Bridgette nodded but didn't say anything. She had so many questions racing through her mind and didn't know where to start.

Linda continued, "This is very hard for both of us, Bridgette. You've lost a father and I've lost the man I loved for almost twenty years."

Bridgette bit her bottom lip to keep her emotions in check. She had only just met this woman and wasn't sure she was someone she could trust.

She held Linda's gaze for a moment and replied, "I'm sorry for your loss too, Linda."

Linda got to her feet and said, "I need a break from crying and there's something I want to show you."

Bridgette got up and followed Linda through a door that led from the kitchen onto a rear porch. The porch was just big enough to accommodate two rustic wooden chairs and a table and had an unencumbered view of the mountain range beyond.

Bridgette stood for a moment at the edge of the porch taking in the view. She looked up at the dense fir trees that rose up the side of the mountain to its peak. It had a calming effect and spirited her away from an evil and chaotic world where she was still unsure how she fitted in.

Without taking her eyes off the view, she said, "It's beautiful."

"Your father and I used to spend a lot of time out here. Sometimes we'd talk, but a lot of the time we just sat and enjoyed the peace and solitude."

Bridgette asked, "How did you meet?"

Linda picked up a large enamel bowl off the table and said, "It will be easier if I show you," as she stepped off the porch.

Bridgette followed Linda as she walked down a short trail that led to a large fenced off vegetable garden. The area was about half the size of a basketball court and contained more vegetables and herbs than Bridgette had seen in most supermarkets. The garden was set out in meticulously neat rows and watered by an intricate sprinkler system.

Linda opened the gate to the garden and took a few steps inside and said, "This is where I met your father."

Bridgette nodded but didn't say anything. She was confused but decided to wait for Linda to continue.

"I used to live in Stanwyck. My husband ran a real estate business until it fell on hard times. He started drinking when he lost the business... and then he started beating me. I used to come out here and stay with my grandfather until he sobered up. Back then, this was only a four-room shack with a much smaller vegetable garden, but even then, I loved the peace and serenity."

Linda sat down on a small rusty metal stool and looked off into the distance as she continued.

"We were only married eighteen months when he was killed in a car crash trying to drive home drunk."

Bridgette wasn't sure how to respond or where Linda was going with the conversation, but responded gently, "I'm sorry, Linda, that must have been very hard for you."

Linda shrugged and replied, "I guess. I wasn't sure how I felt. He'd beaten me up four times by then, and I was making plans to leave him for good. We were effectively bankrupt, and I came out here to live with my grandfather while I figured out what I'd do next. I'd only been here a few weeks when my grandfather had a fatal stroke. He left me the house in his will, and I've been here ever since."

Linda moved the stool closer to a large cherry tomato plant and began to pick some of the ripest fruit as she continued.

237

"I'd come home some nights after working in Stanwyck and walk down here to get fresh vegetables for dinner. I started noticing some of my vegetables were missing. At first, I thought it was animals coming out of the forest, but they usually leave a messy trail."

Linda pointed to a small low-set wooden storage shed at the far end of the garden and continued.

"My grandfather built that shed to store his tools and fertilizer in. I was suspicious and checked it out and noticed a space had been cleared on the floor, almost as if someone was sleeping in there."

Linda put down the bowl and turned to face Bridgette.

"Two mornings later, I saw a man emerging from the shed just as it was getting light. I snuck down here with my grandfather's shotgun and yelled at him to clear off and never come back. To my surprise, he didn't scurry off, but hung his head in shame and apologized. He looked a broken man ..."

Linda stopped for a moment to collect her thoughts. It seemed to Bridgette as if she was reliving that day again.

"I lowered the shotgun and asked him where he was living when he wasn't sleeping in my shed. He said he'd fallen on hard times and was just sleeping in a small shelter he'd made in the forest. I could tell by his voice that he was an educated man. I pushed him to tell me what had happened, and he opened up and told me everything. For twenty minutes, he just stood there and unburdened his soul. He told me all about your mother's murder and how he had been framed and then he told me about you."

Bridgette felt the tears begin to well in her eyes again and took a deep breath to compose herself as Linda continued.

"He broke down as he began to explain how leaving you

behind had been the hardest thing he'd ever done in his life. It was when he started talking about you that I knew he wasn't making up a story."

Bridgette closed her eyes for a moment to keep her composure as Linda continued.

"I knew he was a fugitive, but I didn't think he was a threat to me, so I offered him breakfast. He followed me up onto the back porch and we talked for hours about what he was going to do. At first, I encouraged him to go to the police or even the media, but the more I listened to his story, the more I realized that would put you both in more danger. In the end, I told him I had no close neighbors and he could stay here until he figured out what he was going to do."

Linda paused for a moment and looked back towards the cottage.

"My grandfather had always planned on putting extra rooms on his little house, but he never got any further than drawing up plans and buying the timber. The timber had been stacked on the west side of the house for years. Two days after your father arrived, I came home from work to find him sorting through it. He didn't want charity and offered to build the extra rooms for free—so that was his project for the next few months. By the time he'd finished the house, he had long hair and a bushy beard. We experimented with dyes and decided on red because it made him almost unrecognizable from the man he was before."

Bridgette looked back towards the house, suddenly keen to see her father's wood craftsmanship in more detail. As if sensing this, Linda asked, "Would you like to go back to the house, Bridgette? I can show you the additions Peter built if you like?"

The use of her father's first name prompted Bridgette to ask, "Forgive me for prying, Linda, but when did my father become your partner?"

Linda stiffened for a moment and then replied, "Fair question. The truth is, I'm not exactly sure when I fell in love with him. At first, he slept in a sleeping bag in the middle of the living room until he had finished the construction and then he moved into what is now the spare bedroom. We settled into a routine—I would go into Stanwyck most days to look after my bookkeeping clients and he would either stay here and tend the garden or use the time to investigate what was happening with your mother's murder case. We'd spend our evenings together, and the more I got to know him, the more I liked him. One night I told him how I felt, and we've been together ever since."

Linda lifted up the left sleeve of her jumper to reveal a tattoo on her inner forearm. It was one-half of a heart shape and had tiny Latin words written below it.

"Because of Peter's situation we could never get legally married, so we had our own ceremony here and got matching heart tattoos instead of rings."

Bridgette read out loud the words of the tattoo, "Amor et fides—Latin, for love and loyalty."

Linda nodded as she rolled down her sleeve.

"After what Peter had been through with your mother's murder and losing you, and what I'd been through with an abusive husband, loyalty was as important to us as love."

Bridgette nodded as she thought about what Linda had said. She thought she would resent the woman who had formed a lasting relationship with her father after her mother's murder, but she found herself liking Linda.

"It couldn't have been easy harboring a fugitive and living with the constant fear that there were people that wanted to see your partner dead?"

Linda shrugged and said, "Peter literally turned up on my doorstep one day and everything else that followed just happened. I don't think either of us expected him to stay more than a couple of nights in the beginning and for a long time, he kept saying it wasn't a good idea for me to be involved with him. Eventually, he settled into the little community out here and did odd jobs and a small amount of carpentry. He went under the name of Peter Cash and no one ever suspected who he really was."

Linda paused for a moment and then choked out the words, "I have no regrets about my choices."

The two were silent for a while as they both contemplated their thoughts.

Finally, Linda said, "I need to eat—are you hungry? I'm planning on fixing myself an omelet and it's just as easy to make two as it is one?"

"Thank you, Linda, but I should be getting back to Vancouver I guess."

Linda half smiled as she responded, "I understand if you don't want to spend any more time with me, but if you're hungry, I'd appreciate the company?"

Bridgette had not eaten at all that morning and the thought of an omelet made her feel hungry.

"I don't want to be a bother to you, Linda."

Linda managed a brief smile as she picked up the bowl of tomatoes and said, "I'll take that as a yes."

Bridgette followed Linda out the gate and back up the path towards the cottage. She hadn't known what to expect when she had first knocked on Linda's door, but she was glad she had come.

As they stepped up onto the back porch, Linda said, "Why don't you sit out here and enjoy the view, while I fix us lunch?"

Bridgette thanked Linda as she sat down in one of the chairs and looked up at the imposing view of Catalin Mountain again. She thought about her father again—there were lots of questions she still wanted to ask Linda, but now didn't seem to be the right time. Feeling her phone begin to buzz, she pulled it out of her pocket. She was vaguely aware of Linda's voice in the background, asking her what she liked with her omelet as she listened to the voice message from a missed call.

"Hi, this is Rob from JoLo Promotions. Please call me back so that we can arrange a pickup for your free tickets."

Bridgette put the phone down on the table and took a deep breath. She had hoped the killer would make contact, but the timing couldn't have been worse.

Chapter 35

Bridgette pushed the button for level two and leaned back against the rear wall of the elevator. Closing her eyes, she listened to the hum of the elevator as it gently rose from the basement car park.

She thought back to her brief visit with Linda and wished she could have stayed longer. After receiving the message from the killer to pick up the tickets, Bridgette knew she needed to get back to Vancouver as soon as possible. Linda was disappointed she couldn't stay for lunch but seemed to understand, and they had promised they would catch up again in the next day or two. Linda wasn't at all what Bridgette had expected, and she found herself liking the woman who had taken her mother's place in her father's life.

As the elevator doors opened at level two, she rehearsed in her mind what she would say to Delray. She had called the Chief from the car phone immediately after leaving Linda's cottage, and while he was excited the killer had made contact, Delray seemed reluctant to allow her to continue with the case until she'd had 'adequate bereavement leave'. The conversation had been brief, and she knew better than to argue with him on the phone. She was determined to see the case through to completion and knew she had to choose her words carefully.

After letting out a deep breath, she stopped at his doorway and wasn't surprised to see Hoffman, seated opposite Delray's desk and in deep conversation with his boss. Hoffman seemed to have cooled off a little since leaving her apartment earlier that morning, which she took to be a good sign.

Delray looked up and said gently, "Come in and have a seat, Bridgette," and motioned her to shut the door as she entered.

She complied and settled into the chair next to Hoffman, hoping the conversation with Delray would go a little better than her first conversation of the day with Hoffman.

Delray clasped his hands together and leaned forward slightly in his chair and said, "Firstly, Bridgette, I just want to reiterate what I said on the phone this morning—we're all very sorry to hear the news about your father. I know this must be an incredible shock for you, and we'll do whatever we can to support you."

Bridgette had psyched herself up not to cry, but Delray's words of comfort were making it hard for her to hold back her emotions.

She swallowed and simply responded, "Thanks, Chief."

Delray continued, "You know, Bridgette, while this is an important case we're all working on here, you're now going through a personal tragedy. I've been talking to Lance and frankly, we both think it would be best if you take a few more days bereavement leave to help you get over this."

Hoffman added, "This is not the place to grieve, Bridgette, and that's exactly what you need to do."

Bridgette's heart sank—she had hoped Delray wouldn't side with Hoffman.

Delray continued, "I know you're disappointed, Bridgette, but you've been through enough. It wouldn't be fair to expect you to continue under the circumstances."

Unsure of what to say in response, Bridgette pulled her phone from her pocket and slid it across the desk to Delray as she said, "I haven't responded to his voice message yet. I thought it best that I wait until I got back here."

Delray nodded. "I want to get a plan together before we respond. Also, it will give us an opportunity to organize a replacement for you."

"It's your call, Chief, but to be perfectly honest, I'd prefer to be here doing something useful, rather than sitting at home dwelling on... what happened."

She looked intently at both men and continued, "I haven't known either of you for very long, but neither of you are quitters, which is exactly how I'm going to feel if I'm taken off this case..."

Delray and Hoffman exchanged looks and the room became quiet for a moment while Delray contemplated his response.

"You know, Bridgette; you really have been through a lot in the last two days. You were shot at and nearly killed and now your father? If you don't mind me saying so, I don't think you realize how much stress you're under right now."

"What about if we get a second opinion from one of Vancouver Metro's doctors? If they say I'm fit to work, would that be okay?"

Delray looked at Hoffman who held up his hands in exasperation and said, "It's your call, Felix."

Delray studied Bridgette for a moment and then picked up his desk phone and dialed a phone number from memory. After a short conversation with someone who Bridgette assumed was the chief medical officer, he hung up the phone and withdrew a business card from the top drawer of his desk.

Sliding the card across to Bridgette, he said, "Okay, here's how it's going to play out. I've talked to the CMO, and she's not prepared to give an opinion until you've been examined. Ordinarily, she'd say no dice but given you haven't seen your father in twenty years, there are extenuating circumstances. Her office is three blocks down from here, and she'll see you in twenty minutes."

Delray paused a moment to study Bridgette before he continued.

"If the chief medical officer gives you the all clear, you're back on the case. I can't be fairer than that."

"Thanks, Chief."

Picking up his desk phone again, Delray continued, "I've got a couple of calls to make. Bridgette, come and see me after your appointment. Lance, I'd like you to get McKenzie and Green in here for a meeting in ten minutes. We need to figure out how we want to play this and what we say when we call back to collect the tickets."

Hoffman mumbled, "I'm on it," as he rose from his chair.

Bridgette followed Hoffman to the door and paused to look back at Delray who was busy punching in another phone number from memory.

She said, "Chief, I really appreciate this."

Delray looked up and said, "You know, Bridgette, we all grieve differently. For what it's worth, if it was me in your shoes, I'm not sure I'd want to be sitting at home either."

Bridgette nodded. She found it comforting to know she wasn't alone in her thinking.

Trying to lighten the mood, Delray gave her half a smile and pleaded, "And don't be giving Lance a hard time today, okay? He hasn't had much sleep, and I know from experience how grumpy that makes him."

Bridgette gave a half smile back and said, "I'll do my best."

She looked at the business card for doctor Carol Sanders as she walked out into the corridor. She knew that after being shot at and receiving the news that her father had been murdered, Sanders was going to be a lot more interested in her state of mind than her blood pressure. Bridgette pressed the button for the elevator and thought about what she would say. She had been through all this before after the attempted rape in the Navy and was skeptical of her chances of being cleared to continue to work on the case without taking some leave.

After stepping into the elevator, she pressed the button for the ground floor rather than the underground parking lot. She decided the walk would clear her head and give her a chance to think about what she would say to the doctor.

Chapter 36

Bridgette's medical examination took close to half an hour. After checking her blood pressure, heart rate and re-examining her ear wound for signs of infection, Doctor Carol Sanders used the remainder of the appointment to ask Bridgette a series of probing questions about her mood, state of mind and what she did to cope with stress.

Bridgette had been through all this before in the Navy after the attempted rape and was prepared for the personal nature of the questions. Did she ever have a problem with alcohol, drugs or gambling? No. Was she currently in a relationship? No. Did she have commitment issues? No. Was she gay? No. Was she getting a full night's sleep? Well, not always.

Seemingly satisfied, Sanders moved onto questions about her family, particularly her mother and father. Bridgette did her best to answer honestly and openly but found it difficult to put answers into words since she had effectively been an orphan since the age of seven.

Sanders gave away nothing as she wrote notes in Bridgette's medical file and it was only when she sat in front of her computer and began typing rapidly that she opened up.

"I'm sending an email summary of my examination to Chief Delray. While I'm not giving you a ringing endorsement to continue working, I can't find a good reason to stop you either."

She paused and looked across at Bridgette and said, "I'm trusting you to exercise some of your own judgment on this. If you feel you need to take a day or two off, then you should. Okay?"

Bridgette promised she would as Sanders started typing again.

Without taking her eyes off the screen, Sanders said, "Chief Delray says you're very intelligent, but that doesn't make you smart. If you're not smart, you'll burn out or worse..."

They were silent for a moment while Sanders completed the email.

After pressing send, she turned to Bridgette and asked, "Do you know what the number one cause of death is amongst cops and ex-cops?"

"I'm guessing suicide?"

"You got it. Most of them are preventable, provided the symptoms are diagnosed early and they get the right kind of treatment. The most frustrating thing for me as a doctor is getting cops in here who are on the verge of putting a gun in their mouth when they've never sought any kind of help until their condition is critical."

"Point taken."

Sanders scribbled on a prescription pad and then tore off the page and handed it to Bridgette. "This is a prescription for sleeping pills. Depression and anxiety are compounded by a lack of sleep. I've given you a ten-day supply, but hopefully, you won't need to take them for that long."

Bridgette took the prescription and thanked Sanders for her time.

Sanders gave Bridgette a business card and said, "Here are my contact details. You've been through a lot and it's normal to be feeling a range of emotions. I want to see you again in two weeks, but if you think you need to come back sooner, give me a call, okay?"

Bridgette left Sanders' office and headed to the elevator. She had no desire to wind up on stress leave and knew she would need to heed Sanders' advice. She stepped into the elevator and pressed the button for the ground floor. As the doors began to close, she flinched as a hand reached in to open them again. A burly, young uniformed police officer stepped in and nodded a hello to her. As she began to relax again, she wondered if she would ever feel completely comfortable when on her own again? She made a mental note to speak to Sanders about it at her next appointment.

* * *

The elevator doors opened on level two and Bridgette stepped out and headed for Delray's office. She hoped he'd had time to read the email from Sanders while she had been walking back to the office and would give her the green light to return to normal duty. As she approached Delray's office she slowed slightly and smelt the air—onions, and pastrami. The smell got stronger the closer she got to the office and by the time she reached his office door, it was close to overpowering.

Standing in the doorway, she looked in and wanted to laugh as she saw both Hoffman and Delray with their heads down and totally oblivious to her presence, working overtime on a plate of pastrami and onion sandwiches. She decided not to enter—Delray had a habit of talking with his mouth full and she had no desire to be ducking food missiles if she could avoid it.

Instead, she hovered at the door and said, "Excuse me, gentlemen, just letting you know I'm back from my examination."

Delray looked up at her with a mouth half full of sandwich and said, "I got the email from Sanders," and motioned her to come in and sit down.

"I probably should be getting back to my desk."

Not easily deterred, Delray said, "No, no, come on in, Bridgette."

Reluctantly, Bridgette made her way into the office and politely declined Delray's offer of a sandwich as she sat down. Delray frowned and looked at the clock on his wall.

"It's way after two p.m., Bridgette. You are going to eat something—right?"

"I guess I'm not a big fan of pastrami, Chief," she said tactfully.

"I think I'll get something from the vending machine."

Delray shrugged and said, "Well, all the more for us," as he reached for another sandwich.

After one large bite, he continued, "Sanders has given you the all clear, so provided you're up for this, I'll thank our backup for standing in and release her back to her own team."

"I'm good, Chief."

Delray swallowed and said, "As soon as we're finished here, we'll go over the plan with the team again."

Sliding Bridgette's phone back across to her he said, "I'm done babysitting this. You can monitor it from here on in."

The smell of pastrami and onion was starting to make

Bridgette hungry.

She said, "I think I'll swing by the vending machine and grab a sandwich."

Pointing to the sandwich tray, Delray said, "Two pastramis going begging here, Bridgette?"

Before she had a chance to respond, her phone began to vibrate. She picked it up off Delray's desk and frowned as she checked the caller ID.

"This is a number I don't recognize—it might be him, although I thought he would wait for me to ring..."

She pressed answer as Hoffman and Delray exchanged anxious looks and said, "Hello, this is Bridgette."

There was a moment's silence before a male voice said, "Hi there, this is Rob. I'm the courier for JoLo Promotions. I've got your tickets for the show tomorrow night ..."

Chapter 37

Bridgette signaled Hoffman and Delray that it was the killer who was calling as she stood up and moved into the center of the office.

The male voice said, "Are you still there?"

She replied, "Yeah, sorry—just busy at work."

While Hoffman and Delray were hustling over to get close enough to listen in to the conversation, the voice said, "What do you do for work?"

"I'm a freelance graphic designer."

"Interesting... So, I'm ringing to arrange a time and place for the pickup?"

"Thanks. Is there any chance you could just leave the tickets at the box office?"

"No, I need you to sign a receipt to say I've given them to you."

"Okay. Can you drop them at my work?"

"I'm actually a sub-contractor and I've got a busy sched-ule—you know, lots of deliveries. I'll be making deliveries in the city tomorrow afternoon and will finish about seven. I could meet you close to the theater?"

"I'm actually planning on getting a lift back into the city

with a friend. We could meet you at around seven fifteen?"

Hoffman gave her the thumbs up signal for controlling the conversation.

"Seven-fifteen's getting late for me. Do you work on Saturdays?"

"I'll be working in the city tomorrow - I should finish around four."

"Okay, that might work. Where's your work?"

"On Jollier Street."

"I'll be doing a delivery over on William Street between four and four-thirty—do you know it?"

"Yeah, it's not too far from my work. I could be there shortly after four."

"Okay, I'll call you around four when I know my location. I'll be in a blue van—Rapid Couriers signage on the doors. I'll give you my exact location then."

"Okay, sounds good."

The phone line went dead. Bridgette looked up and said, "He disconnected."

With a slight smile on his face, Delray nodded and said, "Good job, Bridgette."

Hoffman added, "We should get the team going on this right away, Chief."

Delray thought for a moment and said, "Let's sit back down for a minute and review the conversation. I'd like to go through it while it's fresh in my mind."

As he moved back to his chair, he looked at Bridgette and said, "I'm sure you can recall it word for word Bridgette."

"I'll write it down when we're done here, Chief, but it will be good to talk about it first. I've already learned a few things."

When they were settled, Delray said, "Okay, Bridgette, walk

us through it."

Bridgette replayed the opening dialogue back in her mind. "I'm not sure how well you could hear, but he's male, probably mid-to-late thirties, and he has a cultured voice—almost like he's English."

Hoffman said, "I picked that up as well. I gotta say, he doesn't sound like any courier I know."

Recalling the dialogue again, Bridgette said, "He was relaxed and felt in control, although asking me what I did for a living seemed odd."

Delray said, "So, you started by asking him if he could just leave the tickets at the box office?"

"I knew he wouldn't agree to it, but it was a way to start negotiating the time. I didn't think I'd have much of a chance in changing the location—he will have planned that well in advance, but I hoped we could influence the timing a little. I thought if I told him I was coming back into town later with a friend he would look for an earlier time slot for the pickup—one where he thought I'd be alone."

"Just like he had with Monica Travers," added Hoffman.

Bridgette continued, "At four p.m. there will still be plenty of daylight."

"I'm liking it," said Delray as he scratched his chin. "Surveillance is hard at the best of times, but doubly hard after dark. The number one priority has to be your safety, Bridgette. I feel a little easier knowing this is going to happen well before dark."

"I'm not sure my safety's going to be an issue, Chief. Personally, I don't think he's going to go through with it."

Delray asked, "Why?"

"In the early part of the conversation, he used the word

'interesting' when I told him what I did for a living. It's not sitting right with me."

Hoffman said, "I'm not following?"

She frowned and said, "His tone was condescending like he knew it wasn't the truth."

"In which case, he may not show at all," said Delray, as he leaned back in his chair.

Hoffman responded, "Or it might be like the car rental return. He'll be there watching from a hidden location, and we'll be none the wiser..."

Delray folded his arms behind his head. "We'll have to be smart about this. We need to be watching everything that's going on around us."

Hoffman added, "That's not going to be easy, Lance. William Street is always busy."

Delray nodded, "That it is... but this might be our one and only chance to catch this guy."

Chapter 38

Kayne Selwood looked down at the five 6x4 photos of young women he had spread out on the king size bed. They were all similar—young, vivacious and brunette. He paused for a moment and smiled as he picked up the second photo and began to study her features in more detail again.

The phone call had sealed the deal—she would be the one. The photo he had printed from her Facebook account didn't do her justice. Her profile had her listed as Bridgette May, but for a man of his talents, it hadn't taken him long to discover May was her middle name rather than her last name. He picked up a marker pen and wrote the word Casseldhorf at the bottom of the picture and then sat back in his chair and replayed their conversation over in his mind.

She had lied to him about her occupation of course, but that was hardly surprising. After spending most of the previous evening searching the web with his own customized search tools and hacking two government databases, he had learned enough about the young woman to know she was a police detective and probably part of an elaborate plan to catch him.

At first, he had been enraged at the thought that he had

finally been discovered and contemplated abandoning his next performance altogether. But then he got curious—who was she? He had continued to dig into her background, all the way back to when her mother had been murdered when she was seven. Although impressed by her success in martial arts tournaments and her criminology degree, it was a small reference to her that he'd found in an obscure archival file from Vancouver University that intrigued him most.

He swung the roller chair around to face two laptops he had set up on the hotel room credenza and with several swift keystrokes, unlocked the screen on the smaller of the two devices. He shifted the chair in closer and opened up the archive file again. Under the simple title of 'Scholarship Assessments', he re-read the brief bio on his latest target and smiled again as he got to the section covering her IQ assessment. With a score of one-fifty-one and an aptitude for mathematics and the sciences, the university was prepared to offer her admission to any degree course they offered. He thought back to all his previous victims. While they all looked like Elizabeth, none of them were anywhere near as intelligent as she was, which had always been a source of disappointment.

Casseldhorf bore a striking resemblance to Elizabeth, and with her police connection would be more like an adversary than a victim. He switched to the larger laptop and brought up a map of Vancouver's CBD. This would be far riskier than anything he'd ever done before, but the thought of pitting himself against the police and killing one of their own was intoxicating. He zoomed in on the Jollier and William Street location and began to study the side streets and connecting lanes as he formulated a plan. Snatching a woman who was being used as part of an elaborate plan to catch him would be no easy feat, but he was ready for a new challenge.

Pleased that the first part of his plan was starting to come together, he entered several more keystrokes and brought up the map location for Catalin Mountain. He zoomed in on an area just beyond a popular picnic area and began to study the terrain and walking trails in more detail. It was only about a half hour drive out of the city and ideal for his purposes.

He had enough to work with for now and pushed back from the laptop and walked across to the window of his hotel room. He ignored the people milling around on the street eight floors below and focused his attention on the small city parkland on the opposite side of the street. He watched people walking down to the river's edge to feed the ducks and wondered about using the river for his escape but quickly dismissed the idea. His preference had always been to hide in plain sight where it was easier to watch, manipulate and control the outcome.

Closing his eyes, he stood there almost transfixed as he imagined holding the knife again and instantly relaxed as he felt his thrusts plunging deep into the woman's chest and abdomen.

He could feel the terror and smell the blood and whispered to himself, "One more day," as he opened his eyes again.

He checked his watch—he had just over twenty-four hours for the setup and a lot to do. He mentally went through a checklist of things he needed to do and the order in which they needed to be accomplished to make the most effective use of his time. There would be a trip out to his storage unit to swap vehicles and retrieve some of the equipment he would use as props. He also needed to steal a truck, but that could wait until much later that night.

Satisfied with his plan for now, he returned to the bed

259

and picked up the photos of the four women he was no longer interested in. One by one, he patiently fed the photographs through a tiny battery-operated paper shredder. After carefully collecting all the shreddings and putting them into a plastic bag for disposal, he went through his routine of carefully packing up his belongings before leaving the hotel. He generally only stayed one or two nights in any one hotel—any longer and people started remembering you.

After sliding the two laptops into his large backpack, he methodically checked his room to make sure he had left nothing behind. Paying cash and moving frequently, he knew it was highly unlikely that his movements would ever be tracked but being overly cautious had helped make him invisible up until now. He repeated the same process in his hotel bathroom before pausing in front of the mirror to carefully fit his baseball cap. He bought a new one for each performance and always picked one with a long peak to hide his face from security cameras.

Selwood leaned forward and twisted his head slightly to the left and examined the dye job on his hair. While most men who went gray before forty would be dismayed by the way it aged their appearance, he used it to his advantage, applying a dark brown dye to help temporarily alter his appearance. He could see several flecks of gray starting to appear again as the dye began to wash out but knew it would suffice for another twenty-four hours or so.

Satisfied, he left the bathroom and took one final look around the hotel room to make sure everything was in order. It had been advertised as unique, inner city luxury accommodation with a king size bed and adjoining bathroom. To him, it had been just another beige and brown hotel room—not worth the six hundred dollars cash he had paid for two nights, but well worth the investment if everything went to plan tomorrow.

He opened the front door to head for the elevator. He would dump the bag of paper shreddings on his way down to William and Jollier. He had decided to walk to give him time to make several phone calls and carefully explore the surrounding laneways. Like all his previous performances, planning and preparation were everything. If it all went according to plan, by this time tomorrow he would be hiding in plain sight and waiting for the arrival of his next victim.

Chapter 39

The back of the windowless communications van was starting to warm up. With three racks of floor to ceiling communications equipment and a distinct lack of ventilation, Bridgette was finding the confined space increasingly uncomfortable. Seated alongside Danny Collier from the communications team, she had been in position for over two hours waiting for the call. Collier, who was short in stature, seemed at home in the cramped conditions and had said very little to her in the last half an hour as he went through his setup routine. While he had been busy testing communications with each of the four teams, Bridgette had used the time to focus on what was ahead.

After spending most of Saturday morning going over the plan and each team's role, they had traveled in convoy from Vancouver Metro headquarters across the Iron Bridge and into the southern side of Vancouver's CBD. The squad of four unmarked police cars and the communications van had split up and driven to pre-arranged locations around the killer's William Street collection point. As instructed, Collier had parked the van two streets away in Jollier Street to set up and manage mobile communications for the operation.

Now starting to feel slightly nauseous from the warm, stuffy conditions, Bridgette said, "Hey, Danny, I need some fresh air. I'm going to get out of the van for a minute—okay?"

Barely glancing at her, Collier replied, "No problem, Bridgette. When you're out we'll do one last check on your equipment just to make sure everything's still working properly."

Collier's attention to detail was bordering on paranoia, but Bridgette was happy to comply. She'd heard of police officers who had died in stakeouts because their equipment had failed, and they had been blindsided. Collier had given her a range of options for keeping in contact with the team and she had opted for a strap-on radio worn beneath her blouse with a wireless earbud. With her shoulder length hair completely covering her ear, she was confident she could walk in a crowd without the device being detected.

Collier had pre-adjusted the volume of the device and his voice came through loud and clear as she walked away from the van. "Like I said, just one final check Bridgette. Are you hearing me okay?"

She replied softly, "All good, Danny, you're coming in loud and clear," as she walked amongst a few pedestrians.

The voice of Felix Delray broke in on the conversation. "You okay, Bridgette?"

"I'm fine, Chief. It was getting a little stuffy in the van, so I'm out getting some fresh air to clear my head."

"Good idea. How are you feeling about all this?"

Bridgette knew everyone else on the team was listening to the conversation and decided to play down her anxiety.

"I'm okay, Chief. Maybe a little nervous... I don't want to blow this."

"We're all nervous, Bridgette, and if we weren't, I'd be

worried. Just remember we're all here for you and once you get onto William Street, you'll have four of us close by on foot and four cars within a block of you."

Bridgette pictured the setup in William Street. The street was a mix of office blocks, retail and restaurants and was a lot busier on a Saturday than Jollier. It made it easier for the team to blend in, but also a lot harder for them to spot anything out of the ordinary. Delray had insisted on unmarked vehicles and plain clothes for everyone so they wouldn't stand out. She wasn't so sure her two bosses would go unnoticed after changing—Delray looked ready to step onto a golf course and Hoffman looked as if he was one step away from being homeless. Still, it was a lot better than white business shirts and ties, she thought.

Delray's voice came through her earpiece again, "All right everyone, we've got a blue van with Rapid Courier's signage coming up the street..."

Chapter 40

Kayne Selwood casually walked into the men's bathroom and locked himself in one of the two cubicles. He had practiced the routine he was about to follow over and over until he was happy it could be achieved in under ninety seconds. He started by taking off his orange hi-viz vest and then stripped off his electrical contractor overalls to reveal a tan DriGlo Linen Service uniform he had been wearing underneath. Reaching into an internal pocket of the overalls, he produced a large folded white linen bag with a DriGlo logo and quickly stowed the overalls and hi-viz vest in the bag. After carefully removing his baseball cap and the long brown-haired wig he'd been wearing, he placed them in the bag as well and pulled the rope cord tight to close it.

He did a quick check to make sure he'd left nothing behind as he slung the bag over his shoulder. Selwood unlatched the door to the cubicle and paused to check his appearance in the bathroom mirror as he placed a DriGlo cap on his head. Now satisfied that he looked like any other delivery guy for a laundry company, he walked back out into the crowded dining area.

No one paid him any attention even as he discretely dropped

a small envelope on the table of one of the patrons as he walked through the cafe. The man at the table didn't look up or acknowledge Selwood as he deftly slipped the envelope under his newspaper and continued reading.

Selwood paused briefly at the front door and looked back over the sea of patrons. They were all busy talking loudly, eating and drinking and seemed oblivious to his presence, which suited him fine. Ordinarily, he found the thought of being in such a confined space with so many ordinary people repulsive, but sacrifices had to be made. He focused for a moment on the man with long hair, reading the paper at the back of the cafe. Selwood had found him through a group on the dark web—people who were prepared to do almost anything if the price was right. He thought this would be one of the easiest jobs the man had ever scored—five hundred dollars to sit in a cafe for two hours, drinking coffee and pretending to be someone he wasn't. He wasn't a perfect match for Selwood, but with his back to the front door and wearing the same style cap, hi-viz vest, and electrical contractor overalls, he was a close enough match to allay the fears of any suspicious cops trying to track his movements.

Selwood slipped out through the front door of the cafe and looked briefly up William Street. He smiled to himself as he caught sight of the blue delivery van parking on the opposite side of the street exactly where he had instructed. He had seen all he needed and knew everything was proceeding on schedule just as he had planned. He turned and headed down William Street toward Pontefract Drive, casually scanning the street for any sign that he was being followed by plain clothes cops. He was reasonably confident they had no idea about his identity, but he wasn't about to make careless assumptions that could prove costly.

Satisfied that he wasn't being watched as he neared the Pontefract Drive intersection, he focused his attention on the next part of his plan. He had two phone calls to make, the first of which was simple and would be made during the short walk to his next location. After pulling a mobile phone from his pocket, he hit speed dial as he quickened his pace.

Chapter 41

Bridgette's heart began to race as she listened to Delray. She had done some research on Rapid Couriers after the phone call with the killer and found no listed company or business with that name operating in Vancouver. This had initially pleased Hoffman who had remarked, "It will be a lot easier to track a vehicle when there aren't fifty replicas of it running around the city."

Bridgette wasn't so sure. She knew enough about the killer to know he planned everything down to the smallest detail. If he had picked a blue van with a one of a kind company name, there had to be a reason.

As she began to wonder again why he hadn't opted for a plainer color to blend in, Delray's voice broke through again. "Okay, he's parking on the eastern side of the street. It's a loading zone in front of the Jubilee building. Repeat that, out front of the Jubilee building and just down from Collins Lane. I'm going to move across the street and start window shopping and slowly make my way up towards the back of the vehicle."

As his voice trailed off, Bridgette could hear the voice of Lance Hoffman cutting in. His voice was punctuated by his breathing and she could tell he was on the move. "I've got the van in sight. I'm walking down William Street toward it. There's an alfresco coffee shop called 'The Coffee Hut' just up from the Collins Lane entrance. It's close enough for me to see what's going on without getting too close. I'm going to stop there and watch."

Bridgette heard Delray's voice cut back in through her earpiece, "I'm across the street now and moving up slowly towards the back of the van. I can't see what the driver's doing from this position, but so far he hasn't gotten out of the van."

Hoffman replied, "He's just sitting there with his head down, Felix, like he's looking at his phone."

Delray asked, "You get any messages yet, Bridgette?"

"Nothing yet, Chief. I've checked my reception and I've got a strong signal."

"We need to be patient everyone, the next move is his."

Delray did a radio check with the other members of the team and told them to hold their positions for the moment. Bosco and his partner were situated in a car at the top of William Street to cut off any escape via Bridge Street. Smith and Kelly were performing the same task at the bottom of William Street. Bridgette thought they all sounded a little tense as well. It didn't make her feel any better, but it was nice to know she wasn't on her own.

Delray made a final check with Green and Dickson who were both parked on Pontefract Drive. Delray was worried about the lower exit for William Street. Pontefract Drive led back into the city if you turned right off William but out of the city via three separate exits if you turned left. Not wanting to take any chances, he had two cars stationed on Pontefract to better cover the exit.

Bridgette waited for several more minutes, listening to the

occasional burst of conversation from Delray and Hoffman who were both still holding their positions.

She checked her phone again to make sure she had good reception and admonished herself to stay patient. Delray cut in through her earpiece again, "Any message yet, Bridgette?"

"No, Chief, nothing yet."

Delray's voice dropped out for a moment and she wondered whether she was experiencing communication problems.

"Chief—"

In a low voice, Hoffman cut in and said, "Hang on, Bridgette, the driver's just gotten out of the van and the Chief is too close to risk speaking now."

The signal dropped out again. Bridgette imagined Delray doing his best to stay unobtrusive, window shopping or hanging back some distance from the back of the van.

Continuing to speak in a low voice, Hoffman said. "He's opening the side cargo door of the van... He looks to be in his mid-twenties—short brown hair, medium build with a scruffy goatee beard..."

More silence followed and then Hoffman started speaking again, this time in a voice that was almost normal.

"He's got two boxes stacked one on top of the other, and he's carrying them into the building. Repeat, he's just entered the Jubilee building. Does everybody copy that?"

Bridgette could hear a burst of chatter through her earpiece as each of the detectives checked in.

More silence followed before Hoffman asked, "What do you make of that, Felix?"

Delray responded, "I've done a whole bunch of these police stakeouts, and the only thing I can guarantee you is that they never go off according to plan. This one's panning out no different."

More silence followed.

Hoffman's patience seemed to be running thin as he said, "It's been almost two minutes and there's still no sign of him. Are we sure there are no back exits from the building?"

Delray came back straight away, "It's not a corner building, so there's no laneway access. There's probably a fire exit in the rear through to the corresponding building in Elizabeth Street."

"You want me to go in, Felix? He might have spotted us, and this is his way of doing a runner."

Bridgette started walking and said, "I'm near Underwood Lane, which goes from Jollier through to Elizabeth. I can be in Elizabeth in less than a minute to give a visual if I see anyone with that description step out of a building?"

She listened to Delray and Hoffman rapidly discuss what they should do next. They agreed Bridgette was the best option for Elizabeth Street.

Delray said, "Okay, Bridgette, move quickly and keep in constant radio contact. You're on your own right now so make sure you can get to your pistol real quick if anything looks out of the ordinary."

She moved quickly to the entrance of Underwood Lane and paused a moment. "I'm just entering the laneway now. No sign of anyone here."

Bridgette moved quickly past two parked cars and a large dumpster parked out in the laneway at an odd angle. She gave a running commentary to the rest of the team as she went and slowed to a normal walk as she emerged into the sunlight on Elizabeth Street. Feigning confusion as if she was trying to get her bearings, she looked up and down Elizabeth Street for any sign of a man matching Hoffman's description.

"I don't see any sign of him, Chief."

"Okay, just stay where you are for now and keep a lookout for anything unusual. This could all be a setup just like when the van was returned."

Hoffman's voice could be heard again, insisting he should move in and check the building. Delray began to respond that they should wait a few more minutes, but Bridgette was no longer listening. She looked down at her phone as it buzzed to signal an incoming call. She felt a rush of adrenaline surge through her body as the screen showed an unlisted number.

She let out a deep breath and pressed the answer button. "Hello, this is Bridgette."

Bridgette felt a shiver run down her spine as she recognized the voice of the man she had spoken to yesterday.

In the same articulate and almost arrogant voice, he said, "I'm parked in William Street. Are you ready to come and get your tickets?"

Chapter 42

Bridgette took a moment to compose herself. She knew the next few minutes were crucial to their chances of capturing the killer and she wanted to make sure her responses seemed natural.

She relaxed her grip on the phone slightly and said, "Sure, I've just finished work, so the timing is perfect."

"Okay, where are you?"

"I'm on Jollier, near Underwood Lane. Where are you?"

"I'm parked out front of the Jubilee building. If you go down Underwood and across Elizabeth to Collins Lane it will bring you out on William where I'm parked."

"Okay, I'll come now. Blue van, right?"

"I'll be waiting for you."

The phone line went dead. Bridgette said, "Did we all hear that?"

Delray replied, "Perfect, Bridgette. We need you to wait where you are for a couple of minutes to account for walking time from Jollier to Elizabeth."

Bridgette replied, "Okay, Chief," while doing her best to control her breathing. Her heart was pounding so rapidly she wondered if it could be picked up through her microphone.

Hoffman said, "Let's use this time to our advantage, Bridgette. Walk to the edge of Collins and look down to William and tell me what you see."

Bridgette crossed Elizabeth and walked to the edge of Collins Lane and peered down the long thoroughfare. The multi-story buildings on either side cast long shadows making it dark and uninviting. The recent rain had left pools of water on the ground adding the smell of stagnating water to the odor of rotting food that emanated from the dumpsters. Although it wasn't a place she would want to spend any time in, it seemed quiet enough.

"Okay, I'm looking down Collins and I can just see William Street. We have four cars and a truck parked here, all facing towards Elizabeth Street."

Delray asked, "Could it be used for a getaway, Bridgette? It's the closest exit off William Street from where the van's currently parked."

Bridgette looked back down the lane again and said, "We have dumpsters as well as the cars and the truck. You can get through, but it's very narrow. A car couldn't get up any speed, so I don't see it as a smart exit route."

Hoffman broke in, "I'm not liking this, Felix. The position of the van is too open. I don't see how he thinks he's going to pull this off without being seen."

Delray responded, "Right now we have to wait and see what happens. We can't rush in and arrest this guy yet—he's not even parked illegally."

Bridgette could hear Hoffman grumble a response before Delray asked her if she was ready to walk down Collins.

When she didn't respond straight away, Delray yelled, "Bridgette," at such a volume that it made her wince.

"Sorry, Chief, I'm here."

Delray calmed down a little and said, "Don't leave me hanging, Bridgette. I assume the worst if I don't get a response."

Bridgette said, "Lance, can you hear me?"

"Loud and clear."

"How old is the guy in the truck? If you had to put an age on him, what would you say?"

"He's just come out of the building and heading back to the van. I'd guess mid-twenties."

"Not mid-thirties with a baby face?"

"I got a good look at him—this guy is nowhere near thirty."

Bridgette replied, "It's not him. This is a setup, just like at the truck rental company. The man I talked to on the phone is older—easily mid-thirties. I think the guy in the truck is just someone random who's been hired. He probably has no idea what's going on."

Bridgette could hear Delray softly cursing through her earpiece.

In an agitated voice, Hoffman responded, "So if that's not him, then where the hell is he?"

Remaining calm, Delray asked, "Can you see anyone in the laneway, Bridgette?"

Bridgette did another quick scan up and down the laneway and moved her position slightly to see if she could see any sign of someone looking down from an upper window.

"Not that I can see, Chief."

"What about anything out of the ordinary?"

"It all looks quiet. There's a long ladder next to the truck leaning up against the building. It looks like someone's been servicing a power box to one of the buildings, but other than that, nothing out of the ordinary."

"There's no one up on the ladder?"

"No."

Hoffman cut in, "Ron and I walked the street earlier—we saw the truck. It's some sort of electrical contractor's truck. I talked to a couple of the shop keepers and they say the guy's been there working since early this morning."

Delray came back, "It could be our guy just observing to see if we've made the connection?"

Hoffman replied, "Ron watched him get down off the ladder and walk down to a sandwich shop on lower William about twenty minutes ago. I was suspicious and got him to go investigate. The guy's still there eating and there's no rear exit. When he comes back out, we'll see him."

Delray responded, "We've got a lot of moving parts here—"

Hoffman cut in again, "We're being played, Felix. We should get everyone down here and start searching buildings before this guy gets away."

The conversation stopped for a moment. Everyone knew Delray was thinking and didn't want to interrupt.

Finally, Delray came back and said, "Calling everyone down to start blindly searching buildings is a long shot at best. Joel, you copy?"

"I'm here, Chief."

"I want you to move from Pontefract to Elizabeth. Park next to the Collins Lane exit and be ready to block any vehicle if there's an attempted getaway."

Bridgette heard Green respond, "Got it, Chief. I'm moving now. It will take me close to two minutes to get in position."

Delray began to instruct the rest of the team to stay in position, but Bridgette wasn't listening anymore. She cut in over the top of Delray as her phone began to ring again and said, "He's calling again."

She took another deep breath and pressed answer, "Sorry, I'm on my way."

In a slightly annoyed voice, the same man she had spoken to earlier asked, "So what's the holdup? You should have been here by now?"

Thinking on her feet, Bridgette said, "I got another call straight after yours from my friend who's coming into town with me tonight. I'm on my way now—I'll be there in under two minutes."

"You need to hurry, I'm over time here and I don't want a parking ticket."

The man disconnected before she had a chance to respond.

Chapter 43

Kayne Selwood pressed disconnect to end the phone call and stood contemplating what he would do next as he peered out through the storeroom's small security window. She was late—almost certainly stalling for time while surveillance teams got into position. He shifted slightly to his right and leaned in closer to the door's grimy, reinforced glass pane to give himself a better view of the laneway. He wasn't worried about being seen by anyone. He had walked the laneway numerous times during the past forty-eight hours to get familiar with the layout and was confident no one could see him unless they were standing directly in front of the building's recessed rear exit.

Stealing the electrical contractor's truck and the ruse of being a contractor had proven invaluable. After carefully parking the truck in the laneway in the early hours of the morning, he had been able to come and go as a maintenance man going about his business and had observed the police subtly setting up for the operation. He was confident at least two of the plain clothes police officers in William Street had seen him leave the laneway to head to the cafe for lunch and equally as confident they assumed he was still there on a break.

He rested his glove covered hand on the door's handle and mentally went through the remainder of his plan. He knew this was his last opportunity to abort. He was still fairly certain they had no idea of his location. The vacant building had been locked up for six weeks awaiting renovation and the cop he'd seen sitting in a car on Pontefract Drive hadn't taken any notice of him as he walked by in his DriGlo uniform. This was a far greater risk than anything he'd done before, but the thrill of pulling it off was exhilarating. He was confident he could outwit them all—even Bridgette Casseldhorf and smiled to himself as he thought about what he had planned for her during the night ahead.

He took one last look around the small, empty store room and for a moment studied the footprints left by his contractor boots on the filthy floor. He wasn't particularly worried about leaving evidence that he had been here. Like everything else he wore, the boots would be disposed of later that evening after they had served their purpose. He was confident that by the time he left town tomorrow to return to his normal life, no evidence that could link him to his crimes would remain. He turned and patiently looked back out the window. He had learned early on that patience had its own rewards and felt the first rush of adrenaline as he saw movement in the laneway. Silently and gently, he unlocked the door and quietly stepped out into the shadows.

Chapter 44

Bridgette asked, "Did you hear the conversation, Chief?"

"Yeah, I got it. What do you think, Lance?"

Hoffman responded, "The guy in the van didn't make the call. He walked back out of the building just as the conversation was concluding and he wasn't on his phone. Bridgette's right, he's just a prop for whatever the real killer's got planned."

Bridgette heard silence for a few seconds and knew Delray would be thinking about what to do next.

Finally, he said, "We need to see how this plays out, but Bridgette's safety has to be our priority. Lance, I want you to pretend you're taking a call on your phone. Walk down to Collins and casually stop, like you're still talking. Keep an eye on Bridgette as she walks up the laneway."

"I'm on my way, Chief."

Delray continued, "Joel, how close are you?"

"In Elizabeth Street and just about to pull a U-turn to park, Chief."

Bridgette turned and saw the old tan Ford that Joel Green was driving coming up Elizabeth Street. She was slightly relieved to know that she would have cover from both ends of the laneway.

Hoffman broke back in and said, "I'm here at the Collins entrance, Bridgette, but I'm having difficulty seeing all the way up. That truck is obscuring the view."

Bridgette responded, "I'll talk as I walk, so you know exactly where I am."

Hoffman murmured in a low voice, "I've got a bad feeling about this," but said no more.

Delray shot back, "Okay everybody, Bridgette's ready to come down the lane. She will be at the van in sixty-seconds. Lance and I will close in then and we'll see what happens. You should have all heard that we think the guy in the van is just a prop, so keep your eyes open. If you see any sign of anybody looking out of place or watching us, alert the team straight away."

Bridgette stepped into the shadows and slowly began her walk down the laneway. The temperature dropped immediately, and she felt goose bumps forming on her arms. She wasn't sure whether it was the cold or her anxiety that was causing her skin to crawl, but she quickened her pace slightly as she approached the first parked car. She didn't believe in premonitions, but Hoffman's words about him having a bad feeling played on her mind. She would be glad when the short walk was over and she was out on William Street. She mouthed to herself, "Hold it together," before she started her commentary.

In a low voice, she said, "Okay, I'm just passing the first of four cars. It all looks quiet."

Bridgette kept scanning left to right, looking for any sign of anyone watching her from inside a building.

She kept walking and said, "I'm just approaching the second car. I'm keeping a lookout for any sign of anyone watching, but I don't see anything."

Delray murmured some words of encouragement as she walked towards the truck.

She replied, "Okay, I'm close to halfway now—just coming up behind the truck."

She passed beside the long ladder and paused long enough to look up at the electricity box, wondering if the truck was somehow being used as a prop. As she stepped forward again, time seemed to slow to a crawl as her peripheral vision picked up movement on her right-hand side. Even though it only took a fraction of a second for her survival instincts to kick in, Bridgette knew she was in trouble as a dark form rapidly emerged from a recessed doorway. She raised her arms and tried to pivot to shield her face, but her reaction time wasn't quick enough. The dark form turned into a man in his late thirties—tall, lean and devoid of expression. As he lunged forward, she saw his clenched fist swing down towards her skull before her vision exploded into a kaleidoscope of color.

Bridgette saw the laneway and the truck tilt sideways at an odd angle and drift out of focus as her head began to ring with excruciating pain. She felt herself floating and falling all at the same time and then relaxed as everything faded to black.

Chapter 45

Lance Hoffman hadn't stepped foot inside a church since his wife's funeral nine years earlier. He believed in God, but couldn't remember the last time he prayed, only that it was a long time ago. He had a bad feeling about what was happening and whispered a prayer, almost a demand, "God, keep her safe," as he watched Bridgette's silhouetted figure step into the shadows at the top end of the Collins laneway.

He watched her first tenuous steps until his view was blocked by the electrical contractor's truck. Hoffman rarely connected with his partners at anything beyond a superficial level. He almost universally rejected all invitations to socialize; particularly since his wife's death, preferring to keep everything purely on a professional level. Listening to Bridgette's commentary as she passed the first car, he wondered again why Bridgette was different?

Initially, he thought it was because she reminded him of his daughter Megan, but he'd quickly dismissed that idea when he realized how different they were. He wondered whether it was simply because life had dealt her a rough hand and she needed a lucky break? He wasn't sure exactly why he had warmed to the intelligent and stubborn young detective, but he wanted her to succeed and make something of her police career. He whispered, "Keep going, Bridgette," as he heard her through his earpiece say she was coming up behind the truck.

Hoffman focused on the truck and counted off the seconds. His gut began to tighten when Bridgette didn't appear as expected.

At first, he thought she may have a problem with her communications and yelled her name, almost willing her to appear.

Delray cut in with urgency in his voice, "Lance, what's going on? Bridgette, do you copy?"

Hoffman took off down the laneway at a sprint as he answered, "She was hidden from my view behind the truck and hasn't appeared yet. We need everyone down here now!"

Hoffman didn't hear Delray ask Joel Green if he was in position yet, nor Green's response that he was pulling a U-turn as he rounded the front of the truck. Breathing heavily, Hoffman stopped and spun around, scanning the deserted area frantically for any sign of his partner.

Out of desperation, he yelled her name again but was rewarded only with silence.

With rising panic in his voice, Delray cut in, "What's going on, Lance?"

Hoffman responded, "There's no sign of her, Felix," and began frantically trying to open doors that led into buildings, while Delray barked instructions to the team telling them all to close in.

After discovering the four closest doors to the truck were all locked, Hoffman stepped back and looked up the laneway towards Joel Green, who was now out of his car and sprinting down the laneway towards him.

Hoffman yelled, "Have you seen any sign of her?" and swore through gritted teeth as the middle-aged detective shook his head as he ran. Now positive that Bridgette had been taken by the killer, Hoffman knew every second counted if they were to have any hope of getting her back alive.

Hoffman strode back to the first of doors and tried to force it open with a shoulder charge. His considerable body weight made a huge bang on impact but was no match for the steel door frame and he reeled away in agony clutching his right shoulder. Suppressing the pain, Hoffman moved to the second door. This door had a small reinforced window at eye level. Hoffman got up close and looked through the dirty glass into what looked like a small dimly lit storeroom strewn with rubbish. He couldn't see any sign of movement, but some wiring on the floor caught his eye.

Reaching into his pocket, Hoffman withdrew his smart-phone and switched on the device's small flashlight. Doing his best to contain his emotion, he held it up to the glass, just as an out of breath Joel Green reached his side. He ignored Green's questions and moved the light over the wire and held it steady on a small black box that was connected to one end. It only took a fraction of a second for Hoffman to realize he was looking at Bridgette's concealed communication transmitter.

Hoffman yelled to Delray that he'd found the building the killer had used and raised his left elbow to shatter the reinforced glass. The first blow fractured the pane, but it took a second heavy blow for the glass to properly fracture. Hoffman pushed the glass out of the frame with another elbow blow and then reached in and unlocked the door from the inside. With his gun drawn, he took one step back and kicked the door open and quickly scanned the interior of the storeroom before calling, "Clear," when he realized it was empty.

With Green tailing behind him, Hoffman rushed through the storeroom to a door on the opposite side that he presumed led into main part the building. He was relieved to discover it wasn't locked and after pulling it open, stared over the barrel of his gun down a long narrow hallway. The building had an old musty smell and didn't look like it was currently inhabited. Hoffman's attention was drawn to sunlight streaming through window panes in the doors at the far end of the corridor. He knew he was looking out onto Pontefract Drive and put up a hand to shield his eyes from the glare of the late afternoon sun.

He caught a glimpse of a white van pulling away from out the front of the building and cut in over the top of Delray who was still relaying instructions to his team.

"Bill, are you still down on Pontefract?"

Hoffman's earpiece crackled for a moment and then he heard Bill Dickson respond that he was still in position.

Hoffman fired back, "We just had a white van pull out onto Pontefract—it's possible Bridgette's been taken in it."

Dickson responded, "Traffic's heavy, Lance—I got two white vans and a small truck all heading out of—"

Hoffman cut in, "Forget the truck, it's definitely a van. There are two of them?"

"Two, but they're heading for different exits."

Hoffman swore under his breath and turned to Green with his hand out and demanded, "Keys?"

While Green fished in his pants pocket for the keys to his car, Hoffman said to him, "Go through to the front of the building and don't let anybody out until you get reinforcements. Then conduct a full search of the building just to make sure she hasn't been taken upstairs."

Green began to respond with a question, but Hoffman ignored him and said, "Bill, you copy?"

Dickson responded, "I'm on Pontefract. One van is heading for the Catalin exit and the other is heading for the Rochford exit. Which—"

Hoffman was already moving back out through the storeroom toward the laneway and responded, "Take Rochford. I'm at least a minute behind you and with all that heavy traffic you're in the best position to fight the traffic."

Delray cut in, "Okay everyone, I've just pulled the guy out of the van. He's currently sitting in the gutter in handcuffs and doesn't appear to have a clue about what's happening here. Donny, you there?"

The muffled voice response could barely be heard above a car door opening and slamming shut, "I've just picked up Mitch. Where do you want us, Chief?"

"Head out along Rochford to help Bill. Are you there, Pat?"

"Yes, Chief."

"Head out along Rochford as well and keep in radio contact with Bill and Donny. We may lose the van in all that heavy traffic and the road has three major exits. We need to do our best to cover them until I can get a chopper organized to help us."

Hoffman was totally out of breath by the time he reached Green's battered car. Such was his focus as he pulled away from the curb, he didn't hear the remainder of Delray's instruction or notice the pedestrians on Jollier who had turned as one to watch the old Ford, now smoking its tires, as it rapidly changed gears and accelerated towards Pontefract Drive.

Chapter 46

Bridgette began to stir and felt nauseous and disori-entated. She remembered entering the laneway, but nothing more. Fighting back the urge to vomit, she opened her eyes and blinked several times as she stared into darkness. The buzzing sound inside her head was loud but masked by another loud vibrating sound she didn't understand.

She felt uncomfortable and tried to stretch out from the fetal position she currently lay in, but her arms and legs refused to move. Confused and weak, she blinked her eyes again, but everything remained pitch black. She felt dizzy and lay still for a moment as she wondered where she was. Feeling the urge to vomit again, Bridgette twisted her head to get more comfortable and felt a rough cloth pressed up against her face.

She tried to reach up her hand to brush the cloth away, but her arm got tangled in the fabric as well. After breathing in deeply, Bridgette pushed down with her feet. Her heart sank as the heavy cloth began to tighten around her face and she realized she was trapped inside some kind of large bag.

Unable to see anything, Bridgette felt a wave of panic sweep over her and willed herself to stay calm. As she brought her breathing back under control, she felt the fabric again. The bag didn't appear to be air tight, although she knew her oxygen supply would be limited and too much exertion was going to make her groggy and drowsy again.

With her face resting on what she presumed was a floor, she felt vibrations through her cheek and realized she must be in a vehicle. She tried not to think about what lay ahead and attempted to twist onto her back. The bag offered her little room to move and as panic began to set in again, she willed herself to stay calm as she began to think about what she would do next. She reasoned the bag must have a drawstring or zipper somewhere and began to feel around with her hands for any sign of an opening. After almost two minutes she'd found nothing more than a thick seam which resisted all her attempts to prise apart.

Soaked in sweat, she found the conditions stifling, but was relieved the buzzing sound in her head was starting to subside. She wondered if her captor had seen her moving inside the bag. She had heard no sounds other than the road noise. Perhaps she was being held in a separate compartment to the driver? As she began to think about other ways to escape, she noticed the rumbling noise had changed pitch slightly and was now punctuated by a short thumping sound at regular intervals.

She'd heard this rhythmic sound before, but struggled to remember where? Now almost fully awake, she heard a car horn in the distance and realized where she was as she had a flashback to her childhood. With its large steel expansion joints separating the concrete slabs that formed its deck, the Junction Bridge made a sound like no other when crossed in a vehicle. Bridgette remembered her mother and father had taken her on several all-day picnics across the river to the

Catalin Mountain reserve when she was only five or six. Even though it had been over twenty years since she had traveled on the bridge, the distinctive sound the tires made was forever etched in her memory.

She knew what lay ahead and that her only hope of survival was getting out of the bag before the van stopped. She tried to block out what her captor might do to her and she tried to focus on a plan. She felt herself beginning to cramp and pulled her legs tight up against her chest. Now having slightly more room to move, she pushed down with her right hand and shifted her weight to the left and managed to twist and roll into a cramped crawl position. Instead of celebrating the small victory, she braced for the impact of a blow or a kick from her captor, but nothing came. She wondered whether her captor was confident she couldn't get out of the bag, but increasingly she began to sense she was being held in a separate compartment.

With sweat pouring off her face, Bridgette felt the floor of the vehicle with her hands through the bag. It felt cool to touch and as she moved her hands around within the confines of the bag, she sensed the floor was made of metal. Bridgette wondered how big the vehicle was. She listened intently to the engine noise for a moment. It was hard to tell from the confines of the bag, but she thought it sounded more like a car than a truck. She assumed the vehicle wasn't overly large and firmly gripped the fabric of the bag in both hands and began to blindly inch forward in the hope she might bump into something that she could use to rip the bag open.

After several minutes of patiently inching forward, she felt something hard press against her head. Exhausted, she stopped for a moment to get her breath and reached out with her hand to feel the object through the cloth. It was flat and didn't move when she pushed against it. Confused, Bridgette tried to inch around it and then realized she had come up against a wall of the vehicle.

With her clothes now totally soaked in sweat, the confined space of the bag was making her dizzy. She wondered if she was beginning to hallucinate as a rainbow of colors flashed before her eyes. She sensed a new wave of panic beginning to sweep over her and admonished herself to stay calm and then mentally celebrated finding the wall of the van as a small victory.

After taking a moment to clear her mind, she twisted around in the bag to change her direction. With the wall now hard up against her left-hand side, she began to inch forward again and almost let out an audible cry as an excruciating pain shot up through the palm of her left hand.

Rolling onto her right side, she bit down on her bottom lip to conceal her agony and gingerly cradled her left hand. The throbbing was intense, but Bridgette barely noticed it as she felt her right hand beginning to get wet. She knew immediately she was bleeding and felt the palm of her left hand and quickly located a small puncture wound. While laying still to let the pain subside, she wondered what had caused the wound? Bridgette knew whatever it was, it had pierced the bag and could potentially be used to create an opening if she could find it again. Shifting her weight to the left again, she pressed down hard with her right hand again and rolled back up into her crawl position and began cautiously feeling the floor in front of her.

It took her only a few seconds to find a distinctive sharp ridge on the floor. Bridgette figured it was a metal spur—probably made by something large and heavy that had gouged the floor while being loaded or unloaded. As she began to push the bag down hard on either side of the spur, the vehicle rocked, and the road noise became more pronounced. She heard the vehicle change down gears again and knew they were now on a dirt road as the vibrations through the floor intensified. She wondered how much time she had before the vehicle stopped. She remembered Catalin reserve led very quickly into a remote, heavily forested mountain area. If the killer was planning on following his previous pattern of using a grave site close to where people frequented, the road trip was almost over.

With new desperation, Bridgette gripped the bag with her two hands and pressed down hard on the spur as the vehicle changed down gears again. She struggled to maintain her balance as the vehicle began to jolt as it drove over the increasingly rough ground. She whispered to herself to stay calm as the vehicle's engine began to whine as it started up an incline.

Now confident the bag was caught on the sharp ridge again; Bridgette gripped the bag tightly with both hands again and pulled back with all her strength. The jubilation of seeing the bag tear slightly and open up a hole big enough for her to slip her finger through was short lived. As she stared out through the dimly lit hole at the metal floor of the vehicle, Bridgette listened intently as the vehicle changed down gears again and slowed to a crawl.

She envisioned the killer now looking for a suitable place to park and knew her time was almost up. Pushing her right thumb through the hole, she pressed down hard and felt the material give as the vehicle began to brake. She quickly removed her thumb to inspect the size of the hole, but her heart sank as the vehicle pulled up to a halt.

She heard the handbrake being applied and was conscious that any tearing of the fabric she made now might be heard by the killer. She heard the engine switch off and instinctively lay back on her side and worked both hands into the opening she had made as she curled back up into the fetal position. She expected to hear a door open or someone start to move around inside the cabin of the vehicle, but everything remained quiet.

She wondered what the killer was doing as she lay there, still trapped and afraid to move a muscle.

Chapter 47

L ance Hoffman considered himself a good driver, but as
he careened across three lanes of traffic after pulling a
hard left onto Pontefract Drive, none of the motorists
who had to brake suddenly to avoid a collision with the old
Ford would have agreed with him.

Hoffman stole a quick look in the rear-view mirror and
was relieved he hadn't caused any accidents as he listened
to Delray barking instructions over the police radio. No lights,
no sirens and do your best to move through the traffic without
drawing too much attention to yourself was the gist of what
Delray was telling his detectives. Hoffman knew Delray's
reasoning was sound, but as he changed into top gear and
began weaving through traffic, he knew he needed to ignore
the last part of the instruction with so much ground to make
up.

With his wheels squealing hard as he swerved left off Pontefract onto the Catalin exit, he estimated the killer probably
had close to a four-minute head start on him if he had taken
the same turn off. Although the Ford he was driving looked old
and battered, the engine had been fully rebuilt by Vancouver
Metro for undercover work and was capable of top speeds that

would frighten most people. Hoffman wasn't worried about not having the speed to catch the white van, but after passing the third turnoff to outer Vancouver residential areas, he knew staying on the main road was a gamble.

His thoughts were interrupted by Delray's voice breaking through over the police radio again.

"Lance, where are you?"

"About a minute out from the Junction Bridge."

"Any sign of the second van yet?"

"No—he had a couple of minutes head start on me. You get a helicopter yet?"

"I've got one in the air, but it's currently tracking the other van on Rochford. The traffic's heavy and there are too many exits for the guys to fully cover. It's too risky pulling it out of there at present."

"Tell me about it. I've passed three major turnoffs that all lead into residential areas, so I'm gambling I've made the right call by staying on the main road."

"If he's following the same pattern as before, and we have to assume he is, you've made the right decision."

"From memory, when I get over the bridge, the road splits into three not long after I get into the Catalin reserve. It will take me over an hour to explore them all properly and we both know we don't have that much time."

"Hang on a second."

The radio went quiet for a minute and Hoffman guessed Delray had changed back to a regular police frequency to communicate with general dispatch. Hoffman kept his eyes focused on the road ahead and gripped the steering wheel even tighter as he brought the old Ford around a sweeping left-hand bend and down towards the narrow two-lane Junction bridge. He glanced down at the speedometer as the needle crept towards seventy miles an hour and gritted his teeth as the Ford bottomed out with a bang as he drove onto the bridge.

Hoffman knew the combination of speed and the car's stiff suspension would mess with his chronic back condition, but he ignored the pain and focused on what was ahead of him as the Ford sped across the bridge and then shot off the exit into the reserve.

Even though it was relatively close to the city, Hoffman could not recall the last time he had visited the reserve. Thanks to environmentalists, Catalin Mountain continued to remain a pristine, heavily forested, wilderness favored by trekkers and adventurers who were up for the grueling two-day walk through the mountain range to its northern extremity. With the lengthening shadows of the fir trees making visibility of the road harder by the minute, Hoffman switched the lights on as he passed a sign which informed motorists of an unsealed road ahead. As he began changing down gears to slow down, Delray's voice came to life on the police radio again.

"You there, Lance?"

Hoffman adjusted the volume of the police radio and then answered, "I'm here, Felix. The reception's starting to fade—I'm not sure how much longer I'll have radio contact."

"You got the satellite phone with you?"

"In the glove compartment."

"Good. I'll keep this brief. Short answer, I can't get another helicopter for at least an hour, but I've got two squad cars on their way. They'll be out there in about fifteen minutes."

Hoffman knew better than to curse in front of his boss, and instead yelled, "Hang on," as he planted his foot on the brake and brought the old Ford to a skidding halt in the middle of the dirt road.

With the engine still running, Hoffman looked out through the windscreen at the illuminated road sign in front of him and said to Delray, "I've passed the two picnic areas and I'm now at the road junction. Are you familiar with it?"

"It's all dirt from there on in and splits into three, right?"

Hoffman looked out the window and sighed as he responded, "That's the one. I've got three choices. If he's here, he could have taken her up any one of these tracks."

Hoffman heard Delray respond, "I'm in the communications van with Danny Collier now. Let me pull up a map."

The radio went quiet for a moment before Delray came back and said, "None of the roads go anywhere. They get you a little further into the forest but..."

The radio went quiet again. Hoffman could hear Delray mumbling in the background and guessed he was conferring with Danny Collier. Before he had a chance to ask what was happening, Delray came back with urgency in his voice.

"Take the right fork, Lance. It's called the Honeyeater Trail and it leads back around to one of the two picnic areas. If he's following the same pattern as he's done before, he'll be looking for a spot close to where people walk, and the other two trails are dead ends."

Hoffman threw the car into first gear and planted his foot before Delray had finished speaking. With the wheels throwing up gravel as he turned onto the Honeyeater Trail, he replied, "I'm on my way, Felix," and tried not to think about what he would do if he didn't find the van.

Chapter 48

Bridgette lay on her side in the darkness, poised to rip the bag open at her first opportunity. Everything remained quiet and she wondered what the killer was doing. Could he see her? Was he watching her? Being able to manipulate her to walk down the laneway of his choosing and then capture her while under the watchful eye of Vancouver's best detectives showed careful and tactical planning. She knew enough about him now to know what he had planned for her would have been thought through in meticulous detail. She deliberately pushed the thoughts from her mind and tried to calm her nerves.

She wondered where he'd parked. She didn't think he'd had time to drive very far into the Catalin Reserve. Fearful that she would alert the killer to what she was doing, Bridgette resisted the temptation to rip the bag any further and instead listened intently for any sounds that would signal her captor was getting out of the vehicle. At first, she only heard the slow metallic tick of the engine as it cooled, but then she briefly heard the whining sound of a small electric motor. She knew what the sound was before it had stopped and pictured the killer sitting in the front of the vehicle lowering a side window—watching and listening to make sure he was alone and not about to be disturbed.

Keeping her hands firmly gripped around the hole she had made in the fabric, she wondered how much longer she would have to wait? She had no idea of the time, but figured it was late afternoon and began to wonder if he was waiting until it got dark? She sensed the vehicle rocking slightly and began to slowly rip the fabric when she heard a vehicle door begin to open. She hoped the noise she had made would be masked by the sound of the door. Laying still again as everything fell silent, she mouthed the words, 'be patient,' and waited for the sound of the door to close.

The sound she expected never came. As sweat began to sting her eyes, she felt the vehicle rocking slightly again and heard the metallic click of the door being softly pressed closed to avoid making any noise.

Bridgette tensed for what she assumed would follow next and spread the tear in the fabric apart to check the size of the opening she'd made. It was big enough to get her arms through but not her whole body. She debated giving up on stealth and just ripping the fabric and getting out of the bag as quickly as she could but decided she didn't have enough time to escape and be ready to defend herself. Something inside her told her to wait and she continued to lay still with her heart almost beating out of her chest.

She heard the soft fall of what sounded like footsteps. She pictured the man walking around outside. She continued to listen and after about thirty seconds noticed the sound of the footfall becoming softer before it disappeared altogether.

Bridgette had no idea whether the man had simply stopped moving and was still just a few feet away, or if he had moved away from the vehicle. She waited a few more seconds with her hands firmly gripped around the opening in the bag, straining to hear any noise she could.

When everything continued to remain quiet, she whispered to herself, "Now or never," and ripped at the fabric of the bag.

No longer caring about the noise she made, Bridgette continued to rip until she made a hole large enough for her to crawl out through. Desperate to escape, Bridgette reached her arms through the opening and quickly pulled the bag down over her head and body.

After scrambling out of the bag, she rapidly scanned the interior of the vehicle while stretching out her cramped legs. In the fading sunlight, the interior looked like most commercial delivery vans—just a large, square metal box for transporting goods. The storage area was empty apart from two other large white canvas bags that were identical to the one she had just escaped from. They both had the word 'laundry' printed on them in large black letters and appeared to be half full. Leaning forward, Bridgette quickly felt each bag to make sure they didn't contain other victims and was relieved when the contents didn't appear to be anything more than dirty laundry.

The van had both rear and side cargo doors. Bridgette studied the rear door for a moment. It appeared to be hinged at the top and opened outward. Bridgette couldn't see any sign of an internal latch and instead slid across to the side door and got up on her knees. Gripping the door handle, she depressed the latch and pulled hard to slide it open. She wasn't surprised to find the door was locked and bit down on her bottom lip at the setback and suppressed another urge to panic. She looked around again and noticed a small glass window near the top of the panel that separated the cargo area from the driver's area.

Unable to stand up to her full height, Bridgette stood as best she could and cautiously peered through the small window into the cabin area of the vehicle. The vehicle looked new and contained no personal possessions that she could see, with the exception of a small folded up camping shovel that lay on the front passenger seat. She thought of the Travers' grave site and shivered as she realized she was probably staring at the shovel that had been used to dig Monica's grave.

Shaking the image clear from her mind, she examined the window. It wasn't anywhere near big enough even for a small child to crawl through, but it provided her with a reasonable view through the front window of the van to the area outside. As she scanned the area, she could see a dirt track framed on either side by tall fir trees. The killer appeared to have parked in a small clearing and she guessed by the fading sunlight it was around five p.m. Bridgette scanned the road ahead and the forest on both sides of the track looking for any sign of the killer, but she could see no movement.

As she kept a watchful lookout, she wondered what possessed a man to do the things this man had done. How do people end up so evil? How can they do the things they do over and over again? Bridgette's fear began to turn to anger as she thought about Monica and how she might be the next victim. She whispered, "Not without a fight," and turned her attention back to the cargo area of the van.

She carefully scanned the area from top to bottom looking for anything she could use as a weapon but found nothing. She began examining the two laundry bags in more detail but stopped when she thought she heard footsteps.

Sitting perfectly still, Bridgette cocked her head slightly and listened. At first, she thought she might be just hearing things, but after a few seconds she began to discern the unmistakable soft footfall of footsteps again, growing slightly louder with each step as they drew closer to the van. Bridgette had no idea what to expect. She knew she stood little chance of surviving without a gun or a knife and her only real chance of survival was the element of surprise in those first few seconds when the killer opened the door. She willed herself to remain calm and did her best to focus her energy on what was about to come.

She wondered whether he would use the rear or side door and listened closely until the footsteps stopped, and she heard a key being placed in the side door lock. Instinctively, Bridgette grabbed one of the two laundry bags by the carry cord and silently moved across the cargo space to a position just behind the side door. With her heart pounding, Bridgette pressed herself up against the wall, hoping to avoid being seen by the killer when he first opened the door.

Bridgette heard the key turn in the lock and whispered a quick prayer as the door began to slide open.

Chapter 49

Felix Delray watched the driver of the blue van, now in handcuffs, being put into the back of the squad car by the two uniformed police officers. After a brief curbside interview, Delray believed the man's story when he said he'd only been hired the previous day. He had no doubt the man would be released without charge at some point, but right now he was a loose end he didn't have time for.

He felt his phone buzz again as he watched the squad car pull away from the curb and sighed as he saw the number for Assistant Commissioner Leon Cunningham flash up on the screen. It was the third call in less than twenty minutes that he'd ignored from his boss. He wondered whether it was the ordering of the helicopter or the additional squad cars that got his attention? Whatever it was, it would boil down to budget and 'exceeding his authority' like it always did.

Delray let the call go through to voicemail and put the phone back in his pocket. There would be time enough for Cunningham's rebuke later, but for now saving a police officer's life had to take priority. Delray put his wireless earbud back in and spoke into the microphone concealed beneath his shirt.

"You copy, Danny?"

"I'm here, Chief. You want an update?"

Delray replied, "Fire away," as he walked towards a police squad car he had insisted be left behind for his use.

"Okay, Dickson, Bosco, and Smith have been attempting to track the white van along Pontefract. Traffic has been heavy, and they weren't able to get close enough before the Rochford distributor."

Delray feared this would happen and shook his head as he replied, "Let me guess, they lost him?"

"Not quite. They've ended up following three similar looking white vans. Bosco and Smith's cars followed two vans that didn't take the Rochford freeway exit. Both vans have been pulled over for searches and driver interviews and have been given the all clear. The detectives are now heading back here. The van that Smith and Kelly have been following left the freeway and drove into a residential estate. It's just pulling up out front of a house as we speak. You want me to patch you in so you can hear what happens?"

Delray replied as he opened the door of the squad car, "Just let me know when it's done, Danny. If it's parked out front of a house in a residential area, it's highly unlikely to be our guy."

Delray politely listened as Collier promised to keep him fully informed of all developments as he got into the vehicle. He sat for a moment lightly drumming his fingers on the steering wheel while he debated what to do. Cunningham would be expecting a call, but he wasn't confident he could hold a civil conversation with his boss right now without calling him a moron or worse.

"Hey, Danny, you copy?"

"Right here, Chief."

"You hear anything from Detective Hoffman since I last spoke to him?"

"No, Chief. He's out of range right now. Our network range doesn't extend far into the Catalin Mountain region, and I haven't heard him on the satellite service yet."

"I'm going to head out there now. I've got two squad cars on their way out there, but there's a lot of ground to cover. Tell Bosco and Smith to head out there as well. It will be dark soon and Lance can use all the help he can get."

Delray started the engine and as an afterthought said, "Hey, Danny?"

"I'm here, Chief."

"If Assistant Commissioner Cunningham somehow manages to get in touch with you trying to find out where I am, tell him I'm on my way to Catalin Reserve and my comms access will be limited."

"Got it, Chief. Do You want me to pass on the satellite phone number for the car you're in?"

"Only if he specifically asks you for it."

"Got it."

Delray pulled a fast U-turn and headed towards Pontefract Drive. He figured it would take him close to thirty minutes to get out to where Hoffman was now searching and tried not to think about what the killer could do to Bridgette in the meantime. He recalled his last conversation with Hoffman and hoped he had guessed right on the location.

Chapter 50

Bridgette braced herself as the door of the van began to slide open. She decided to keep herself pressed up against the side wall as long as possible, knowing her slim chances of survival might be slightly improved if she could at least see the killer and any weapon he carried before she reacted.

From her concealed position, she could see part of the killer's torso as the sliding door clicked into the open position. The killer took one step forward and began to raise his right arm. Bridgette's eyes locked onto a small black pistol he held in his hand.

As the weapon came into full view, Bridgette knew there was no time to hesitate and swung the laundry bag in an arcing loop hoping to dislodge the gun from the killer's hand. Despite the adrenaline rush she felt coursing through her body, the bag swung more slowly through the air than she expected. She knew she was weak and still recovering from the blow to the head and hadn't counted on the killer's reflexes. The killer pivoted and fired two rounds as the laundry bag struck his right arm.

With the sound of the gunshots ringing in her ears, Bridgette launched herself forward and out of the vehicle as the killer fired the gun a third time. She felt no pain as she felt herself collapsing onto the man. As they hit the ground, she brought her right knee up into the man's groin with all the strength she could muster. The man groaned and his eyes rolled momentarily into the back of his head. Bridgette knew she was still too weak to fight any further and rolled off the man and started running for the cover of the forest. She heard the gun discharge again as she reached the tree line, but didn't dare look back. She knew most small handguns were notoriously inaccurate at any distance beyond a few paces and right now distance was her friend. She felt her legs begin to cramp as she raced through the forest but willed herself to keep moving.

After two minutes and near exhaustion, she tripped on an exposed tree root as she came into a small clearing. Tumbling forward, she landed heavily and clutched at her left ankle as a sharp bolt of pain ran up her leg. She looked back along the trail expecting to see the killer right behind her, but apart from the sound of her labored breathing, the forest remained still and quiet.

Her left ankle began to throb immediately, and Bridgette doubted she could continue at anything more than a hobbling pace. She quickly lifted the leg of her jeans to examine the ankle. She was relieved to see there was no bone protruding, but as the ankle began to swell and turn a purple blue before her eyes, she knew running any further would be almost impossible. She looked around and noticed a large fallen tree surrounded by undergrowth on the other side of the clearing. With nightfall approaching, she hoped she could use this as a hiding place at least until it got dark.

Knowing every second counted, Bridgette tried to get to her

feet and test the ankle, but the pain was excruciating. She felt nauseous all over again and began to drag herself across the clearing towards the fallen tree instead. Her heart sank as a voice broke the stillness.

"I knew you were going to be something special even before I started profiling you."

She looked up and saw a man in his late thirties standing next to the fallen tree. Wearing a DriGlo uniform, the man showed no ill-effects from their encounter at the van. He was average height and build and had a relaxed, almost amused look on his face as he stared down at Bridgette from over the barrel of his gun. His narrow face was accentuated by a short haircut and olive features, giving him a cruel, sadistic look. The killer didn't seem to be out of breath from running and looked totally in control. He radiated evil and the gun pointed at her forehead almost seemed superfluous.

Bridgette knew she was in no shape to run or fight back and doubted anyone from Vancouver Metro had any idea where she was. Although terrified, she refused to show him any fear.

In as defiant a voice as she could muster, she replied, "You're not the only one who's been profiling."

Without taking his eyes off Bridgette, the killer bent down and picked up the small camping shovel she had last seen on the front seat of the van.

Tossing the implement towards her, he said, "You succeeded where everyone else failed. I'd almost given up hope that any law enforcement agency would ever make the link between me and my performances."

As fear slightly gave way to anger, Bridgette held the man's gaze and replied, "You call murdering defenseless women performances?"

The killer responded with a smile. It gave her a brief look into the soul of a man who fed off violence and murder. Bridgette held his stare but didn't move to pick up the shovel. As terrified as she was of being shot, she decided it was preferable to being stabbed or beaten to death.

"I'm not digging my own grave."

The killer let out a short laugh and then replied, "You dug your own grave the moment you replied to my competition."

His face darkened again as he asked, "Who do you think you're dealing with? How stupid do you think I am?"

He easily held Bridgette's glare and kept the gun pointed at her forehead.

"I check everyone thoroughly when I make my final selection. Your Facebook history showed a lot of gaps and a lot of inactivity which made me curious. Also, you used a surname which sounds like a middle name..."

Without taking his eyes or the gun off Bridgette, the killer moved sideways to sit down on the trunk of the fallen tree.

Seemingly comfortable and in control of his anger again, he continued.

"I'm a cyber security consultant and tracking people through the internet is one of the things I do best. Within half a day I knew almost as much about you as you know yourself..."

He cocked his head slightly and looked at Bridgette as if she were a specimen under a microscope.

"You've had an interesting professional life. A career in the Navy, then study to be a criminologist and now... a detective for the Vancouver Metropolitan Police."

Bridgette wasn't about to give the killer any reaction and said nothing as she continued to glare back.

"It was when I discovered you had an IQ of over one-fifty that I got really interested."

Despite her dire position, Bridgette couldn't help herself and asked, "Why do you always choose brunettes?"

Bridgette was surprised when the killer responded with a question.

"Why do you want to know?"

"I'm curious—smart people generally are."

The killer nodded once and asked, "I have a condition called hypospadias. I'm sure someone as smart as you knows what that is?"

Bridgette vaguely remembered reading somewhere about the birth defect that could leave a male with a range of life-long deformities to his penis. She wasn't sure where the conversation was going, but every moment she managed to stay alive gave her hope. She decided to steer the conversation back to her question.

"I've heard of the condition, but I don't understand how that relates to selecting brunette victims?"

The killer laughed and said, "You're very ballsy for someone in your position. All the others... well, let's just say there was a lot of begging and screaming—all very undignified."

The killer paused and scratched his chin for a moment and then said, "You're not going to live long enough to tell anyone and I enjoy talking to people with a similar intellect, so I'll indulge you with an answer. But then it will be time to dig..."

The killer paused for effect and smiled as he said softly, "You don't dig—I will shoot you."

To prolong the conversation, Bridgette nodded.

The killer didn't seem at all embarrassed about his personal revelation as he continued.

311

"Because of my condition, I was never very good with women—until I met Elizabeth..."

The killer shifted his position slightly and said, "She had dark hair and was incredibly beautiful. We dated for a while and she seemed to have no issue with my condition. We'd made plans to marry and then I became suspicious over some of her behavior and started following her. I found out she was having an affair behind my back and confronted her. After telling me I wasn't a real man she broke off our relationship."

The killer paused for a moment and then said, "That was of course totally unacceptable and couldn't go unpunished... so I killed the boyfriend. It was easier than I thought. I stole a car, ran him down and dumped the body. I made sure he would never be found and watched as the grief slowly and surely started to consume Elizabeth. But I wasn't satisfied..."

The killer looked at the gun in his hands for a moment and said, "So I bought this gun..."

Returning his gaze to Bridgette, he continued.

"Suffice to say, I planned on shooting her but ended up stabbing her instead. I won't bore you with all the details, but it was the most uplifting experience of my life."

The killer paused and waited for a response, but Bridgette gave him nothing. She wanted to yell and scream that he was a monster, but refrained, knowing it would be the last thing she ever said.

The killer continued. "I was in a state of euphoria for months. I would think fondly about how I killed Elizabeth almost every waking minute of my life... and then it began to wear off. I'd go and visit the location where I'd buried her and that helped for a while..."

The killer paused for a moment and then continued in a

voice barely above a whisper.

"And now I have my performances... My encores as I call them, where I kill Elizabeth over and over again. I shall enjoy telling her about you."

Bridgette watched with trepidation as the killer's top lip began to curl upwards. She knew the conceited smile meant the conversation was over and braced herself for what was to come as the killer slowly re-positioned the gun so that it pointed at her left leg.

"You're more than just another Elizabeth. You've raised the bar."

Silence followed for several seconds and then the killer said, "You have two choices—either start digging, or I put a bullet in your leg. One way or another, you will do as I say."

In an instant, Bridgette knew what she needed to do. With her heart almost beating out of her chest, she struggled to her feet and picked up the shovel.

Ignoring the intense pain in her left ankle, she held the shovel up and defiantly shouted, "I'm not digging my own grave," as she rushed towards the killer.

She expected the gunfire that followed. It would be over soon enough and at least she would die without having to beg for her life. She was confused as the killer swung the gun away from her. In the chaos and noise that followed, she saw the fire flash from his gun as it discharged twice, but puzzled as she heard four gunshots, not two.

In an instant, the killer disappeared into the darkness of the forest as two more shots rang out. Conscious of a presence behind her, she turned around to see Lance Hoffman standing on the other side of the clearing. In the fading light, he was not much more than a dark silhouette holding a gun loosely by his right side. He said nothing and seemed slightly unsteady on his feet. Bridgette's relief instantly turned to shock as she watched a dark stain quickly begin to spread across the front of his shirt.

Chapter 51

Felix Delray came over the rise in the road faster than he expected and took the right-hand bend with two wheels in the gravel. He breathed a sigh of relief when all four wheels were back on the tarred road and slowed the car down for the long sweeping left hand bend that led onto the Junction Bridge. He figured another two minutes and he would be in the forest and looking for Hoffman and Bridgette.

Delray knew he would lose normal communications with Danny Collier soon and decided to get a final update on the situation before he crossed the bridge.

"You copy, Danny."

"Right here, Chief."

"I'm just about to head over the Junction Bridge—you hear anything from Hoffman yet?"

"Nothing yet, Chief. I've tried contacting his satellite phone, but no response. Before we go any further, Chief, I've got Assistant Commissioner Cunningham on another line. He says he wants to speak to you ASAP. To put it bluntly, he's pissed and says he won't be releasing a chopper for the search until he's spoken to you..."

Delray shook his head. It was a typical Cunningham stunt

to reinforce his control, regardless of what was on the line.

"Patch him through, Danny."

Delray waited a few seconds before he heard Cunningham's voice through the car's communication system.

"I could have your badge for what you've tried to pull here, Chief Detective. How dare you undermine my authority."

Delray rolled his eyes. He'd heard it all before and would no doubt hear it again.

"Sir, I'm sure you've been briefed on the situation with Detective Casseldhorf. I'm currently en-route to—"

"You've got a lot of explaining to do. Deliberately excluding McKellar and the federal team from any operation connected to the Travers' case is going to cause considerable embarrassment to the Commissioner. You don't seem to have any idea of the mess you've gotten—"

Delray shot back, "Sir, for your information I called McKellar and he wasn't interested. I even followed it up with an email summarizing our conversation."

"We'll talk about it tomorrow morning. I expect to see you in my office at eight o'clock sharp. You've got a lot of explaining to do."

"Sir, we have an officer missing and we have grave fears for her safety. We need a helicopter to search Catalin Mountain as soon as—"

"Are you sure she's out there?"

Delray shook his head again and kept his anger in check as he responded.

"Sir, I can't give you any guarantees. Hoffman saw a white van on Pontefract Drive just after Detective Casseldhorf was taken captive. The traffic was heavy, but we believe she's in the back of that van."

Delray went on to explain the results of the other searches as he pulled off the road on the far side of the bridge. He wanted nothing more than to continue on into the Catalin Reserve but didn't want to risk a communications dropout with Cunningham before he had a helicopter committed to the search team.

After finishing his update, he added, "So that leaves Hoffman, Sir. He hasn't sighted the van on any of the road exits and the killer's pattern fits with a location near the reserve."

"So, let me get this straight, nobody has actually seen a white van in the area? Detective Hoffman is just following a hunch?"

Delray knew Cunningham's summary was reasonably accurate but wasn't about to give him any reason to say no.

"A woman's life is in danger, Sir—one of our own. I can't give you a guarantee she's here, but I can almost certainly guarantee you she'll be dead by morning if we don't find her."

Delray didn't get a response straight away, and waited patiently, wondering what Cunningham was up to. After almost a minute of waiting, he got his answer.

"We have one helicopter in the air, but you can't have it. It's currently tracking suspects on the southern highway that are suspected of robbing a convenience store at gunpoint half an hour ago. The attendant took one in the stomach and may not pull through. I'm getting a second helicopter organized, but the night shift pilot has called in sick, so it will be at least half an hour, maybe longer, before it's airborne."

With urgency in his voice, Delray pleaded, "Sir, with all due respect, can't we leave it to the squad cars to chase down the suspects? A police officer's life is at stake."

"And what happens if she's not there, Chief Detective? What

happens if we pull the helicopter and do a search and find nothing? How do I explain to the media that a hunch about a police officer is more important than someone who took a bullet doing his job in a convenience store?"

Delray knew it was pointless wasting any more time on an argument he wasn't going to win.

"Sir, if someone could keep Officer Collier informed of progress with the helicopter that would be appreciated. I'll be off the grid in about two minutes but will keep in contact via satellite phone."

"My office at eight o'clock tomorrow morning and be ready to explain yourself to the Commissioner... Delray, are you still there?"

Delray rolled his eyes again in frustration—Cunningham was wasting precious seconds they couldn't afford.

"I'm still here."

"I'm tired of you exceeding your authority. If she dies, I'm holding you personally responsible. I've seen the Commissioner ask for badges for far less than this—and they've all been better cops than you'll ever be. You need to think about that and if you believe in a God, start praying she'll be found alive."

The line went dead, and Delray thumped the steering wheel in anger.

He put the car into gear and said, "You still there, Danny?"

"Right here, Chief."

Delray planted his foot, and as the car screeched back onto the road again, he said, "I'll be in the Catalin Reserve in under two minutes to help with the search. Contact me on the satellite phone as soon as you get an update on that helicopter and keep trying Hoffman for me."

"Will do, Chief."

Delray relayed several more instructions about getting the remaining team members to meet in the picnic area to start coordinating the search, but he got no response from Collier and knew he was now off the grid.

He thought about Cunningham's threat as he sped past a signpost directing him to the Catalin Reserve picnic area. Maybe Cunningham would get his way? Right now, he didn't care. There was a lot more at stake tonight than his career.

Chapter 52

Bridgette watched in horror as Lance Hoffman let go of his gun and collapsed to his knees. She limped over to her partner and gently lowered him to the ground. She feared the worst as she looked at the front of his shirt, which was now fully soaked in blood.

She could only see one bullet hole mid-way down the right side of his chest and felt helpless as she watched Hoffman begin to cough up blood.

She knew he would die without immediate medical help and said, "Do you have a phone on you, Lance?"

Already struggling for breath, Hoffman managed to reply, "Not on me. There's a satellite phone back in the car."

"Which way is it, Lance? I need to get you help immediately."

Hoffman shook his head and replied, "I'm not going to make it."

Bridgette thought about Hoffman's response for a moment. He had always been a straight shooter, and it seemed disingenuous for her to start pretending to be optimistic about his chances of survival.

She gently took his left hand and replied softly, "I've got to at least try, Lance."

Hoffman seemed to rally a little and said, "I parked right be-hind his van, but you'll get yourself killed if you go anywhere near there."

It was now almost completely dark, and Bridgette felt frustrated that she couldn't see Hoffman properly anymore. She put her hand on his forehead—it was clammy, but his skin felt cool to touch. She felt the burly detective starting to shiver as his body temperature dropped.

Bridgette pulled her jacket off and laid it gently across his body and said, "Is there anything I can do to make you more comfortable?"

Hoffman coughed again and with labored breathing an-swered, "I'm not in much pain. You should grab my gun and get out of here. He could return at any moment."

Bridgette reached across and picked up the gun. She settled back down beside Hoffman and held his hand again.

With a trace of irritability in his voice Hoffman said, "I want you to get out of here. The longer you stay the more likely—"

"I'm not leaving you, Lance. I've got your gun and if he comes back, I'll be ready."

They were quiet for a moment and then Hoffman said, "I saw his gun as I was getting into position—a snub nose Rossi—fires six shots. It's completely inaccurate beyond a few paces unless you hold it with both hands and practice regularly. I can't believe the bastard managed to hit me."

"I'm sorry I let myself get captured, Lance. This is my fault."

Hoffman coughed again and said, "It's nobody's fault, Bridgette. We're all in this together."

"If I had been more careful in the laneway—"

"Don't beat yourself up over this—we all knew the risks."

Bridgette began to ask Hoffman how he had found her but stopped as Hoffman began to groan softly.

"Can I make you more comfortable, Lance?"

In a weaker voice, he replied, "I feel like I'm drowning—I'm having trouble breathing ..."

"We need to elevate your head."

After putting the gun down, Bridgette got up on her knees and gently lifted the burly man up by the shoulders and slid her right leg in under his head. She moved forward until Hoffman's head was cradled in her lap.

In a weary voice, Hoffman whispered, "Thank you, Bridgette... thank you for staying with me."

Bridgette fought back tears as she realized Hoffman's time was short. She had started to grow fond of the man few people seemed to understand. She was discovering he was far more sensitive than most people gave him credit for, and she would be forever grateful for the way he had saved her life.

Feeling helpless as she watched his life ebb away, she asked softly, "Is there anybody you would like me to give a message to?"

Hoffman was silent apart from his labored breathing and wheezing. Bridgette began to wonder if he was too weak to talk before, he whispered, "Tell my daughter, Megan, I love her and I'm sorry."

Bridgette was about to tell Hoffman she would but stopped as Hoffman continued in a weak voice.

"And tell Felix I enjoyed working with him..."

"I will, Lance."

"You're going to be a great detective, Bridgette, but you gotta fight for your parents. Their murders can't go..."

"I won't—I promise."

Hoffman coughed again and said, "You can trust Felix, but I'm not sure who else."

They were quiet again for a moment. Hoffman's raspy breath was becoming shallower. She decided she needed to say what she needed to say now before it was too late.

Fighting back tears, she whispered, "Thank you for being my partner, Lance. I didn't know what to expect at first, but you've taught me a lot—more than you'll ever know."

Hoffman coughed weakly and in a wheezy voice whispered, "I only wish..."

Bridgette couldn't decipher any of the other words he spoke. He became quiet again and then his raspy breathing stopped. Bridgette leaned forward to check his breathing but couldn't detect anything. She reached up her left hand and felt for the carotid artery in his neck. There was no pulse and Bridgette knew he was gone.

She sat for a moment and continued to cradle Hoffman's head in her lap as she felt consumed by a mixture of grief and anger. It seemed such a pointless waste of life.

She breathed in and out deeply and whispered to herself, "Not now, Bridgette," as she fought to keep her emotions in check.

Finally, she pulled away from Hoffman's body and laid his head gently on the ground. She looked around as she picked up the gun but couldn't see or hear anything in the darkness. Bridgette got to her feet and debated whether or not to put her blood-soaked jacket back on. Ordinarily, she would have left it behind, but it was already cold, and she had no idea what was ahead of her. Blood soaked or not, if she had to spend a night in the forest, it would help keep her warm.

She picked up the jacket and thought back about the number

of shots Hoffman had fired as she put it on. Hoffman was old school and had refused to upgrade to one of the modern Glock handguns now favored by Vancouver Metro. She recalled him firing four shots, which meant his gun should have still had two live rounds.

She wondered if he had any spare bullets in his pockets. Two rounds were better than none but not as good as a fully loaded weapon. After pocketing Hoffman's gun, she bent over his body and quickly searched his pockets. She found no bullets, but pocketed his car keys and a half-used pocket book of matches that she found in his jacket pocket.

Bridgette did a quick search of the ground with her hands and quickly located the small shovel. She leaned on it slightly and took two steps forward, testing to see if she could use it as a crutch. Satisfied that it would serve the purpose, she pulled the gun back out of her jacket and hobbled to the edge of the clearing. Everything remained quiet as she looked back at the still, dark form of Hoffman's body.

She whispered, "I'll be back soon, Lance," and then disappeared into the forest.

Chapter 53

Bridgette stood in the darkness thinking about what she would do next. She could barely see two or three steps in front of her and knew the killer could be just a few feet away—watching and waiting. She took comfort in the gun she carried in her right hand. While she had a weapon, it was no longer a totally one-sided contest.

She thought through her options. Her foot had swollen considerably in the last twenty minutes and every step was agony. She knew walking out of the forest in the dark wasn't possible and contemplated finding a suitable hiding place to spend the night. Close to exhaustion from everything that had happened, she didn't trust herself to stay awake the whole night in the freezing conditions. The thought of being that vulnerable while the killer was still out there made the decision easy—she needed a different strategy.

She tried to think like the killer. Would he have cut his losses and headed back to his van to escape? She hadn't heard any vehicle driving off, but maybe she had missed it? After the gunfight, her focus had been solely on Hoffman and trying to keep him comfortable during the last few minutes of his life. She decided it was wishful thinking to believe the killer had simply driven off. Everything she had learned about him so far led her to believe he wouldn't be leaving any loose ends behind.

Bridgette started to formulate a plan. It was far from bulletproof, but it was better than staying here. Using the shovel as a crutch, she took a few tentative steps forward and stopped to listen for any signs of the killer's presence. She did her best to control her breathing as the throbbing pain in her ankle shot up her leg again. She listened intently but heard nothing beyond a few crickets. With the gun clenched tightly in her right hand, she moved off down the path again.

* * *

Bridgette cautiously worked her way back towards the small clearing where she had escaped from the van. With constant stopping to rest her swollen ankle and to check that she wasn't being followed, the journey took her close to an hour. She half expected to encounter the killer on the trail somewhere and as a precaution, circled wide to make her final approach from the opposite direction. Although it was dark, her eyes had adjusted to the low light and she was able to move almost silently through the forest. As she approached the edge of the clearing, she stopped for a moment and leaned on the shovel to rest her swollen ankle. She could just make out the light-colored shape of the killer's van parked exactly where he had left it.

Although not surprised to see the vehicle, Bridgette shuddered at the thought that the killer was almost certainly still here. She looked into the darkness to her left and to her right before focusing on the van again. It was hard to tell in the dim light, but there didn't seem to be anyone inside the vehicle. She switched her attention to Hoffman's car, which was parked almost directly behind the van. She thought about the satellite phone in the glove-box. Just a few steps away, one quick phone call could end this nightmare. She judged the distance from the edge of the clearing to the car to be about ten paces. Even hobbling quickly would leave her exposed for too long.

Using the trees for cover, she stood still for several more minutes, patiently watching and listening for any sound or movement that would indicate she wasn't alone. Even though the forest remained silent, she felt an oppressive force surrounding her. The chill she felt running down her spine had nothing to do with her physical condition—she felt his presence and knew he was here somewhere.

She mentally went through her plan again. It was far from foolproof, but she hoped it would flush the killer out and give her some control over what happened next. Ignoring the cold, she took off her jacket and threaded one sleeve down over the handle of the shovel. Crouching down, she scooped up handfuls of dry pine needles from the forest floor and wedged them inside the sleeve. When satisfied she had enough of the debris pushed into the sleeve, she wrapped the remainder of the jacket around the lower part of the handle and used the other jacket sleeve to tie it off. She had tried to be as quiet as possible, and after completing the task, stayed in the crouched position to watch and listen again.

She took no solace from eerie stillness as she turned her attention to the van's front passenger window again. The window was close but there was no room for error. She looked around again as she pulled Hoffman's pocket book of matches

327

out of her jeans pocket. There would be no turning back once she started what she had planned. She took a deep breath knowing what she was about to do would expose her. She had rehearsed each step over in her mind, visualizing each tiny detail until she was confident, she could execute the whole sequence in just a few seconds. If it took much longer, she knew if the killer was here, he would have time to react and get the upper hand.

She struck the match against the pocket book and watched as the phosphorous head exploded into a tiny blue flame. Working quickly, Bridgette brought the match into contact with the pine needles wedged into the sleeve of her coat and was relieved when they immediately caught on fire. Satisfied, she quickly picked up the gun and aimed at the window of the van and pulled the trigger in one seamless movement. As the boom from the gun pierced the quiet evening, Bridgette stood up and grabbed the shovel by the handle. Hobbling two steps forward, she threw the shovel like a javelin towards the broken window. The distance was only about six paces, but there was no room for error. Bridgette's heart caught in her mouth for a split second as she watched the flaming shovel hit the shattered window. Her greatest fear was that it would simply bounce off and fall harmlessly to the ground. To her relief, the shovel's blade pierced the broken glass and the implement disappeared somewhere inside the front of the vehicle.

As she stepped back towards the cover of the forest again, Bridgette watched the darkened interior of the van for several anxious seconds. The dim glow seemed to almost die out completely until she saw a small flicker of flame rising up just above the window line. Satisfied that the van would be fully engulfed in flame within a minute, Bridgette went to step back when a familiar voice called out from behind.

"I have my gun pointed at your head. You try and run, and I'll turn you into Swiss cheese."

As she silently cursed herself for not moving back into the forest quicker, Bridgette felt the cold steel of the killer's gun pressed firmly into the small of her neck.

In a voice barely above a whisper, he hissed, "Drop the gun and walk out into the clearing."

Instead of dropping the gun, Bridgette tossed the gun into the clearing and hobbled forward as the killer shouted, "Put your hands in the air."

Bridgette walked forward three more steps and stopped next to her gun.

After raising her hands, she said, "I'm turning around," and then slowly turned to face the killer.

The killer smiled and said to her, "That little trick of throwing the gun out to where you're standing won't do you any good. You know as well as I do that I can cut you down before you've even finished thinking about going for the gun."

Bridgette noticed something different about the killer's voice. The confidence and bravado that had been natural earlier, now seemed to be forced as he said, "I want your partner's car keys."

Without taking her eyes off the man, Bridgette slowly lowered one hand and reached into the pocket of her jeans. Carefully, she withdrew the keys and held them out in front of her.

The killer remained at the edge of the clearing and was little more than a silhouette standing in the shadows.

He made no move to come any further towards her as he

demanded, "Toss them at my feet and then turn around and face the van."

Bridgette could feel the heat from the van rising rapidly as the fire took hold. The whole clearing was now fully illuminated by the burning vehicle and she saw the shadows from the flames begin to dance across the trees. She knew the likelihood of the fuel tank exploding was low, but that didn't make her feel any better about her situation. She had no idea what the killer was planning but decided to stand her ground.

Swallowing hard, she tossed the keys at the killer's feet and defiantly held his stare.

Something inside her made her say, "If you're going to shoot, shoot me now."

The killer laughed and said, "I'm going to do a lot more than shoot you."

Bridgette frowned to herself—it was almost as if he was stalling for time.

Emboldened, she replied, "It's interesting."

"What's interesting?"

"Your van. After I got out of the bag, I looked through the small window into the front. All I could see was the shovel you use to bury your victims and nothing else. No coffee cups, no food wrappers—nothing that would incriminate you if it were left behind."

"I'm very careful, that's why I've never been caught."

Feeling increasingly uncomfortable as her clothes began to heat up, Bridgette paused a moment as she looked directly down the barrel of the killer's gun. She knew what she was about to say was a huge gamble but decided to press the point.

"You've got one major flaw... you're predictable."

The killer's features hardened, "Predictable?"

Bridgette flinched as the killer pulled back the hammer to manually cock the pistol. "If I'm not mistaken, it's you that's looking down the barrel of a gun?"

Undeterred, Bridgette replied, "As I walked back through the forest, I thought about all your previous murders. You intimidated all your victims to do exactly what you wanted. You said it yourself earlier, they all begged and screamed for mercy. I don't think any of them ever had a chance to fight back and it got me thinking."

Bridgette waited for a reaction. When none was forthcoming, she swallowed and continued. "Before today, you've never had to use your gun…"

"Your point being?"

"You fired four shots at me. Two when I was in the van, one as I leapt out and one as I ran into the forest. And then you fired two at Detective Hoffman… six in total."

The killer held her stare but said nothing.

"Before he died, my partner told me about your gun. A six shot Rossi. It got me wondering if you carry spare bullets. You've never had to fire the weapon, so why would you?"

The killer continued to hold her stare but said nothing.

Bridgette knew she couldn't hold her current position for much longer. She could feel sweat dripping down her face as the heat radiating from the burning vehicle behind her became intense. She wondered if keeping her in this position as long as possible was part of the killer's strategy to weaken her? With her clothes now becoming unbearably hot, she knew she needed to move quickly before she succumbed to the heat.

Keeping her voice as level as she possibly could, she continued, "You plan everything in advance and only bring exactly what you need. You're methodical and predictable."

331

The killer grinned momentarily as he kept the gun pointed at her head.

In a soft voice, he replied, "Are you game enough to gamble? I only need to be carrying one spare bullet and you lose."

Bridgette's back and legs now felt as if they were on fire. She knew she would collapse shortly if she didn't move away from the heat. With only one round left in her weapon, reaching down for her gun might be suicide, but standing where she was any longer was also a death sentence.

Keeping her hands in the air, she said, "It's hot, I need to move," and shifted her right foot slightly until she felt the gun up against the side of her shoe.

Ignoring the killer's screams at her not to move, Bridgette dropped to her knees to grab the gun. As the darkened form of the killer rushed towards her from the shadows, she brought the gun up into the firing position and fired blindly as she was crash tackled to the ground. Bridgette felt like her whole body was now engulfed in flames as she lay on the ground only a few feet from the inferno. Totally winded, she went into survival mode and ignored the searing heat as she watched the killer's right arm swing a short-bladed steel knife down towards her throat.

Chapter 54

Bridgette knew she could never halt the swing of a knife wielded by a man who weighed almost twice her body weight. Instinctively, she thrust her left arm upwards to parry the weapon as the blade swung down towards her neck. Life or death would be measured in fractions of a second. A millisecond too slow and she knew she would become the killer's latest victim.

She felt her elbow make contact with the attacker's forearm and saw the blur of the blade as it slid by, barely an inch from the left ear. It wasn't the initial strike that worried her, but what happened from here. With his full body weight now on top of her, she had almost no hope of holding the killer off and desperately swung the gun she still held in her right hand at the killer's temple.

The killer let out a groan as the gun struck him hard. She hoped the blow would have knocked the man out or at least disabled him, but to her horror, the killer shook it off and began to raise the knife to strike again. Bridgette knew the odds of parrying a second thrust were slim and desperately grabbed at the man's right wrist after letting go of the gun.

Time almost seemed to be suspended for Bridgette as the

knife hovered inches from her face. Keeping her hands gripped as firmly as she could around the killer's right hand, she pushed back with all her strength.

She felt the man's warm breath washing across her face as he leaned down and whispered, "It's time to die, bitch."

She refused to give in and focused every fiber in her body on holding the knife away from her face. The stalemate continued for what seemed like minutes to Bridgette until she felt an explosion of pain as the killer punched her in the rib-cage with his left fist. Ignoring the urge to cry out in pain, Bridgette kept her concentration fixed on the knife which now swayed menacingly, barely an inch from her nose. Emboldened, the killer punched her a second time. She felt her body going into shutdown as the pain from the second blow barely registered.

Bridgette knew the fight was almost over. She felt her strength waning and knew she couldn't hold the knife away for much longer. Keeping her grip around the killer's wrist as firmly as she could, she looked into the man's eyes expecting to see the triumphant jubilation of a murderer who knew he was just seconds away from killing again. Instead, she saw the killer's eyes briefly roll into the back of his head as he began to cough up blood.

She instantly felt the strength draining from his right hand and began to push the knife further away from her face as the killer coughed up more blood. Bridgette was unsure whether the man was just feigning before he struck hard again, but as the man's cold and calculating features began to dissolve, she realized something was wrong. She felt the killer's body go limp as the knife fell out of his grip and landed harmlessly on her chest. The man seemed to pass out and Bridgette quickly rolled his dead weight off her before grabbing the knife.

Scrambling into a kneeling position, she looked down at the killer who now lay on his back with his arms outstretched in a crucifix position. Bridgette could see blood oozing from a small hole, low down on the man's shirt and realized her last bullet had found its mark.

The killer opened his eyes and coughed up blood again but made no move to get up. On her hands and knees, Bridgette crawled away from the searing heat and watched as Hoffman's car caught on fire. Exhausted and now unable to call anyone for help, Bridgette lay on her back and stared up at the starlit sky. She watched the sparks from the flaming vehicles as they shot skyward like miniature fireworks. She remembered holding her mother and father's hands as she watched fireworks as a child. She was tired and glad they had brought her home and tucked her into bed. The fireworks began to fade, and she whispered goodnight to them as she drifted off to sleep.

Chapter 55

B ridgette opened her eyes and blinked as she heard her name being called.

"Bridgette, are you okay? You're covered in blood."

She let out a gasp but then relaxed, as her eyes began to focus on the face of Felix Delray who was looking down at her with real concern.

"Have I been out long?"

Delray replied, "I'm not sure," as he gently helped her up into a sitting position.

Bridgette felt dizzy but tried to ignore it as she stared at the two burning vehicles. The killer's van was now not much more than a blackened, smoldering metal shell, but Hoffman's car was still a hot ball of flame.

"Detective Hoffman's car caught fire just before I passed out, so I can't have been out for long..."

Delray put his arm around her and said, "It's not safe here—we're too close to the fire," as he helped her to her feet.

With Delray's help, Bridgette hobbled a few more feet away from the inferno before they sat down again.

Taking off his coat, he said, "You're shivering and going into shock," as he gently placed the garment around her shoulders to keep her warm.

In a voice that tried to hide his anxiety, he asked, "Have you seen, Lance?"

Bridgette bit her bottom lip and nodded once. Delray sat down beside her. The grim expression on his face suggested he knew bad news was coming.

He put an arm gently around her shoulders and gently said, "Take your time, Bridgette."

Bridgette was quiet for a moment as she relived what happened in the forest.

"I don't remember much about the alleyway. I remember waking up in the van inside a laundry bag..."

Bridgette went on to recount how she had managed to escape from the bag and flee into the forest. Delray listened patiently without interrupting. She began to struggle as she got to the point where Hoffman had stepped in and saved her life.

"I was never going to give in. I ran at him swinging the shovel, expecting him to shoot me dead... that was when Lance stepped in..."

Bridgette went on to explain how Hoffman had been shot in the gunfight before the killer escaped. She found it difficult to put into words how helpless she felt as Hoffman lay dying.

"I tried to make him comfortable, but I felt so useless. There was nothing I could do to stop what was happening—he wasn't bitter, he seemed to accept what was happening."

Bridgette paused for a moment and then looked directly at Delray as she continued. "He asked me to tell you that he had really enjoyed working with you."

Delray went to say something in response but choked on

his words and simply nodded as he stared off at Hoffman's burning car.

They were quiet for a moment before Delray nodded at the burning vehicles and asked, "So what happened here?"

"Before he died, Lance told me he'd parked here. I wasn't sure what to do after he... My ankle was in no shape to walk out of the forest, so I thought I'd come back here and use the satellite phone to call for help."

"But he was here waiting for you."

Bridgette nodded and said, "Part of me was scared when I saw the van and realized he was probably still here somewhere... but part of me wanted revenge."

"That's a natural reaction."

Bridgette went on to explain how she had started the fire in the van to flush the killer out.

She paused for a moment when she got to the part where the killer had discovered her location and forced her to walk into the clearing at gunpoint and then said, "Lance saved my life twice tonight..."

Delray looked slightly confused as he asked, "How so?"

"Before he died, he told me he got a good look at the killer's gun—a six shot Rossi. I remembered at the time thinking he'll need to reload because he'd already fired six shots—four at me and two at Lance. As I was making my way back through the forest, I started thinking about that. Lance hadn't wanted me to stay with him after he'd been shot. He insisted I leave because he thought the killer would come back at any moment to finish us off."

Delray nodded in agreement and added, "People like that won't think twice about taking advantage of a situation where you're vulnerable."

"I was never going to leave Lance to die alone, but I thought about what he'd said as I walked back through the forest. I reached the same conclusion you had and wondered why he hadn't come back and shot me while I sat there caring for Lance. I thought then that maybe his gun was empty."

Delray nodded and said, "But coming back here was still one heck of a gamble to take. He could have had a box of bullets back here in the van."

"Yes, he could have. I circled wide and approached from the opposite side I had escaped from, hoping I could set the van on fire before I was discovered. I thought I'd have the element of surprise, but he must have heard me coming."

Bridgette went on to explain how she had called the killer's bluff at gunpoint and the struggle with the knife that followed before she had passed out.

Delray grimaced and said, "If he'd carried just one spare bullet, Bridgette... you wouldn't be here now."

"I managed to peek through a small window into the front driver's compartment while I was still locked in the van. The van was pristine. Apart from his shovel, the vehicle was clean—not even a gum wrapper. That didn't surprise me. You don't get to murder as many people as he has by leaving clues. It got me thinking—he only brings what he needs and nothing more."

Delray got to his feet and walked over to the killer. He was still lying on the ground where he'd collapsed in a pool of his own blood and didn't appear to be moving. He shook his head as he looked down at the face of a man he knew had killed at least half a dozen people.

"He looks just like anyone else you'd see on the street."

"Do you recognize him?"

339

Delray shook his head and said, "No. He probably isn't in our system. If he's as smart as we think he is, he won't even have a parking ticket against his name."

Bridgette said, "If he's still alive we should call an ambulance."

Delray bent down and placed his index finger on the man's carotid artery for a moment and then rose to his full height again.

As he walked back to Bridgette he said, "I called in the location of the fire to the uniform guys who are also out here looking for you. They'll be here in a couple of minutes..."

Delray sat down next to Bridgette again and said, "I'll get one of them to call it in when they get here."

They sat in silence for a few moments and watched as the fire in Hoffman's car started to die down.

"You took a big gamble, Bridgette. I'm not sure what I would have done in your shoes."

"Better for it to be over quickly with a gun than the alternative, Chief."

They were silent again for a while until Delray spoke.

"I'm going to miss him. He was the grumpiest son of a bitch I ever had to work with, but he was as honest and as trustworthy as the day is long."

"This is my fault, Chief, I'm sorry."

Delray put his arm around her again and said, "No, Bridgette, this is nobody's fault. We were all doing our jobs, and sometimes it's risky. I lost one good officer today, but it could easily have been two. If anybody should be hung out to dry it should be me."

They were quiet again and then heard the faint sound of a siren.

Delray got to his feet and said, "That's one of the squad cars now. When they get here, I'll get you to give us directions so that we can go and recover Lance's body. I'll leave one of the uniforms here with you, and they can call an ambulance."

Bridgette said firmly, "I'm coming with you," as Delray helped her to her feet.

"Bridgette, you can barely walk."

Fighting back tears, she said, "I promised Lance I would come back for him."

Delray nodded and said, "Okay, I understand."

As they watched the squad car drive slowly up the trail towards them, Delray looked briefly across at the body of the killer, before returning his focus to Bridgette.

He said, "The next few weeks are going to be rough on us all, Bridgette, but especially you. I know it's cold comfort, but you need to remember that if it wasn't for you, that maniac would still be running around killing people."

Bridgette was unsure what to say in response. She thought about Lance Hoffman lying dead in the forest, a ten-minute walk from where she currently stood and wondered whether it had all been worth it.

Chapter 56

B ridgette stared at her reflection in the bathroom mirror. With almost no sleep in the forty-eight hours since the ordeal on Catalin Mountain, she barely recognized the face that stared back at her. The mood amongst the team when they had returned to Vancouver Metro after capturing the killer had been somber—everyone was taking Hoffman's death hard. Delray had been hauled off almost immediately by Cunningham for a late-night meeting with the Commissioner to explain why he had left the federal task force out of the operation, and she had been left to explain to internal affairs why one of Vancouver's longest serving and most decorated police officers was now dead.

After coming home, she'd found sleep impossible. Closing her eyes reminded her too much of being trapped in the bag. She couldn't remember how long she had been standing in her bathroom studying her reflection in the mirror. The face that had stared back at her an hour ago was frustrated and angry. The aggressive three-hour interrogation by internal affairs kept returning like a nightmare. She couldn't understand what motivated them to want to bring down honest cops.

As the rage subsided, the face in the mirror began to change.

Anger and frustration gave way to sadness and despair as she realized she was fighting a system she could never beat. The exhausted face that stared back at her now was lonely, confused and crying out for it all to be over. Nothing made sense—her second career was going the way of the first. What was the point? Did it really matter and with her father gone now, who really cared anyway?

She held up her service issue Glock 19 pistol and turned it slowly in front of her face. She studied the weapon from various angles in the mirror's reflection and then placed the weapon against her right temple. As she stared at her reflection, she tried to imagine what it would be like to pull the trigger. She doubted she would feel anything and wondered if there was an afterlife, or would it all fade to black?

Bridgette had learned enough from her training to know that people intent on suicide sometimes survived shots to the temple if they didn't get the angle right. Slowly, she moved the barrel of the gun around until it was pointing directly at her. She opened her mouth and moved the gun forward until she felt the cold metallic taste of steel on her tongue. She closed her mouth around the barrel and began to breathe heavily as she closed her eyes. Bridgett put her index finger over the trigger and felt like she was hovering between life and death as a single tear began to trickle down her left cheek. Just a few more micro-grams of pressure and it would all be over. In a fraction of a second, the pain and agony would be gone forever.

The sound of her phone vibrating startled her. She opened her eyes and looked down at the device nestled amongst her cosmetics on the shelf below her bathroom mirror—it was Delray. Bridgette ignored the call and looked up at her reflection in the mirror again but found it difficult to concentrate as the phone continued to vibrate. Her heart began to race when the phone finally became silent—she knew she'd reached a crossroad. She withdrew the weapon from her mouth and frowned as she studied her reflection. The image of an exhausted young woman with disheveled hair and holding a gun close to her head seemed surreal. Was this a dream?

Her phone buzzed a second time—it was Delray again. He had never been a fan of leaving messages and she knew he would keep ringing until he finally got through. Bridgette let out a deep breath and composed herself as she picked up the phone with her left hand and pressed answer.

"I hope I didn't wake you?"

"No."

There was silence for a moment before Delray asked, "Have you been sleeping, Bridgette?"

Bridgette closed her eyes for a moment as she thought about her response. She didn't want this conversation right now, but she knew Delray meant well.

"Bridgette?"

Bridgette lowered the gun as she replied, "I'm still here."

"Are you sleeping?"

"Not really."

More silence followed before Delray replied, "You know, none of us function well without sleep."

Bridgette gently placed the gun on the shelf and then turned and limped back into her living room.

"You still there, Bridgette?"

"Yes."

Despite wanting the phone conversation to be over as soon as possible, she found comfort in Delray's voice.

"If you're anything like me, sleep's going to be hard to come by for a while..."

Delray said no more. In the silence that followed, it was clear he wanted her to do the talking. Bridgette wanted to end the phone call as quickly as possible but found herself opening up to the only person she still trusted in Vancouver Metro.

Barely holding her composure, she managed, "Why are they so hostile?"

"I'm assuming you mean internal affairs. They're all hand-picked by—"

Bridgette cut in and angrily said, "They questioned me for almost three hours and made me sound like a criminal. They twisted everything I said. There was almost no acknowledgment that we had actually caught a serial killer, or that I had been abducted and almost killed. All they were interested in..."

Bridgette couldn't finish. She closed her eyes and breathed deeply while she regained her composure.

Finally, she said, "Sorry, Chief, I didn't mean to take that out on you."

In a calm voice, Delray replied, "No apology necessary. You have every right to be angry."

"They were like a pack of dogs."

"Cunningham hand picks every one of those assholes who now work in internal affairs. They all want to get to the top as quickly as possible and don't mind what they do to get there."

Bridgette let out a sigh. She'd said her piece and didn't want to talk anymore and waited patiently for Delray to wrap the phone call up.

Delray had other ideas and confided, "I'm not sure how much you've worked out, Bridgette, but Cunningham doesn't like me either. For me, it's always been about doing whatever it takes to get the job done, even if that means taking personal risks and occasionally bending the rules. That's never sat well with him, so now he's using you to get to me."

Bridgette wasn't sure what to say. She hadn't expected this much honesty from Delray. She looked back towards her bathroom and wondered what she could say to end the conversation without appearing rude.

Her boss continued. "This is his chance to get rid of two for the price of one, and he's taking it. All they're interested in is finding a way to make you and me responsible for Lance's death to get us suspended. And if that doesn't work, they'll use the fact that we didn't involve the federal task force as plan B."

"But why, Chief? Isn't it our job to catch the bad guys?"

"Absolutely, but internal affairs have a whole different agenda—when we look bad, they look good. It's insidious and made worse by the people Cunningham has put in there to run it. Was it Aaron Sterling that interviewed you?"

Bridgette closed her eyes as images of Aaron Sterling, with his oily hair and over-sized Adam's apple sitting across the interview table from her returned.

Delray added, "He's a piece of work, isn't he?"

Bridgette opened her eyes again to get rid of Sterling's image and said, "He ran most of the interview. I was lucky if I could finish a sentence without being interrupted. In the end, it became nothing more than a shouting match with him constantly accusing me of being a liar."

"I'm sorry you were treated like that, Bridgette. I got the lowdown on what happened from McKenzie and Bosco, and I'm personally taking it up with the Commissioner tomorrow. They were way out of line interviewing you on your own

346

without me or someone else being there as your advocate."

Suddenly tired of standing, Bridgette slumped into her favorite easy chair and asked, "I thought we all worked for the one team?"

Bridgette could hear the sadness in Delray's voice as he responded. "We used to be a team, Bridgette, but Cunningham changed that. Our new Commissioner's only been in the job a few months, and he's come from another state police force, so he's still feeling his way. Word has it, he detests Cunningham, so we're all hopeful he'll find a way to get rid of him sooner rather than later."

Bridgette was having trouble concentrating. Normally, she would have found what Delray said very interesting, but all she could think about was the gun she'd left in the bathroom.

As if realizing he wasn't cutting through, Delray changed the subject slightly.

"You know, Bridgette; you've got a lot to be proud of. If it wasn't for you, Kayne Selwood would be still out there looking for the next young woman to murder. To catch a guy like that, you have to take risks."

Bridgette thought about Delray's comment. She was glad they had caught Selwood, but Hoffman's death had made it impossible for her to be proud of what had happened.

"Why do you stay, Chief? With your experience, surely you could get a job in security or consulting that pays way more than what you're getting with only half the grief?"

"Let me ask you a question, Bridgette. Why did you join? Your IQ is off the charts. You could have been anything you wanted to be and earn a whole lot more money in the process."

Bridgette contemplated the question and then responded, "I asked you first."

Delray let out a brief chuckle and replied, "I think we joined for similar reasons. For me, it was never about the money—it was about making a difference, even if it means working for fools like Cunningham."

"The man is such an asshole."

Delray chuckled again and said, "You'd be surprised at how often I hear that, Bridgette. All I can say is Vancouver Metro is more than just one man. It's a community and most of them are really good people. I have a lot of faith in our new Commissioner, and when Cunningham finally falls, I want both you and me to be around to watch."

"Will we survive that long?"

"This will blow over, Bridgette. We lost one of our best officers, but bottom line, we got a killer off the street who has killed eight people that we know of. Trust me, I've been in this position before and while it's horrible right now, we'll get through it. The Commissioner isn't stupid and no amount of whining from Cunningham or Internal affairs will change what we've achieved."

Bridgette sat for a moment and wondered if she could really get through this? Would it be really any different in a few months' time?

Delray continued. "You know, Bridgette, it doesn't get any tougher than this. You get through this; you can survive anything."

Bridgette found herself saying, "I'm not sure I'm cut out for this. It feels like I'm stuck in a nightmare that won't end."

"It will pass, Bridgette—you just need time and lots of rest."

"How can you be so sure?"

"In the thirty odd years I knew Lance Hoffman, I'd seen him make plenty of mistakes. Most of them involved him opening his mouth when he should have kept it shut. He never understood tact and diplomacy, but the one area I could never fault him on was his judgment of people. He could read people better than anyone else I've ever worked with, and his judgment was almost flawless.

After the shooting incident in the basement and your father's murder, I asked him point blank whether he thought you'd be able to get through it. His response surprised me."

"What did he say?"

"He said you're a survivor and was positive you could ride out the rough patches if you learned to trust people."

"But Lance didn't trust people."

"Not quite true. Lance didn't trust many people. I know he trusted me at least. Over the years, we've both leaned on each other pretty heavily in times of crisis, and right now, I'm hoping you'll lean on me. You don't have to do this on your own, Bridgette."

Bridgette closed her eyes for a moment and shook her head. She didn't want to be rude to Delray, but neither did she want to continue the conversation.

"I know this is incredibly hard for you, Bridgette, but there are people here for you..."

Tactfully, she replied, "I think I need to get some rest."

"That sounds like a good idea. Before you go, I just thought you'd like to know that Lance's funeral is the day after tomorrow. We're organizing a police guard, and we'd like you to attend."

Bridgette thought about the gun in the bathroom as she responded, "I'm not sure that's such a good idea. If it wasn't for me, he'd still be alive."

"You know that's not true."

"To be honest, Chief, I'm not sure I'd be welcome."

"Everyone in the squad wants you there, Bridgette. They're all concerned for you, and they think you showed a lot of courage volunteering like you did even though you're just a rookie. Nobody on the team is blaming you or anybody else for that matter. We can't change what happened, but we all have to stick together if we're going to get through this."

Bridgette didn't have the energy to respond and waited for Delray to say something else.

"Promise me you'll consider it, Bridgette?"

Bridgette found herself nodding as she said, "I promise."

"Good. I'll call you about the same time tomorrow to see how you're doing. For now, get some rest, okay?"

"Okay."

Bridgette disconnected the call and put the phone down. She stood for a moment trying to think through what Delray had said, but nothing was making any sense. She thought about her gun again and walked back into the bathroom.

Epilogue

B
ridgette sipped her peppermint tea as she sat alone in a booth at the rear of her favorite coffee shop. It was still early and there were only a handful of other patrons in the classic New York style diner. She liked the atmosphere at this time of the day. The subdued background noise of people chatting quietly over breakfast, and the kitchen staff preparing for the day ahead was soothing and allowed her time to think without distraction. She reflected on how fragile life was as she remembered the last time she had been here two weeks ago with Lance Hoffman. Her father and Hoffman had both been alive then—fit and healthy with every chance of living to old age if it were not for the violent intervention of other men.

Her rage still simmered below the surface, but with each passing day, she found it a little easier to control. News of Kayne Selwood's death from gunshot wounds had provided her with some comfort, but her father's murder still ate away at her.

"Bridgette?"

Slightly startled, Bridgette looked up and saw Felix Delray standing by her booth dressed in a suit and tie and carrying a leather satchel.

"Sorry, Chief, I was a million miles away..."

Delray replied, "No problem," as he slid into the opposite side of the booth. A waitress appeared from nowhere and took Delray's breakfast order of eggs, bacon, and coffee.

Delray waited until the waitress headed back to the kitchen, and then asked, "How are you doing?"

"Each day is a little better than the last, Chief. I'm sleeping eight hours a night now without any tablets."

Delray nodded and said, "We were all worried about you there for a while. Ever since Lance's funeral, I've had just about everyone from the squad in my office each day asking me how you're getting on."

Bridgette managed half a smile and said, "That's sweet."

"If you don't mind me saying so, I was worried too... particularly when you weren't keeping appointments with Doctor Sanders or returning some of my calls."

Bridgette put down her peppermint tea and replied, "I was in a dark place for a while... it was hard to make sense of what was happening."

Delray nodded thoughtfully and replied, "That's not surprising. You've been through more in the last month than most cops experience in a lifetime."

Bridgette held Delray's gaze for a moment. Her boss was a picture of concentration, and she knew his concern was genuine.

In a quiet voice, she said, "There was one night... I was standing in my bathroom staring at my reflection in the mirror. I must have stood there for two hours trying to get my head around everything that had happened. I was angry, sad and confused all at the one time. I was no longer sure about anything and felt totally worn down. I got so low... I had a to be or not to be moment."

Delray looked stunned by, Bridgette's admission but waited for, Bridgette to continue.

"It was after the internal affairs interview. I was angry and depressed and looking back on it now, probably still in shock. I've never felt so alone or isolated in my whole life, and the murders of both Lance and my father were weighing heavily on my mind."

Delray leaned forward and said, "Bridgette, promise me you'll call me if you ever get that low again?"

"While I was standing in the bathroom I took a call on my phone. I had a conversation with someone I trust and it kind of drew me out of my funk. I'm not sure what would have happened if I hadn't answered the call, but I knew he would keep ringing, so..."

Delray nodded as he realized who, Bridgette was talking about and replied, "I've never been good at leaving messages."

Bridgette reached across and squeezed Delray's hand for a moment and murmured, "Thank you."

She noticed the burly detective's eyes starting to moisten as he seemed momentarily lost for words.

"After I got off the phone from you, Linda called. She was very down herself. We must have talked for an hour or more, and we both started to feel a little better. She invited me to come out and stay with her, and I found myself saying yes. I drove out to her cottage and ended up spending the next three days there. It was good therapy for both of us."

"I take it you've become good friends then?"

Bridgette nodded as she looked out the window, "Neither of us have close relatives here in Vancouver, so we're leaning on each other a lot to get through our grief."

"Well, I'm glad you can help each other. God knows we all need someone to support us in times of trouble."

Bridgette turned back to face Delray and said, "I've learned something very important out of all this."

"And what's that?"

To Delray's surprise, Bridgette unbuttoned the cuff of her shirt sleeve and began rolling it up to reveal her left forearm.

"I've never been a fan of tattoos, but I never ever want to be in that place again. No matter how dark things get, there's always a reason to live. I've been thinking a lot about my mother and father and even though they're both gone now, I know they loved me. Not everyone can say that about their parents, so for that I'm thankful."

Bridgette turned her arm slightly towards Delray to reveal a ring-shaped tattoo on her inner forearm. Delray leaned forward and read the word 'Family' written in tiny cursive script inside the concentric circles.

"Neither of them would have ever given up like I almost did, and I want a constant reminder of that. This will be with me forever. When I wake up in the morning, it will be the first thing I see."

Delray replied, "It looks like you've got room for a few more words."

Bridgette smiled briefly as she rolled her sleeve down again and said, "I'm a work in progress, Chief. I may be twenty-seven, but I've still got a lot to learn."

Delray answered, "We never stop learning," as he withdrew a document from his satchel.

After flattening the document out in front of him he continued, "I had a long chat with the Commissioner yesterday—one on one without Cunningham."

"I didn't think that was allowed."

"Cunningham didn't like it much, but the Commissioner wanted to hear my side of the story on why the federal task force wasn't included in the take-down of Kayne Selwood. I told him McKellar was more interested in finding another body, and I even showed him a copy of the email I sent to prove it. The Commissioner was more than satisfied. He strikes me as the kind of guy who's not big on letting red tape get in the way of good police work."

"So, you get to keep your job?"

Delray smiled and said, "Better than that, we both get to keep our jobs."

Delray slid the document across the table and said, "The Commissioner is convinced you'll make a very good detective and has waived any further probationary period. This is the official letter of offer, although you will still have to attend an official swearing in ceremony as well."

Bridgette was taken aback and stared down at the document. She had dreamed of this day for years and wasn't sure what to say.

Delray continued, "I know you've been through a lot, and you may need time to think about it... "

She responded, "No. This is what I want. It's just that after the shootout in the basement, I thought internal affairs would have had more than enough ammunition to see me thrown out for good."

Delray smiled knowingly and said, "Cunningham over-played his hand. His whole argument was built around you being in a compromised position while your father was still at large. Now that your father is no longer alive, his case has fallen to pieces, and he's been officially told to back off by the Commissioner."

Delray leaned in close again and said, "I'm not supposed to be telling you this, but the Commissioner plans on presenting you with a bravery medal at the ceremony. After he read my report, he said a promotion simply wasn't enough."

Delray touched his nose and continued, "But you didn't hear that from me."

Bridgette looked slightly overcome as she replied, "Thanks, Chief. This is a surprise—I'm not sure what to say."

"You don't have to say anything for now, but my advice would be to have a few words ready for the Commissioner at the ceremony."

They were quiet for a moment before Delray asked, "Speaking of surprises, I picked up your contract from Human Resources yesterday and thought they had misprinted your surname, but they said you have officially changed it to Cash?"

Bridgette nodded and replied, "I found out a lot about my father while I was staying with Linda. She was able to fill in some of the gaps, which I really appreciated. She told me my father started using the surname Cash shortly after he met her and had been using that name ever since. I asked her why he hadn't picked a totally different name, which would have been far less risky."

"And what did she say?"

As tears began to well in Bridgette's eyes, she replied, "She said he deliberately picked an abbreviation of our name so that he could still have a small connection to me."

Bridgette paused and frowned slightly before she continued. "I know he's innocent of my mother's murder, and someday I'll prove it. This is my way of saying I'm not ashamed of who he was or what he had become."

"Well, I'm sure your father would be touched by that and Cash does have a nice ring to it."

Bridgette picked up her tea again and asked, "Can I change the subject for a moment?"

"Sure."

She took a sip and then asked, "Should I be feeling guilty about killing Kayne Selwood?"

Delray frowned and replied, "It was self-defense, Bridgette. You just did what you needed to stop him killing you, and nobody should ever feel guilty about that."

Bridgette nodded but didn't respond as she took another sip of peppermint tea.

Delray continued, "Do you feel guilty?"

She thought for a moment and then said, "I feel guilty about not feeling guilty—if that makes sense?"

Delray scratched his chin and thought for a moment.

"You know; I've never had to kill anyone in the line of duty. I've wounded two guys in shootouts, but no one ever died. I can't honestly answer the question other than to say, I think it's healthy that you can't simply dismiss what happened."

Bridgette nodded again as she thought about Delray's answer.

Delray added, "Vancouver Metro has counseling for situations like this. It can't hurt to check it out?"

Bridgette replied, "Doctor Sanders has already set me up. It's a condition of my return to work that I get a psychological evaluation. I'll ask, but your answer makes sense."

"I know you've got a couple more days leave, Bridgette, but the subject of your return came up when I spoke with the Commissioner yesterday."

Bridgette did her best to keep her response measured, "Okay."

Delray clasped his hands together and thought for a moment before he responded.

"Both the Commissioner and I are worried—very worried in fact, about your safety. You could have easily been killed in that shootout in the basement, and right now we have someone on the inside of the department who is clearly working against us."

Bridgette responded, "Now that my father is dead, maybe the threat is over?"

Delray nodded and replied, "Maybe? But nobody knows for sure. Bottom line is, the Commissioner wants whoever did this caught and prosecuted. We all take corruption very seriously, and nobody wants to see a repeat of what happened to you or worse."

Delray paused as the waitress returned with his coffee and breakfast. He waited until she had left and then continued as he stabbed a piece of bacon with his fork.

"Both the Commissioner and I think it would be wise for you to spend as little time as possible at the office until we've got a better idea about who's responsible for all this. We've lost one good officer this month, and no one wants to see you become another statistic."

Bridgette responded, "I'm not sure I can stand being on leave for too much longer," as she watched Delray begin to shovel bacon and egg into his mouth.

Delray swallowed and then reached into his leather satchel again. He pulled out a manila file and passed it across the table. He motioned Bridgette to open it as he ate more of his breakfast.

Bridgette read the hand-printed name John Tyson on the front cover, before opening the file and scanning the first page.

When she realized she was reading the bio of a fellow police officer from Vancouver Metro, she looked up and said, "Okay, who is John Tyson?"

Delray stopped chomping and after taking another large sip of coffee, replied, "John Tyson is a Vancouver Metro detective. Years back, he worked Homicide with me, but more recently he's been working on computer fraud and organized crime."

Delray wiped his mouth with a napkin and then added, "His life fell apart about twelve months ago. His wife moved out and filed for divorce, and he took it pretty hard. They have an eight-year-old son and when she got custody, he started drinking and it all went downhill from there. Eventually, we got him in a program, and he started to get better. About five months ago he returned to work, although he was still finding life pretty tough."

Delray paused and took another sip of coffee and then continued. "Three months ago, we had a request from Sanbury Police Force—"

"Sanbury, as in the town up near the ski fields?"

"That's the one. Sanbury only has a small police force, and one of their senior detectives had a car accident and broke his leg badly. He needed multiple surgeries and was going to be off work for twelve months or more, and Sanbury reached out to us for a detective to take his place during his recovery. Tyson was looking for a change and put his hand up and got the job. He was only there a month when he disappeared—he just didn't show up for work one Monday morning."

"So, he's been missing for two months?"

Delray nodded and added, "The police up there have him listed as a missing person and have conducted their own investigation, but they haven't gotten any closer to finding him."

"Could he have just had another breakdown and gone off the grid?"

Delray grimaced and replied, "Possibly, but unlikely. His bank accounts haven't been touched and he hasn't contacted his son, which is totally unlike him."

Delray studied Bridgette for a moment and then continued, "The Commissioner wants some answers and isn't getting a lot of cooperation from the local authorities. He wants one of us to go up there for a few days and conduct an independent investigation."

Bridgette raised her eyebrows and replied, "Me?"

Delray responded, "After what you managed to achieve with the Monica Travers' case, the Commissioner is convinced you've got a better chance than most of getting to the bottom of what happened. Maybe this is a way to give you something challenging to do without exposing you to any more risk here until we get a better handle on who attacked you?"

Bridgette nodded and asked, "Do the local police have any theories?"

"Not really, which is why the Commissioner wants one of us to investigate. There was no sign of forced entry or a struggle in the house he was renting, and his car was still parked in the driveway when he was reported missing. They think he may have just gone hiking on Sacred Mountain and got lost. It wouldn't be the first time that's happened."

Bridgette studied Delray's face for a moment and then responded, "Only, you don't buy that?"

Shaking his head, Delray said, "I've known John Tyson for over twenty years. You'd be far more likely to find him in a sports bar watching a football game than wandering around on a mountain enjoying the scenery."

They were both quiet while Delray finished the remainder of his breakfast.

After draining the last of his coffee, Delray wiped his mouth with a napkin and said, "I have a nine o'clock meeting with the Commissioner and need to get going. Promise me you'll think about running the investigation at Sanbury?"

"I've already thought about it, Chief. A change of scenery might be good for me."

Delray smiled and said, "I think it's a good move for you, Bridgette. I'll organize a briefing for you after you get your medical clearance, so you'll know as much as we do before you go."

Bridgette reached into her bag and withdrew a folded sheet of paper and said, "Before you go, I want to give you this."

She slid the paper across to Delray and said, "When I was reviewing my mother's murder file on the microfilm, I came across this just before I was shot at."

Delray held up the paper and studied the grainy image printed on the page and replied, "A witness list?

"Yes, it's the original witness list for my mother's murder investigation. I came across it as I was scrolling through the microfilm. There were inconsistencies with the list, so I took a photo of it on my smartphone to check later."

Now intrigued, Delray asked, "Inconsistencies?"

"There are two witnesses on that original list that don't show up in the computer records."

Delray raised his eyebrows, "Well that's interesting."

"It may be nothing. The data entry operators may have simply missed them when they were entering the information into the computer record."

Delray scratched his chin and said, "The fact that the microfilm was stolen at gunpoint and the physical record for the same file is missing makes me think this isn't likely to be just a simple data entry error."

Waving the piece of paper, Delray continued, "This could potentially help us make the breakthrough. If the two witnesses on this list are still alive and can be found, who knows what they might be able to tell us?"

Bridgette held Delray's gaze and said, "I'm not ready to go back to investigating this just yet. But when I am, this list will be where I start."

Delray frowned and asked, "Does anybody else know about this."

Bridgette shook her head but didn't say anything.

Holding her gaze, Delray continued, "You don't know who to trust, do you?"

"I certainly don't trust anyone from internal affairs with this information."

"But you trust me? For all you know, I could be the bad guy?"

Bridgette half smiled and said, "Chief, you dragged me away from a burning car on Catalin Mountain and besides, you said Lance Hoffman was a great judge of people... He said to me more than once that you're the one person at Vancouver I can trust."

Delray's face became momentarily downcast at the mention of Hoffman's name. Bridgette knew she was not the only one who had been personally impacted by what had happened. She watched in silence as he carefully folded the paper and put it in his satchel.

After closing his satchel, Delray tapped it with a finger and said, "That goes into my office safe as soon as I get to work. I think it's a smart move not telling anyone else about it for now. We should wait and see how the investigation pans out before we make our next move."

"Thanks, Chief, but I wasn't expecting anyone to help with this. This is something I had planned to do on my own time."

Delray frowned and said, "When one of my officers is fired upon, I take that personally."

As he stood up, Delray left a twenty dollar note on the table and said, "I gotta fly. I'll let the Commissioner know you're happy to run the Sanbury investigation. I know he'll be happy."

Bridgette went to say thank you to the burly man for all he'd done for her, but he interrupted her and said, "By the way, you need to watch the news today. The Feds will be announcing they've just found the body of another one of Kayne Selwood's victims buried off a walking trail on a horse ranch."

Bridgette raised her eyebrows and said, "They?" as she realized her theory about Selwood's sixth murder victim had been right.

Delray smiled and responded, "We all know who really made the breakthrough Bridgette, but the Commissioner's prepared to let them have this one seeing as how Vancouver Metro got all the glory for catching Selwood himself."

With a small wry smile, Bridgette responded, "I've got a lot to learn about politics."

Delray returned the smile and said, "Call me when you get the all clear from Sanders."

Bridgette watched Delray as he walked out of the diner. Now alone again, she sipped the last of her peppermint tea and thought about the day ahead. With no doctor's visits or other appointments to attend to, she finally had a free day to herself.

She smiled as she whispered, "Bridgette, you need some pampering."

She would start with a manicure and then a massage. Later, there would be some retail therapy to buy a new coat. Winter was coming and Sanbury would be cold at this time of year.

About the Author

Trevor Douglas lives in Brisbane, Australia. After a long and successful career as an IT Consultant, Trevor published his debut novel, The Catalin Code, in early 2014. Trevor is married with two adult sons and when he is not writing, enjoys bush walking, watching AFL and discovering the best coffee shops in Brisbane with his wife. He is currently writing his eighth novel, The Catalin Connection, the second book in the Catalin Mystery Thriller series, which is due for release in late 2023.

You can connect with me on:
🌐 https://www.trevordouglasauthor.com
❑ https://www.facebook.com/trevordouglasauthor

Subscribe to my newsletter:
✉ https://www.trevordouglasauthor.com

Also by Trevor Douglas

I hope you enjoyed the book. If you would like more information about my other books, or would like to be notified when the next Bridgette Cash novel will be released, please visit my website. Also, word of mouth has always been my best form of promotion. If you could spare a moment to leave an honest review at your favorite digital bookstore, that would be much appreciated.

Until next time, best wishes,

Trevor.

Other Books By Trevor Douglas

Links to all my other books can be found on the books page of my website: www.trevordouglasauthor.com/books

Cold Comfort

(Bridgette Cash Mystery Thriller Series – Book 1)

How do you catch a killer who never leaves a clue?

Bridgette Cash is a rookie detective working her first murder case. The circumstances surrounding the murder of a young woman lead her to believe it's the work of a serial killer, but nobody is listening. Convinced the killer will strike again shortly, can Bridgette find enough evidence to catch the killer before another young woman is murdered?

Cold Trail

(Bridgette Cash Mystery Thriller Series – Book 2)

Murder, meltdown, or misadventure?

Police officer John Tyson has disappeared on a remote mountain range, and Detective Bridgette Cash has been sent to investigate. Hampered by local police as she tries to discover the truth, Bridgette becomes the target of a syndicate as she uncovers secrets about the nearby town of Sanbury.

Racing against the clock, a town that refuses to help, and a huge snowstorm, can Bridgette find the answers before it's too late?

Cold Hard Cash

(Bridgette Cash Mystery Thriller Series – Book 3)

The bodies are just the beginning...

The gruesome discovery of a skeleton and a body in an underwater cave become Detective Bridgette Cash's greatest mystery when forensics reveal they have more in common than just fatal gunshot wounds. As Bridgette seeks answers, she is drawn deep into an underworld from which she has little hope of escape. Alone and exposed, can she survive long enough to expose the truth and bring justice to the victims?

The Cold Light Of Day

(Bridgette Cash Mystery Thriller Series – Book 4)

How many times can one man die?

The body of an unidentified man is discovered floating in a lake. The coroner's report concludes the man has been dead for no more than a week, but police records confirm the man was murdered ten years earlier. As Bridgette seeks answers and the release of a man wrongly imprisoned for murder, she uncovers secrets old and new. Will she survive as the murderer shakes her resolve and make her question everything she stands for?

Out In The Cold

(Bridgette Cash Mystery Thriller Series – Book 5)

A cop desperate for a vacation. A killer desperate for revenge...

A remote cabin in the picturesque Cascade Mountains is the perfect spot for a vacation. Or is it? Cutoff from the rest of the world, Detective Bridgette Cash is unaware that psychopath, Alex Hellyer, has escaped from a prison hospital. Hellyer has unfinished business on his mind and Bridgette is at the top of his list.

The Catalin Code

What would you be prepared to risk for a friend?

Robbie Mayne returns home from a business trip to Europe to find his best friend has been killed in a hit-and-run accident. Not convinced that his friend's death was an accident, Robbie sets out to discover the truth, triggering a deadly sequence of events that force him into hiding and a fight for his life as he is pitted against a notorious organized crime figure. Robbie is no longer sure who his friends are as he races to find the truth before he becomes the next victim.

The Final Proposition

Three million dollars or someone's life... Which would you choose?

After being exonerated for a crime he did not commit, Adam Wells leaves prison as the only living person who knows the location of a hidden cash fortune. Desperate to help a young friend who will soon die without an expensive and risky operation, Adam must weigh up the risk as he learns the money belongs to a drug syndicate who will stop at nothing to get their money back.